CHECK MATES

STEWART FOSTER

SIMON & SCHUSTER

For Dad

First published in Great Britain in 2019 by Simon & Schuster UK Ltd
A CBS COMPANY

Copyright © 2019 Stewart Foster

5 7 9 10 8 6 4

Simon & Schuster UK Ltd
1st Floor
222 Gray's Inn Road
London WC1X 8HB

www.simonandschuster.co.uk
www.simonandschuster.com.au
www.simonandschuster.co.in

Simon & Schuster Australia, Sydney
Simon & Schuster India, New Delhi

A CIP catalogue record for this book is available from the British Library.

PB ISBN 978-1-4711-7223-6
eBook ISBN 978-1-4711-7224-3

Typeset in Times by M Rules
Printed and bound by CPI Group (UK) Ltd, Croydon, CR0 4YY

1

The Staring at the Wall Club

I stare at the wall. It's as wide as my cubicle and stretches up to the ceiling. A white blank space full of nothing. Mrs Ewens says it's supposed to help me think about what I've done, the effect it has on the class, the effect it has on me. But staring at the wall doesn't feel like it helps me. It feels like punishment.

All I did was ask Mr Fields if he was wearing a wig.

My class laughed, but he didn't think it was funny. What did him wearing a wig have to do with geography?

'Nothing,' I said.

'Yes, nothing, Felix. So get on with your work.'

But I couldn't concentrate. Jake, my best friend, was sitting next to me laughing and that made me worse.

'Sir, do you like crumpets?' I asked. I don't know why it was crumpets; it could have been anything – last week it was beetles, orange peel, fishing nets, but this morning it was the word 'crumpet' that randomly jumped into my head and out of my mouth.

'What?' Mr Fields looked as confused as the kids in my class.

'Do you like crumpets? I don't. They're full of holes like they've been eaten by worms.'

That's when Mr Fields snapped. That's when he said, 'Felix, out!'

So that's how I got to talk to Mrs Ewens.

That's how I ended up here in the Staring at the Wall Club again.

It's actually called the Isolation Room, but we call it the Staring at the Wall Club, because that's what we do – stare at the wall. It's my second time this week, the ninth time this month. It's not because I do anything really bad, it's just that I can't concentrate or keep still. Apparently it's called ADHD – attention deficit hyperactivity disorder, which my mum and dad say is a complicated way of saying I've got ants in my pants. All I know is that I can't help it, but it does mean I get sent to stare at the wall a lot. But not as often as James King in Year Nine. He tells me he gets sent here every day. He's sitting the other side of the partition wall right now, tapping his foot against his chair leg. And there are four other kids here – two boys from Year Eight, two girls from Year Nine. We don't talk to each other, but sometimes we smile or nod like we're members of a secret club. But most of the time we sit in our cubicles and stare at the white wall, thinking about the things we've done, except all I can think of is going home with Jake to fight the cavalry.

Tap. Tap. Tap.

2

Tap. Tap. Tap.

'James, I think we've had enough of that!'

Tap. Tap. Tap.

Tap. Tap. Tap.

'James.' Mrs Ewens looks over the top of her computer. 'Can you stop it?'

'But, miss, I've been here for ages.'

'And whose fault is that?'

'Mine.' James King sighs.

Tap. Tap. Tap.

I stare at the wall.

Tap. Tap. Tap.

'Hey, you!' James King whispers like we're in prison. I ignore him. He's always in here because he's been fighting, or has sworn at a teacher. I'm only in here because of crumpets. I try to concentrate but I can't stop getting carried away by my imagination or the tiniest thing that grabs my attention, like cars going by outside and a spider crawling down the wall, along the floor. I slide my shoe across the carpet tile. The spider crawls up the toe of my shoe, over my laces.

'Oi!'

'What?' I jump out of my thoughts as James King pokes his head round the edge of the partition. I don't want to talk to him and get in more trouble, but Jake says the worst thing you can do is ignore James King because he'll think you're scared of him.

'What?' I whisper back.

'Did you get sent to Mr Mclugash?' James King talks like he's my friend but he never says my name.

3

'No,' I whisper back.

'I did,' he boasts. 'Says he's going to expel me if I do it again. What did you do?'

'Nothing much. Just couldn't sit still.'

He pulls a face like that's no big deal then says, 'You're the kid with the weird granddad, right?'

'You say this every time we're in here,' I sigh.

'I know I do – that's because he *is* weird.'

'You don't know him.'

'Don't have to,' James King says. 'But picking you up every day in a pink car is weird.'

'He's just my granddad,' I say.

'James, move along, away from Felix.'

'Get him to move.'

'No,' says Mrs Ewens. 'I asked you.'

James King huffs, then picks up his bag and moves.

It's only a few seconds before he starts tapping again.

I stare at the wall, and try to block him out. Some kids do homework in here, some read books. Jake said he fell asleep once, but I just stare at the wall to make time go quicker, to forget where I am. If I stare long enough, I see colours and shapes and they merge together and it's like I'm watching a film – my house, Jake's house, my granddad's house, around the edge of a grass square. And in the middle of the square is my and Jake's tree.

In the winter we're soldiers crawling across the grass on our bellies with guns, talking on a two-way radio, and when the coast is clear we fix our bayonets and run through the snow. In the summer we load cannons and fire them at the horizon where the enemy are camped. Sometimes I get grazed by a bullet; sometimes they hit me full on, right between my ribs. I can still feel the stabbing pain in my heart, and if I lift up my shirt I can run my fingers over the ridge in my skin where the scab fell off.

Me and Jake take everyone on. It doesn't matter who they are or what country they come from, it's any soldier who dares to come near us and threaten our tree. I imagine I'm there now and I can see them advancing through my binoculars. There's a sniper on top of Mrs Flower's roof, sweeping around the square, over the parked cars at the front doors of our houses. He keeps sweeping, sweeping, until he suddenly stops dead in line with our tree. I need to stop him. I need to . . .

I pick up my rifle and rest the butt against my shoulder.

Snap!

The sniper locks right onto me and I'm locked onto him. We're two eyes at the opposite ends of a giant telescope.

'Don't shoot!' he whispers.

'Don't shoot!' I whisper back.

Click.

He's pulled his trigger.

Click.

I've pulled mine.

I duck as a bullet whizzes past my ear.

Ha. Got you! The sniper's head explodes like a giant tomato.

'Felix! Felix!' Someone taps me on my shoulder.

I jump and turn around. Mrs Ewens is looking at me weird.

'Yes, miss . . . I was just . . .' My brain scrambles back to this world. Mrs Ewens taps the table.

'Felix,' she says. 'Your granddad is here.'

2

The Pink Car

James King says a lot of things – some of them are funny, most of them are nasty. Luckily, because he's two years above me, I don't get to hear everything he says, but unfortunately for me the things he says about my granddad are true. No, he's not weird, but he really has got a pink car and he's just picked me up from school in it. My grandma used to pick me up from primary school, but when she got ill, Granddad took over, and he kept going even after she died. I thought he would stop this year when I got to secondary, but he kept turning up. I told Mum that it was embarrassing, but she said it gives Granddad something to do, a routine and company. I go to his house for tea each evening too, but that's only temporary while Mum does double shifts at work. I think Granddad does enjoy picking me up, but not when I get sent home early, because he misses his favourite programmes on TV.

'You must concentrate, Felix!' he shouts over the crashing of the gears. 'You can't be getting sent home from school all the time!'

'It's not all the time, Granddad,' I say. 'It's only twice this week.'

'And that's twice too many!' Granddad looks at me sternly. 'Maybe they should think of tying you to a chair.'

'Bit drastic, Granddad,' I say brightly, trying to cheer him up.

Granddad shakes his head slowly then looks ahead at the road.

I hug my bag as he drives on. I do love my granddad loads, but I wish he didn't have a pink car. People can see it for miles. Even Jake says it looks like an ice-cream van. Granddad doesn't even like pink. Sometimes I wonder if he bought it because he's so short-sighted, but I know he got it because it was my grandma's favourite colour. One day I woke up, looked out of my bedroom window and saw it parked across the square outside their house. Grandma loved it and drove it everywhere – to the shops, to the bowls club, to rumba classes, to the cinema when she took me there for a treat once a month. After she died, Granddad put an advert in the local paper and a for sale sticker in the back window of the car. But nobody telephoned him and the only people who stopped by were those that stopped to let their dogs pee on the wheels. But I don't think he wanted to sell the car anyway, because after four days he took the sticker down and sold his blue Ford Fiesta instead.

Granddad winces as he pushes the gearstick again.

'Should have bought an automatic!' he says. He seems to be getting louder and madder the closer we get to home. I think maybe he's had a bad day with his diabetes. When his sugar levels go weird it makes him short-tempered, or maybe he really is getting fed up with picking me up early. Maybe he's getting bored of picking me up full stop. I don't like it when he looks tired and he looks tired a lot since Grandma died. I told him once that he didn't have to, that I would walk home with Jake. He said he'd promised, but I'm not sure if he meant he'd promised Grandma or me.

As we drive past the shops I think about what I can do for the rest of the afternoon. I don't like being sent home because it makes the teachers annoyed with me and Mum and Dad mad. But it did get me out of double English and *Romeo and Juliet*! I'll have to catch up, but it's hard when I'm already behind. Last term I tried to catch up in the holidays, but it's like starting a race after the starter gun has gone. All I want to do now is go up the tree and wait for Jake to come home. Or I could just play Angry Birds, but Granddad took my phone off me yesterday evening when he discovered me playing it behind my maths book.

I glance across at him. We're now past the chip shop and his grumpiness is making me nervous. It gets even worse when we're stuck in traffic at the lights. I wish the school hadn't bothered him. If only I'd sat still and not said anything about a wig.

'Granddad,' I say cautiously. 'Have I made you miss the snooker on TV?'

He stares at the lights.

'Granddad.' I lean forward to get his attention. 'I'm sorry I made you miss the snooker.'

'What's that?' Granddad blinks like I've just woken him up.

'I said, I'm sorry if you missed the snooker.'

'Ha!' He shakes his head. 'I am not caring about snoooka! I just care about the things going on in there!' He takes his hand off the steering wheel and raps his knuckles on my head. 'Now, let's get back to base.'

He knocks my head again. Grandma used to tell him not to do it. He'd tell her he was only messing. He is, but he doesn't know how much it hurts.

I rub the spot as tears well in my eyes.

I love my granddad and I think he loves me, but sometimes it's hard to tell.

3

Teatime in Germany

It's not just my granddad's car that is pink; lots of other things in his house are pink too. All the walls are pink, and the bathroom carpet is as bright as a flamingo. The cake mixer is light pink, so is the toilet roll and so is the flowery duvet on their bed. Mum says it's like Grandma has gone but there are still pieces of her everywhere; even her pink raincoat hangs on the coat hook next to Granddad's hat. The only room that isn't pink is the sitting room, where the curtains are always pulled over, making it as dark as a cinema. Mum is always asking Granddad to open them – wouldn't he be happier if he let the light in? But Granddad just barks that he prefers them closed. So that's where me and Granddad sit and eat our tea every evening, in the dark, while he watches the German news on TV.

'Do you want more bread?' he asks.

'No thank you,' I reply.

'But I am thinking you must eat something.'

11

'I'm full up, Granddad,' I say.

'Just another sausage.'

I sigh as Granddad slides another sausage onto my plate. Grandma used to bake fruit cake and cook shepherd's pie and fry the best chips ever. Now all Granddad seems to eat is tinned sausages and tinned beans and packets of ham and bread from Lidl and Tesco.

I don't like sausages, but luckily Samson, Granddad's ginger cat, loves them. I squeak him over, listen for the clink of Granddad washing the plates in the sink, then I break the sausage into three pieces and feed it to Samson, who gobbles it up.

'Have you homework?'

I jump as Granddad walks back in.

'Yes, Granddad,' I say, trying not to look guilty.

'Then I am thinking you should get on with it.' He nods at my bag beside me on the table.

I sigh. I wish I'd tried harder and stayed at school. All my work would be done and I could be watching TV or talking to Mum and Dad – if they were in. They've been working stacks since Dad's plumbing business went bust last year. Mum says we need the money, and I know we do, but I'd like to see them too.

I slide the bag towards me and get my books out.

'Did you want more light?' asks Granddad.

'No, I'm okay,' I lie.

It doesn't matter if the room was lit by football lights, I still won't be able to concentrate long enough to read what's on the page. Mum and Dad are right when they say I've got ants in my pants. I've always been that way, but since last year it's like I've got a colony

12

of them crawling all over my body and niggling at my brain. I must concentrate, but the harder I try, the worse it gets. At primary school I used to get extra help from Mrs Lowes – she helped everyone in my class, so nobody really noticed. But at secondary school it's different; I didn't get help at all in the first term. After Christmas, Mrs Hudson, the support assistant, thought it would be a good idea to sit with me in maths and English, but it felt like everyone was staring at me, which made concentrating even harder. I told her I didn't need her help. All I wanted to do was get rid of her, because having her sitting beside me was more embarrassing than going to town with your mum. So now I just have 'catch-up' lessons instead.

I open my maths book as Granddad sits in his chair and flicks through the TV channels – Das Erste, Bayerischer Rundfunk, ZDFneo, RTL. There are pictures of floods in Bremen, people marching down the street in Munich, and bolts of lightning flashing across the sky and hitting the TV tower in Hamburg. Then the picture switches to a reporter talking outside the parliament building in Berlin. I see it every day of the week because Granddad has a satellite dish that beams all the German TV channels into his sitting room. He can get English channels too, but mostly he just watches the German news. He says it's one way he keeps in touch with Germany. The only other way is when he goes to meet his friends at the German Friendship Group every Tuesday. He took me once when I was little and I thought it was scary because it was full of strangers talking in a language I didn't understand. Grandma said I came home crying, but I don't remember that bit.

Back on the TV, the picture changes back to the floods with people being rescued from their houses by firemen in yellow dinghies. Then the picture flicks to people gathered in a hall with blankets around their shoulders. It's like . . . It's like Noah and . . .

'How big was the ark, Granddad?'

'What?' Granddad turns round.

'Noah's ark, Granddad,' I say. 'Was it as big as an ocean liner? Or bigger . . . like an aircraft carrier?'

Granddad shakes his head. 'Felix,' he says. 'Sometimes you are really confusing me.'

'I know, Granddad, but just say how big you think it might have been. Would have to be massive to get two of every animal on.'

'Felix, I am watching the news. This is serious – people are in trouble.'

'I know, I'm only asking.'

Granddad turns back to the TV. I think of asking him again, but he seems very worried about what is happening in Germany. I'd like to chat to him about it, but he hardly ever talks to me about his country. I think that's a bit strange. I don't know where he lived or worked. I don't even know the city where he was born. The only time he talks about growing up is when he tells me how he met Grandma at a dance at Bühlers Balhaus, a famous dance hall in Berlin. Then his eyes light up like a disco ball. He says he noticed her because she was wearing a pink flowery dress, but most of all he remembers she was sitting on her own reading *The Little Prince* in the corner of the room. There is nothing before. My dad says that's just Granddad being Granddad and no one can change him, but I find it weird that Granddad's life only seemed to start when he was eighteen.

I rest my head on my hand and look around the room. It's so dark and quiet that all I can hear is the sound of my breath and the ticking of the clocks. There are clocks everywhere. There's a big wooden one on the mantelpiece, and another on the sideboard, and another on the shelf by the door, and there's a giant grandfather clock with a pendulum, which *knock-knock-knocks* in the hall. It's another hour until Jake is back. Maybe I could just go home and watch *The Amazing Spider-Man*, or play Fortnite on my PS4. No. I have to try. I need to work or otherwise he'll tell Mum and Dad when they get back. They'll get annoyed, but they'll be even madder once they find out I've been sent home early again. Mum said I was running out of chances – and that was two weeks ago.

Granddad turns the TV off and picks up his giant chess book. It's the thickest book I've ever seen, even thicker than the Bible, and Granddad seems to read a page of it every day.

I shuffle along the table so I can catch the tiny bit of sunlight shining through a gap in the curtains. My maths book is full of my scrawly blue ink, and in the margins Mr Andrews's scrawly red. Every page seems to have more of his ink than mine. I blow out my cheeks. In the corner of my eye I see Granddad peering at me over the top of his book.

'You okay?' Like he's telling me I am, not asking me a question.

'Yes, Granddad,' I nod.

He looks back at his book. He doesn't understand how I feel, like everyone else.

I open my exercise book to page sixty-three.

Simultaneous equations.

Complicated equations.

Too-hard-for-me-to-do equations.

The Amazing Spider-Man?

Fortnite?

Angry Birds on my phone?

I shake them all out of my head. I have to concentrate, all my teachers say it. I must concentrate. I must sit still. But I can't. Last week in cookery, Mrs Lennon said I'm so easily distracted I'd follow a bee out of the window.

I push the maths books aside and switch to history.

Question 1: Imagine you are a suffragette. Write an account of what it would be like if people did not have the right to vote. What would it feel like not to be heard or have a voice? What actions would you take so that people took notice of your opinion?

I wonder what's for tea?

Oh. I already had it.

Imagine you are a suffragette ...

Granddad turns the TV up louder.

It's still raining in Germany. The floods are getting worse.

Imagine you are a suffragette ...

I hear a faint tinkle of a bell and look up. Samson slinks through the hall.

'Would you like me to feed Samson, Granddad?' I say this like it's the most exciting thing I could do.

'No.' Granddad shakes his head. 'I think you should work.'

I sigh. It never used to be boring like this when Grandma was alive. I glance at the picture of her smiling face on the mantelpiece

16

and imagine her voice when she used to sing along to the radio in the kitchen in the mornings and her hugging me every time I walked through the door, even if I'd only gone to the shops for bread. I'd go to give her the change and she'd press the coins into my palm, telling me to save them for a rainy day or spend it on sweets, spend it on one of those computer game things, spend it on anything you like. But since she's been gone it's like it's raining all the time, like the closed curtains have drained all the colour and her laughter from the house. All that's left is her pink car, German TV and the *tick-tick-ticking* clocks. She didn't look like my grandma when she was ill, not even in her pink dressing gown. But she still smelled of roses and told me stories about when I was born, when I was growing up, how she and Grandma used to dress me in a furry zip-up suit that made me look like a seal and then take me for a walk in the park.

Granddad doesn't talk about things like that. All he does is talk about the news or the weather, or spend his time cutting the garden hedge or mending the hinges on doors.

Imagine you are a suffragette . . .

Imagine . . .

Imagine . . .

Imagine the person you loved loads isn't around any more.

4

Writing for Dummies

'Felix,' says Mrs Hudson with a concerned look on her face. 'Where's your coloured overlay?'

'I forgot it.'

'But you're always forgetting it.'

'And I forgot my lunch,' I say.

Mrs Hudson shakes her head. 'Have you done like I said – put notes on your bedroom door and on the fridge?'

'Yes, but I forget to look at them too.'

Mrs Hudson sighs. 'Use this one,' she says, sliding a yellow overlay across the desk.

'It doesn't work.' I slide the overlay back to her.

'It might help,' says Mrs Hudson.

'It doesn't,' I say. 'I'm not dyslexic.'

'No.' Mrs Hudson pushes the overlay back to me. 'But you *are* behind in English.'

She's got me there. I didn't do any work at Granddad's and I didn't get to do any when I got home because Mum was giving me earache about getting sent to the Isolation Room. She went on and on, things like, 'Can't you just be quiet and sit still ... you won't learn anything from staring at a wall ... was it Jake's doing ...? is he a bad influence ...? because if he is I will go down the school ...' I told her it was nothing to do with Jake, it was just me. She just shook her head and went downstairs and said she'd talk to Dad when he came home, but luckily for me I was asleep when he did. Or at least I pretended I was when I heard his van pull up outside.

Mrs Hudson tells us to open our books. As I skim through the pages I glance at the others in the student support group – Michael, Ross and Laura all have yellow overlays in front of them to help them read. They never forget their overlays, but then neither did I. I left it behind on purpose, because I'm not like them. I can read okay, it's just I can't concentrate. People try to help and I know that they and Mum and Dad care. I've had loads of tests – a reading test, a reasoning test, a hearing test. One time Mum even took me to get my eyes tested at Specsavers. I had to rest my chin on a piece of plastic and look through mini binoculars and read letters through the lenses. The person doing the test said I had perfect twenty-twenty vision, so the next month they sent me for a hearing test instead. But there's nothing wrong with my ears or my eyes. I can hear dogs barking in the park from my bedroom window and I can see that fly landing on Mrs Hudson's book from here.

'So,' she says, brushing the fly away. 'Laura, if you read the first page, then Ross can take over.'

I look down at my book and follow the words as Laura reads slowly. We are all behind in our work but for different reasons. Michael gets stuck on words with silent letters like the C in muscle and scent. Ross can read okay in his head but stutters when he reads out aloud, and Laura gets stuck on words with three or more syllables, which makes her sound like a broken-down robot, like she does now . . .

'Tran . . . Tran . . . Tran . . .' She looks up from her book.

'Break it down into parts.' Mrs Hudson leans over and places her finger on Laura's book. 'Tran . . .'

'Tran . . . Tran . . . Tran-sit-on. Transiton!' Laura smiles.

I glance at Ross and Michael, but their heads are down, looking at their books. They used to laugh at each other's mistakes and sometimes they are funny, like when Ross reads 'limp noodles' instead of 'lymph nodes', but now they just keep reading, staying serious, like they really want to get better at it. And so do I, it's just that I can't sit still long enough to do it.

'Transition,' says Laura.

'Do you watch *Transformers*?'

'What?' Mrs Hudson looks at me, startled. 'Felix, where did that come from?'

'No idea.' I shrug. 'But do you watch them – *Transformers*? You know, the robots that turn into cars and machines.'

'We all know what they are.' Mrs Hudson looks around the table. 'But, Felix, we all need to concentrate on this.'

'It's good.' I lift up my fists and bring them together. 'They all smash into each other like this and—'

'Felix!' snaps Mrs Hudson. 'We need to concentrate.'

'Sorry.' I sit back in my seat. 'I was only saying.'

Mrs Hudson takes a deep breath, then says, 'Well done, Laura, now, Michael, you take over from there.'

Michael starts reading, but he immediately gets stuck.

'Invis . . . Invis . . .'

'Keep trying,' says Mrs Hudson.

'Invisible,' says Michael, reading on.

I try to follow the words, but it's hard when Optimus Prime, Bumblebee and Megatron are now smashing into each other inside my head. There's metal grating, grinding, sparks flying everywhere. Optimus Prime turns into a sports car, Megatron into a massive truck, Bumblebee into a helicopter, and they chase each other along streets between giant cranes and skyscrapers. *Crash! Bang! Smash!* Shards of glass fly through the air between the helicopter's rotor blades. Optimus Prime changes into a—

'Felix?'

'Tank,' I say, without thinking.

'What?' Mrs Hudson narrows her brow. Michael, Ross and Laura are looking at me like I just walked off an alien spacecraft.

'Oh! Nothing.'

Mrs Hudson shakes her head. 'Felix, it's a pity you can't use your imagination in your writing.' She looks at me for a long time, like the longer she looks, the more chance her words will go into my head. I shrug and look at the ground. It's pointless worrying about something that can't happen.

'Okay,' Mrs Hudson says eventually. 'You can go now. That's us done for this week.'

We all pack our books in our bags and I follow Laura towards the door until Mrs Hudson says, 'No, Felix, not you. I'd like a quick word.'

'But I've got cookery,' I say.

'I know. But I wanted a word about what happened yesterday with Mr Fields in geography.

I smile.

'It's not funny,' says Mrs Hudson, catching up with me. 'You can't just shout out random things – you might think it's humorous, but you're affecting the rest of the group.'

'I'm not laughing at that, and I don't mean to get into trouble, it's just geography – Mr Fields. See?'

'You're avoiding the issue.'

'Am I?' I say brightly, trying to make the situation less serious. 'Sorry, I won't do it again.'

'But you said that last week, and the week before that.'

'I know, but I mean it this time.'

'Do you?'

'Yes,' I say with my serious look. People think I don't care, but I do, it's just I can't help what I say or the funny expression they say I have on my face.

Mrs Hudson looks at me for a long time, like she's wondering if I mean it, then she says quietly, 'Felix, is there anything in particular that's bothering you? I know you have trouble concentrating, but some of your teachers tell me your behaviour has been getting worse lately. Like just now.'

I shrug.

'So is there anything?'

22

'Nope.'

'Are you sure? Do you think it would help if we sat down and had a chat with your mum and dad? What do you think?'

I think they are too stressed. I think they can't afford to take time off work.

'I'm okay,' I say. 'I'll just try harder.'

'Promise?'

'Yes. So can I go now?'

Mrs Hudson smiles wearily as she takes her hand off the door frame. 'Yes,' she says. 'You can go now.'

I walk out into the corridor. Everyone seems to think there's something wrong. I don't know if there is, but I do know I'm getting into more trouble. Just like Mum said last night. I went up to my room to get away from her, but she still went on, saying that if I don't behave I'll end up having to work long hours packing at the factory like she does, or have to stay on an extra year to pass my exams. She started to say something else about Dad, but I didn't hear because I closed the door.

When I get to cookery class, everyone has their heads down kneading dough on the benches. I look around for Jake, but he's already paired up with Rebecca, which is weird because he doesn't really like her.

'Ah, Felix!' Mrs Lennon turns round from an oven. 'You're too late to start, so just join a pair.'

'Over here, Felix.' Jake waves his floured hands at me like a clown. Rebecca shakes her head, like she thinks Jake's an idiot.

I drop my bag by the door and walk over to them.

'Where have you been?' Jake asks.

'Nowhere.' I shrug.

'Reading for dummies?'

'Don't call it that,' I say.

'Writing for dummies then.' Jake grins. He's my best friend, but best friends can be annoying sometimes.

'Don't listen to him, Felix,' says Rebecca. 'Just check the instructions and turn the oven on.'

Rebecca is always on my side, trying to keep me calm. She's one of the brainiest in the class and was my best friend in primary school. She used to come round my house lots, but her mum and mine fell out, so she doesn't any more. She still is a best friend, but not as best as Jake now.

I look at the oven temperature on the recipe: 'Temp 210 for 35 min'.

I walk over to the oven.

Jake's mixing flour with his hands, like he's forgotten what he just said. Writing for dummies. Reading for dummies. I was doing both, but everyone doesn't have to know about it. I can read. And there's nothing else wrong.

I bend down and turn the oven dial. The smell of gas stings my nose, reminds me of making bread with Grandma. When I'd sit on the kitchen floor and watch the bread rise through the glass and start to daydream of catching a train or a plane. And Grandma would join in and somehow we'd always end up in Nova Scotia, where neither of us had ever been, but it was always there because Grandma liked the name. And because it's got coloured wooden houses – most of them are blue or red, but she remembered seeing a picture of a pink one in a magazine.

Was it two hundred and ten or two hundred and fifty? Thirty-five minutes or forty-five?

Two hundred and fifty?

Yes. Two hundred and fifty.

I set the dial.

Behind me I can hear Jake and Rebecca talking, something about the mix being too thick, but all I can think of is wishing I could go to Nova Scotia with Grandma again.

'It's okay, Felix,' says Jake. 'Maybe we just feed them to the birds.'

'No, better not do that,' says Rebecca.

'No, don't want to kill them.' Jake laughs.

Rebecca puts her hand over her mouth, trying to stop herself doing the same, but I can see the water in her eyes and the creases in her cheeks. 'I'm sorry,' she says, 'but they are as hard as bullets.'

'It's okay,' I say. 'I meant to do it. Something had to get us out of that lesson early.'

'Yeah,' says Jake. 'But setting off the fire alarm?'

I laugh even though I know I shouldn't as we walk out of the school gates.

'Maybe I could cut the tops off,' says Rebecca, looking down at the burnt rolls in her container.

'You're joking,' says Jake. 'A shark couldn't bite through those.'

We laugh again, but all the time I'm wishing Rebecca had thrown them in the bin. She said she couldn't because her mum told her it's bad to waste food, but I really wish she had. I'm making out that I meant to do it, that it was a joke, but all the bread rolls do is remind

25

me that I was daydreaming about making bread with Grandma when I should have been checking the oven.

We reach the zebra crossing. Rebecca looks down at her container again.

'Tell your mum I'm sorry,' I say. 'I'll pay for the ingredients.'

'It's okay. I'll tell her I did it.'

'No, you don't have to,' I say.

'It's fine, Felix.' She smiles. 'Don't worry about it.' She looks at me like somehow she knows I am. I try to force a smile back. 'I'll see you both tomorrow,' she says as she turns away. Since she stopped coming around my house, she doesn't hang out with me so much at school either. I think it might be because I irritate her now – I know Jake definitely does, because he's always going on about her being brainy and he hated it when last term when me and Rebecca did a school project on the Romans together. Mum says I should try to work with her again, because I concentrated better when I did and got better marks, but now I think I'd mess around too much and put her off her work.

As me and Jake turn the corner, I think for a moment that Granddad hasn't turned up and I feel bad for hoping that he won't. Now I get to talk to Jake about the things we did at school and the tactics we can use against the enemy later, but just as I'm about to say something a white van pulls away and I see Granddad's pink car parked tight against the kerb.

Jake steps into the road.

'I'll see you later,' he says.

I nod. I used to ask if he wanted a lift, but he said he didn't want to be seen anywhere near my granddad's pink car, let alone get in it. I've got no choice. He's my granddad. He smiles and waves as I get closer. I check around. I know Granddad made someone a promise to keep picking me up, but it is embarrassing getting into Bristol's only pink car.

5

I've Got Problems

The TV weatherman is pointing at a map. Tomorrow it's going to be raining in Hamburg, sunny in Frankfurt and Stuttgart, and raining in Dresden and Berlin.

I'm stuck with Granddad again. I thought this was only going to be temporary while Mum took extra shifts, but she seems to be working them every night. Dad is always working, but I'm used to that.

Granddad sighs like the rain is falling on him in his chair. I don't know why he watches the weather for any country. Since Grandma died, he hardly ever goes out in England, let alone Germany.

I open my books. The trouble with not doing my homework yesterday evening is that the same question is staring at me now:

Imagine you are a suffragette. Write an account of what it would be like if people did not have the right to vote. What would it feel like not to be heard or have a voice? What actions would you take so that people took notice of your opinion?

Underneath there's a drawing of a woman running in front of a horse, and another chained to the railings outside the Houses of Parliament, and another in a prison cell. I look around the room. It's as dark as a prison in here and I'm so hungry my stomach is rumbling, but Granddad hasn't heard because he's busy ripping up envelopes and bills into tiny pieces. He does it to everything that comes through the letter box. Dad told me Granddad has always done it, because he is scared people will find out his bank balance or how much his gas bill is, or they might use his identity like people do on the internet, but why would anyone want to steal the identity of someone who is seventy-two years old?

I sneak a look through the gap in the curtains. The sun is shining on the grass, between the branches of my tree, on the roof of my house. I wish I was out there, but Granddad will go mad if I just get up and disappear. I could pretend I need the toilet. A pee wouldn't give me long enough; it'd have to be a number two. That would give me ten minutes. I could push it to fifteen if I pretend I've got constipation like Aunt Sophie. I could run across the grass, take cover behind the tree, then bolt as fast as I can for my house. I'm so hungry that I'd grab anything from the cupboards – crisps, chocolate, yoghurt, Ryvita even – anything but tinned sausages. I'd stash it all in my bag then grab Mum's iPad and run back before Granddad had a chance to notice I'd gone. I'd put the iPad between the covers of my book and pretend I was reading when I'd actually be watching police car chases on YouTube.

I could do it. If I slide my chair back quietly, I could be—

'How is it going?'

'Uh! What?' I jump like I've been hit by an arrow.

'I said, how is it going?'

Granddad is standing right behind me.

'Erm, it's okay, Granddad,' I say.

'But this page is blank.'

'Yeah, umm ... er ... It's because it's too dark, Granddad,' I say. 'I can't see what I'm doing.'

'But we can solve that.' He bends down and flicks a switch on the wall. A side lamp flashes in my face.

I cover my eyes.

'Sorry.' Granddad directs the beam down to my book. 'There,' he says. 'I am thinking this is better.' He reaches across the table and picks up *Of Mice and Men*.

'Umm,' he says. 'I have not seen this one. Is it any good?'

'It's okay,' I say. 'But it's better when someone else reads it out.'

Granddad chuckles. 'You are crafty,' he says. I screw my eyes as he raps his knuckles on my head. 'Come on,' he says. 'I will try to help you. Start here.'

'It's okay, Granddad,' I say. 'I can do it.'

'But I know you have problems.'

'Problems?'

'Your mother said when she came over last night. She said she was telling you to behave at school, but you wouldn't listen. You locked yourself in your room.'

'I didn't lock it. I just closed it.' Granddad nods but I'm not sure he believes me. 'It's true, Granddad – my door hasn't even got a lock ... So what did she say?'

'Oh, it was nothing,' says Granddad. 'Just things like this – that you don't settle to do anything and of course that you are having special lessons at school.'

'But I don't actually need them,' I say. 'And what does Mum know anyway? She's always too busy working at the factory. Nobody's got any time since Dad's business went bust and Grandma di—'

I stop myself.

Granddad looks up at me. I think we both know the word I was going to say, but we've never spoken it since Grandma *went*. We never say the D word, we always say 'gone', like she has just *gone* to the shops for a paper, or like she *went* to see Mrs Danes next door. We don't say she never came back.

Granddad looks at my book.

'Maybe we should just try,' he says softly.

I take a deep breath. Maybe I should at least have a go because he is making an effort to help.

Granddad taps his finger on the first word and starts to read.

'*The bunkhouse was a long, rectangular building. Inside, the walls were whitewashed and the floor unpainted.*' His words come out slowly and loudly but I'm not hearing them. Problems? Did Granddad really just say that *I've* got problems? Who's been talking about me? Mum, Dad, the teachers! The neighbours! Is that why Mrs Flower looks at me weird when I go past her gate? Is that why the woman in the chip shop counts my change out slowly? Is that what the teachers say about me when I walk past the staffroom? Felix has got 'problems'? Is that what I am? A problem child? My only problem is I can't sit still. It doesn't matter where I try to read – in English, in

31

the library, in my bedroom, at Granddad's – you can put me in any room, anywhere in the whole world, but the problem is still there.

'*In three walls there were small, square windows*,' Granddad continues, '*and in the fourth, a solid door with a wooden latch. Against the walls were eight bunks—*' Granddad stops suddenly. 'Now you,' he says, like I'm five years old (at least that's how old I feel). A five-year-old with problems!

I look at the next sentence.

On the wall there were pegs, on which hung broken harnesses ...

I say it once more in my head, then out loud:

'*On the wall there ... On the wall there ...*'

Problems? I've got problems?

'I can't do it,' I say.

'You can,' says Granddad, 'you just have to—'

'I said I can't do it!' I push the book away and stand up. 'My brain's all wrong.'

'What?' Granddad chuckles.

'It's not funny,' I yell. I turn and run out into the hall.

Granddad shouts, 'Felix, come back now,' and then something else, but I'm too far down the garden path to hear.

6

Up Our Tree

The soldiers are creeping like cardboard cut-outs across the sun and there's smoke billowing on top of the hill.

I'm up in the tree after storming out on Granddad an hour ago. I've got 'problems' he said and now I've got another one, because even though I've been fighting hard, the enemy has me surrounded. There's a spotter on the horizon, between the new office block and the sports centre. I need to get the cannons ready, pack the magazines with powder and load the ball, but I can't take them on my own.

I look across the square to Jake's house. I need his help. I need a whole platoon, but all I can see is Mrs Flower walking her old dog. Can't she see what's happening? The enemy is coming and I'm the only gunner here.

I jam the powder down the barrel, and then add some hay. I stand, pick up a cannonball and heave it in. Then I turn the wheels and aim the barrel at forty-five degrees.

Ready?

Ready.

I light the fuse; crouch down with my hands over my ears.

BANG!

BOOM!

BA—

'Felix! Felix!'

'What? Where? When—' My head scrambles back. 'Mum! How did you get there?'

'Walked of course. What did you think?' Mum's at the base of the tree with a pizza box in her hand.

'Doesn't matter,' I say, trying to shake all the problems and the cannons and the soldiers out of my head.

'Just come home and eat this.'

'Can't I eat it up here?'

'No, me and your dad have something we want to discuss with you.'

'What is it? I didn't get sent out of class today.'

'It's not that.'

'Have you spoken to Granddad then? I didn't mean to—'

'Felix!' Mum snaps. 'I'm not going to talk about it while you're up in the tree. Just eat this.'

'So I can eat it up here?'

'Yes! I'm too tired to argue,' she sighs. 'But then come straight home.' She places the pizza box against the tree and walks away.

I look across at Granddad's house. I wonder if he's snitched on me and told Mum I stormed out. But I don't know how he could, because he's not gone over to ours and he hates using the phone as he thinks anyone could be listening in.

Out of the corner of my eye, I spot Jake running across the grass towards me like a bloodhound, with his hair flopping up and down on his head. He can smell pizza from miles away.

'All right?' He grins up at me. 'I'm starving.' Jake stuffs the pizza box up his sweatshirt as I throw the rope over the side.

'Have the enemy advanced?' he asks as he climbs. 'Ouch! This pizza's burning through my belly!' He throws the box ahead, then scrambles onto the platform.

'How was it at your granddad's?'

He said I've got problems.

'Just the usual,' I say. 'Did some classwork, watched German TV.'

'God, that *is* dull!'

'Then he tried to make me read and I stormed out.'

'Don't blame you for getting out of there. That place gives me the creeps!' He looks across at my granddad's house. 'Why do you reckon he does it?'

'What?'

Jake chews on pizza. 'Your granddad. Why do you reckon he keeps his curtains closed?'

I shrug and break off a piece of pizza.

'My mum says it's because he's depressed after your gran died,' says Jake.

'Don't think so. He did it when she was alive. Grandma used to say it was like living in a chapel of rest, whatever that is.'

'Maybe it's because he's sensitive to light.' Jake licks tomato from his lips. 'Or he's a werewolf and comes out at night.'

'He's not a werewolf,' I say. 'He goes to the shops and doctors in the day.'

'That's just his cover,' says Jake. 'He's a werewolf with a pink car.' Jake laughs. I smile, but as I look at Grandma's car it reminds me that I miss her loads, that if she were alive maybe she'd be taking me to the cinema this weekend.

Jake throws the empty pizza box over the side and looks up at the hill. He says something about the enemy coming down both sides of the hill into the valley, but I'm not really listening because I'm looking across the park, at Granddad's pink car, then the green front door of his house.

I wish I hadn't stormed out and left him on his own. He'll be sitting in his armchair in the dark now, watching TV. It must be really lonely. I wish I hadn't shouted at him. I wish I could go back and—

'What do you reckon? Felix!' Jake punches me on the arm.

'Ouch!' I say. 'That hurt.'

'Yeah, but you were miles away. I asked if you're going to help me load the cannons or not?'

'Okay,' I sigh. I crawl across the platform and pull out the cannons. Jake elevates them to forty-five degrees, then jams the powder in. I pick up a ball and roll it down the barrel, then we take aim at a point between the electricity pylon and the water tower, where we last saw the smoke last night. Sometimes I think I'm too old to play games like this, that if anyone found out at school they'd laugh at us. Jake says it doesn't matter what they think, but we swore to each other that

36

we would never tell, just in case. I don't think he'd ever say anything anyway, because from the smile on his face I know he likes escaping up here as much as me.

'Light the fuse,' he says.

'Lighting fuse,' I repeat.

'Stand back.'

'Stand back.'

'Fire!'

'Fire!'

Me and Jake cover our ears and go back to war.

7

No Way!

'Well, I think you're being very unreasonable, Felix. It's only two days.'

'Two days! That's forever! I can't, Mum. All he does is read his chess book and watch German TV.'

'Well, that's mean.' Mum drops some clean clothes on the end of my bed. 'You know your granddad has been lonely since your gran died. He needs company and, besides, it'll be good for you.'

'Good for me? How? What good will it do me to know it's raining in Germany?' I get up off my bed. 'And two days, Mum?' I plead. 'Do I have to? Can't I have a sleepover at Jake's?'

'No. Just think how your granddad would feel – him all on his own and you over at Jake's or up your tree.'

'But—'

'No, Felix!' Mum holds up her hand, like a stop sign. 'That's enough. You need to stop being so selfish. Me and Dad have been working so much that we need a break.'

'What about me? We haven't been away together in ages.'

'I know, but another time. Dad and I need some time on our own. Besides, it's only Cornwall – it's not like we'll be on the other side of the world.' Mum looks at me like I should know why they need to go away. And I do – it's because they argue loads, sometimes about me and my behaviour, but mostly about money. And it's got worse since Dad's business went bust.

'When are you going?' I say eventually.

'Tomorrow afternoon. Dad's finishing work early, so we'll be gone by the time you get back from school.'

'So it's actually *three* days!' I huff. 'My head will be aching where he raps his knuckles all the time.'

'Just tell him it hurts,' says Mum. 'Anyway, it's only two and a bit ... And your granddad can't pick you up tomorrow – he's got an appointment at the clinic.'

Mum closes my door. The poster of Astro Boy stares back at me. It's an old black and white one that Dad gave me. I wish I was Astro Boy, because then I could fight crime and get out of this mess. When Mum said she and Dad were going away, I thought I was going too. For a second I dreamed we were going to Center Parcs or even Disneyland Paris. I've never been to either, but last year Freya in my class went to both. But no, they're going without me and leaving me with Granddad.

I put my head in my hands.

It's going to be terrible. I can't stay with him. Not all weekend. I'll die of boredom, counting every second on his clocks. I've got to do something to get out of it or make it more bearable. I've got to—

I've got it. I've got it!

'Mum!' I stand up and shout.

'What?'

'Can I take my PS4?'

'No!'

8

I Hear Voices

'Maybe it won't be as bad as you think,' says Jake as we walk into our square.

'It will be,' I say. 'He'll be watching *Ein Platz in der Sonne,* now.'

'What's *Ein Platz . . .* whatever you said?'

'*Ein Platz in der Sonne.* I made it up. It's the same as *A Place in the Sun*, but in German.'

Jake laughs.

'It's not funny, Jake. He's going to be so grumpy because I haven't apologized for shouting at him last night.'

'Oh, that's easy.' Jake beams. 'Just say sorry, like I do. You don't actually have to mean it.'

I look around the square. The sun is shining on the grass, on our tree, on the roofs of the parked cars. Mrs Flower is out in her front garden. She's pretending to cut her roses but all she's really doing is nosing around, checking what other people are doing. She won't be able to see much of Granddad though because his curtains are clamped shut as usual. It's Friday. I should be looking forward to a weekend in the tree, but instead I've got to spend it at Granddad's. All day at school I've been thinking of ways to get out of it. I asked Rebecca if I could go to hers, but she said it might be weird because our mums aren't talking and she thought I was being mean to Granddad anyway. Jake said I could stop at his, but his dad doesn't speak to me. I would be okay if parents, including mine, didn't interfere. So there's nothing for it, I have to stay with Granddad, but the hardest thing is that I have to apologize for storming out on him first.

The red numbers on the cooker are flashing 0 0 0 0 0 as I open Granddad's back door. Samson is in the corner licking the last bits of jelly meat from his bowl. I bend down and give him a stroke. He purrs and rubs his head against my legs. I listen for the rumble of the TV or music from the radio, but there's nothing, just the sound of my breath as I creep through the kitchen into the hall. Granddad must have fallen asleep in front of the TV. I hope so. That way I can just sneak up the stairs to my room, go without tea and hope that everything will be okay in the morning.

I creep past one of the clocks, then the radiator, then peer around the frame of the door.

The tiny spotlight is on and Granddad's leaning forward in the shadows with his head in his hands like he's crying. The only time I've seen him cry was at Grandma's funeral, but then everyone cried at Grandma's funeral, including me. I don't want to see him cry. I don't think he'd like me to see him cry either.

I go to lift my left foot and creep past the doorway. Granddad raises his head. I step back.

'So,' he murmurs, 'that is what I did today. Went to Tesco, chatted over the fence to Mrs Danes, and that is about it. Oh and of course I went to the clinic.'

I peer into the room. Who is he talking to? One of his friends from the German Friendship Group? He'd be talking in German if it was and I never saw anyone come into the square anyway. And he can't be on the telephone, because he hates using it. Maybe he's just talking to Sampson, but he's still eating in the kitchen.

'Felix is fine. But I am thinking he misses you as much as I do.'

Granddad turns his head towards the mantelpiece. He's talking to the picture of Grandma; the one where she's sitting on the seafront wall licking an ice cream. He must be missing her as much as me. More even. I saw her lots, but he lived with her for over fifty years and saw her every day.

I lean back. My shoulder knocks against the clock and the clock knocks against the wall.

'Felix! Is that you? Felix!'

'Uh ... Yes, Granddad,' I say, panicking.

'Good,' he says. 'I was wondering where you were.' He peers round the door, smiling. He doesn't seem to care that I might have heard him talking to Grandma. 'Come in,' he says. 'I've been thinking.'

'M-me too, Granddad,' I stammer. 'I'm sorry about last night.'

'Pwah!' Granddad waves his hand like when he flicks a midge off his tea. 'That doesn't matter. I have not been feeling myself lately.'

43

'But I shouldn't have shouted,' I say. 'And it's not you I was mad with. I was mad with myself.'

Granddad nods as he gets comfy in his chair. 'I know,' he says. 'But forcing you to read is not the best way ... So I have been sitting here thinking to myself.'

And talking to Grandma!

'I am thinking, what can we ... I mean, what *I* can do with Felix.'

'Are you going to buy me something, Granddad?' I sit down next to him, thinking this weekend might not be so bad after all.

'No.'

'Because if you are, can I choose? I don't need any more woolly jumpers – Grandma knitted me a whole wardrobe already.'

Granddad chuckles.

'No, I am not buying you anything. You will just have to wait and see tomorrow morning when you wake up. But it will be something that helps you keep still, helps you concentrate.'

'A DVD, Granddad? A game for my PS4?'

'No ... No ... Nothing like that. Now,' he grunts as he pushes himself out of his chair. 'I think it is time for tea.'

'Okay,' I say. 'I'll get the knives and forks.'

'Good, you do that.' Granddad ruffles my hair. 'I am glad we have talked.'

'Me too, Granddad,' I say. 'And I am sorry.'

'It's okay. *Neuer morgen, neuanfang,*' he says sharply.

'What does that mean?' I ask.

'New morning, new start.'

9

Ten Things

The whole house seems to shake when Granddad gets up in the morning, not because of his heavy footsteps but because all the clock alarms go off at the same time, including the two cuckoo clocks on the landing. I can hear his footsteps thudding as he rushes around the house turning them all off.

There isn't one in the guest room though; Grandma told me that a guest should always feel like they are on holiday and be able to rest. So that's what I'm doing, resting in the pink bed with pink pillows and pink duvet surrounded by pink walls and pink curtains, which make every day start like the sun is out (my grandma said that too, not me).

I pull on my socks and trousers. Granddad's radio is playing German brass band music in the kitchen and the smell of bacon is wafting up the stairs. I puff out my cheeks. I wonder what Granddad has planned for me today – probably just a trip to Aldi! If it was Mum or Dad, I'd be going to the cinema or something – one time Dad even took me to the Memorial Stadium to watch Bristol Rovers. I wish I was going to watch Rovers, even if Dad did get annoyed last time because I kept fidgeting – and when I did sit still I daydreamed so much that I missed two goals.

I pull my sweatshirt on and head downstairs. On every step the music grows louder, but when I reach the bottom there's no sign of Granddad in the kitchen. I walk into the dining room. He's not there either. Maybe he's forgotten about it. Maybe he's not only talking to himself but he's wandered off on his own like Mrs Gough did last year. She only went to the shops, but a day later the police found her walking along the M4 motorway towards the Severn Bridge.

My heart skips when I see a note on the dining room table. Please, Granddad, not you, not when Mum and Dad aren't here to look for you.

I pick up the note and start to read.

Ten things I'd like to teach Felix.

The writing turns blurry. I wipe the sleep from my eyes and start again.

Ten things I'd like to teach Felix.

1. *How to clean brass.*
2. *How to do the Bavarian Schuhplatter Knee Dance.*
3. *How to do clean the patio slabs.*
4. *How to mow a straight line on the lawn.*
5. *How to play chess.*

6. *How to make Rouladen.*
7. *How to play 'Hoppe, Hoppe, Reiter' on the glockenspiel.*
8. *How to shred paper.*
9. *How to read a book without losing your temper.*
10. *How to clean mould from the shower curtain.*

How to clean the patio? How to mow the lawn? What sort of list is this?

I walk over to the window. But even with more light it still doesn't make sense.

Shred paper; read a book without losing your temper?

'Ah, I see you have found it.'

I jump as Granddad walks in.

'My list.' He puts his cup of tea down on the table.

'Yes,' I say. 'But what is it? It's just chores!'

'I'm thinking it's not.'

'It is, Granddad – clean the patio, mow the lawn, clean mood from the curtains.'

'Mould,' says Granddad.

'I don't care what it is,' I say, 'it's still cleaning.'

'No. No,' says Granddad. 'It is a list of ten things I'd like to teach you.'

'But why?'

'Because it would be good for you. You think about it while I am going to the toilet and check my levels.' He turns away from me and walks out into the hall. Granddad goes to the toilet loads and when he does he checks his levels. If he doesn't keep his sugar level up, he gets all shaky and sometimes even grumpier.

I look at the list – how to clean brass, how to cut a straight line on the lawn, how to play chess, how to … how to … This isn't a list of ten things to teach Felix. It's a list of the ten most boring things in the world.

There must be some mistake. I turn the paper over to see if there is anything more exciting on the back, but it's blank.

I walk out into the hall and shout up the stairs, 'Granddad, are you sure you've given me the right list?'

I hear a thud on the ceiling. He said he was going to the toilet, but this noise came from his bedroom. I listen for another thud or the sound of his footsteps.

Nothing.

'Granddad,' I shout. 'Are you okay?' I turn my head and listen, but all I can hear is the pendulum knocking inside the grandfather clock.

'Granddad?' I put my foot on the first stair.

'Ah! I see you cannot wait.'

I look up. Granddad's looking at me sternly with a box in his hand.

'What is it?' I ask.

'It is not my best set,' he says, 'but it is a start.'

'What? No, Granddad. Not chess!'

'But you used to play ludo with your grandma.'

'I know, Granddad, but chess! Only swots play chess, and it takes longer than Monopoly!'

'But it is a game of craft,' he says.

'No, it's the most boring game in the world. Can't you just play on your own and I'll go and get my PS4?'

'No,' says Granddad. 'That's all children do all day – play computer games. Chess is a real game where you're not staring at a TV all the time.'

'Well, I'm still not playing.'

Granddad looks down at the box like he's disappointed, but why couldn't he get something more exciting, like a football or the new *Spider-Man* DVD or a BMX bike? I should know better. Even when Grandma was alive, my birthday presents were always something 'practical' like a new duvet or a woolly jumper. Mum would make me wear it all day, just so I didn't upset Grandma, even though I'd get really hot and itchy because my birthday is in the middle of the summer.

Granddad pushes past me in the hall and is headed for the dining room.

'Clear the table,' he says.

'I will,' I say, 'but I'm still not playing.'

Granddad sighs. 'Felix, I know you don't like coming here so much now,' he says with a sad look in his eyes, 'but I am trying to do something with you.'

'I do, Granddad. It's just . . .' I look back at the list and see if I've missed anything, but it gets worse every time I look. It's not just me who would think that – none of my friends would want to shred paper or make Rouladen, whatever that is. I think of saying that to Granddad, but he's now sitting in his chair flicking through the pages of his chess book like he's given up on me.

I sit down at the table and turn a page of *Of Mice and Men*, just to make Granddad think I'm *actually* reading, but I don't know why I bother because he's not turned a page over either. Maybe he's as fed up as I am and he's gone to sleep with his eyes open. I saw a documentary about dolphins doing that – one side of their brains goes to sleep while the other side stays awake so they remember to breathe. I think it was a documentary – or maybe it was in *Finding Nemo*. I wish I could do something with Granddad, but there's nothing we like doing together. If Grandma made a list, she'd fill it with twenty things. Twenty brilliant things, like taking me to the cinema and a coach trip to Legoland. I'm too old for that now, but if she was alive I bet she'd take me to Thorpe Park.

I look back at Granddad's list.

Ten things I'd like to teach Felix.

It's bad enough having extra lessons at school without having them at home. *Ten! TEN! Why couldn't he have just made five? One even?*

I rest my head on my hand and I stare at the clock on the mantelpiece. It's only five past nine. I could be playing Tekken on my PlayStation, or prepping the guns to find the enemy with Jake, or I could just be at home on my own in bed. The rest of my class aren't stuck in all weekend like this – Rebecca will be going to town with her sister, Tom Jenkins will be going to the cricket with his dad, Harry Giles will be—

'If you had to do one of them, which one would you choose?'

'Wha-what?' I jump out of my daydream.

Granddad's stopped being a dolphin and is staring right at me.

'My list of chores – if you had to do one, which would you choose?'

'So it is a list of chores?'

Granddad grins as he pushes himself out of his chair.

'Yes,' he says. 'And if you had to do one, which would it be? I'm not saying you have to do one, just . . .'

'Hypothetically?'

'Yes.' Granddad looks surprised.

'It's okay, Granddad,' I say. 'I'm not dumb – I know what "hypothetically" means, I just can't spell it.'

'I know this,' he says. 'So . . . hypothetically, which one would you choose? But we must discount cutting the grass because it is wet.'

'Okay.' I peer across at the list. It would be good to do something outside just to get out of here, but if we can't cut the grass . . . 'Okay,' I say. 'If I really, really had to . . . I'd . . . clean the patio slabs.'

'Excellent!' Granddad claps his hands. 'Excellent! You get the detergent and the buckets and I will get the overalls.'

'What? No! You said "hypothetically"! And you were asleep!'

'I know this.' Granddad grins. 'But I also know that you are bored.'

'Yeah, but—'

'But nothing. Come on. Your grandma would be pleased.'

'That I'm cleaning the patio?'

'That you are doing something with me.'

I look at my books.

Of Mice and Men *or clean the patio.*

Algebra or clean the patio.

History or clean the patio.

'Of course we could always try che—'

'Okay! Okay!' I jump up. 'I'll clean the patio.'

'Wonderful!' Granddad smiles.

I follow him into the kitchen and we put our shoes on by the back door. I stop.

What am I doing?

He said 'hypothetically'.

Granddad whistles happily as he walks down the garden path.

I shake my head.

How did I fall for that?

10

Early Alarm

'One kilo of round steak, four tablespoons of stone ground mustard, six slices of bacon, two onions (chopped), four cloves of garlic (minced), and cabbage, cabbage, lots of cabbage – you can never have enough cabbage, Felix. Now chop it into tiny pieces.'

I chop a cabbage, then another, then another. I look to my left – more cabbages, hundreds of cabbages, all rolling towards me. Rolling, rolling on a conveyor belt full of cabbages on an endless production line.

'Six slices of bacon, two onions, and cabbage, lots of cabbage. Chop, Felix. Chop!'

'No, Granddad. No. No more cabbage.'

'Felix ... Felix!'

'No, Granddad. No more!'

'Felix!'

'No—'

I open my eyes. Granddad's standing over me in his striped pyjamas, shaking me awake.

I look around for the cabbages, but all I see is the wardrobe, curtains and the clock on the table.

'I think you have been dreaming.'

'Yes, Granddad.' I smile with relief.

It wasn't a dream, it was a cabbage-chopping nightmare, repeating over and over again what me and Granddad did last night. I didn't want to make Rouladen, but after spending hours cleaning the patio I was so hungry I'd have eaten sprouts! We stood in the kitchen for hours and made stacks of it to go in the freezer. I can still smell it stinking up the whole house.

I rest my head back on the pillow, but my head is still ringing with the *ping* of the notes of the glockenspiel, because somehow he got me playing 'Hoppe, Hoppe, Reiter' last thing before I went to bed. But at least now I've done it I won't have to do it again.

Granddad puts a cup of tea down on my bedside table.

'Drink this,' he says. 'Then we will decide what we will do next.'

'Next, Granddad? Don't I get a rest?'

'Rest? We haven't got time to rest; we've still got seven things to do.' He holds up his list. 'There is too much dew on the grass to cut the lawn, but we could do number one or two. I am not fussy, you choose.'

'Later, Granddad.' I pull the duvet up to my chin. 'I'm going back to sleep.'

'No, you can't,' says Granddad. 'You will be back at school

tomorrow. I want to teach you all these things this weekend. Tell you what, we can choose something quiet and inside. Number one or two?'

'Remind me what was number one, Granddad?' I peer over the duvet.

'How to clean brass!'

'No, Granddad.' I shake my head. 'My arms are still aching from the slabs. What's number two?'

'To teach you the Bavarian Schuhplatter Knee Dance.'

I wince. 'Granddad, I'm not wearing those funny trousers and frilly shirts like I saw on YouTube.'

'Umm . . .' Granddad taps his index finger on his lip. 'Of course, we could always play ch—'

'No.' I put my hands on my head. 'Granddad, I'm not playing chess!'

'Okay,' says Granddad, 'just look at my list and you decide while I make breakfast.'

'Argh!' I slump back on my bed.

Granddad turns out of my room. *This is terrible. Why did he do his list? Why did Mum and Dad have to go away? It's Sunday. I'm not working on a Sunday. Even God took Sundays off.* I glance at the clock again. *Five past eight. Five past eight!* I'm supposed to be asleep and dreaming, not waking up to a nightmare.

11

The Grass Cutters

I stand by the front door, squinting in the sun.

'Ah! There you are,' says Granddad, peering at my fingers. 'Have you washed it all off like I said?'

I show Granddad my hands.

'Umm,' he says. 'You still have some brass cleaner under your nails, but you can wash them again when we've done this.' He points at the lawn of long grass and daisies. 'I am thinking we start here, at our bottom left corner.'

'But, Granddad,' I huff. 'It's so hot and I'm so tired.'

'Then we should get it done before it gets hotter.'

Granddad turns away from me and walks to the corner in his blue gardening overalls. He hasn't worn them since last summer. When Grandma was alive they used to walk around the garden together, pruning the roses, and when she got too ill to do that he used to cut the roses and put them in a vase in their bedroom.

I look across at my house. All the windows are closed and there's an empty space where Mum and Dad's car should be parked. I feel bad for wishing they would come back, because Granddad hasn't looked this happy in ages.

'So, we start here. Come on.' He smiles as he beckons me. 'Oh, can you move the gnomes first?'

I look at Grandma's gnomes, four of them posted like guards on every corner. Me and Grandma gave them names – Boris, Horace and Morris, and the fourth one is called Francke (after Granddad) because he looks grumpy, like he'd never let anyone through the garden gate. I laughed when Grandma told me that. But I'm not laughing now as walk around the lawn picking them off the grass and putting them safely in the flower borders.

'Wonderful,' says Granddad. 'Now we can start.'

I trudge across the lawn to where the grass meets the garden path. Granddad takes a tape measure out of his pocket and crouches down.

'The blade is sixty-six centimetres wide, but we measure in sixty centimetres to allow for the overlap.' He holds one end of the tape against the path and measures sixty centimetres out from it. 'Right, now you put one of your sticks in the ground, right there.'

I look at the two sticks in my hand, joined together by a long piece of string.

'Come on, Felix,' says Granddad. 'It does not matter which one.'

I press one stick into the ground.

'This is good,' says Granddad. 'Now we walk up the other end of the lawn.'

I sigh and look at the mower on the path.

'Granddad, can't we just turn it on and push it like everyone else does?' I point at the gardens around the square. 'It's just grass, Granddad, everyone has got it.'

'Yes,' says Granddad, 'and look what a mess some of them make of it.' He nods at the gardens where the grass has gone bare from people's trampolines or from people parking their cars in front of their sitting room windows like Jake's dad does.

'But at least they don't waste time measuring like we are,' I say.

'Preparation,' says Granddad. 'You should always prepare. Now follow me to the other end – you can hold onto the string as we walk.'

I follow Granddad with the string trailing out behind me. I've seen him mowing the lawn loads of times, but he seems happier and has twice as much energy today. I thought he just got the mower out of the shed, plugged it into the mains and pushed it. But he plans it like he does everything else. My dad says many Germans are meticulous and thorough. That's why they've got straight autobahns and fast cars that don't break down.

'Okay.' Granddad's bending down with his tape measure again. 'Now put the stick in the ground, pull the string tight and tie it to the stick.'

I do as he says and we both stand up.

'There.' Granddad wipes his hands on his overalls. 'A perfect straight line. Now all we have to do is mow it.'

We walk back to the mower and Granddad puts it at the beginning of the line. 'Remember we always start here,' he says. 'This is a1.'

'What do you mean, a1?'

'It will become clear,' he says. 'Now you push the mower, keep

58

it tight against the string and I'll hold the cable so we do not cut it by mistake.'

I put my hands on the mower's handles and pull the yellow controller towards me. My hands start to vibrate as the blade turns. Granddad nods for me to start walking. I push the mower slowly across the grass, keeping the right edge close against the string, just like he said. It's not as much fun as washing the car, but it's way better than playing the glockenspiel.

I reach the end of the lawn where it stops by a rose bush. Granddad reaches across, taps my hand to let go of the throttle and takes over. I watch as he swivels the mower round then turns it off.

'There.' He smiles as he looks down the line I've just mown. 'You have just mown your first file.'

'You mean row,' I say.

'No,' he says. 'I mean *file*. And remember where you are?'

I look around me.

'In the corner by the rose bush?'

'No. This is a8.'

I give him a confused look, kind of the same as the one I pulled when Mr Groves tried to explain Archimedes' principle in science.

'Never mind,' says Granddad. 'I will explain as we go.'

'Granddad,' I sigh. 'Do we have to prepare so much? This is Monkton Park, not Wembley.'

'But we've only just started.'

'Let's do something else. I could go to the shops and get you a newspaper. Or ... or ...' I point across the square. 'Or I could walk Mrs Downes's dog. She's been ill and not walked it for ages.'

'Felix!' Granddad snaps. 'For once just concentrate on the thing you are doing.' He sounds like the teachers at school. 'Now, we turn the mower round and start another file, but see we are also starting a rank.'

'Granddad,' I say. 'I've no idea what you are talking about.'

'Never mind,' says Granddad. 'Listen now, understand later.'

I go to argue but Granddad's already pushed the mower to the end of the lawn.

'This is b1,' he says, shutting the mower off. 'Now I mark another sixty centimetres on the ground.'

'Have we got to do this every time?' I ask.

'Yes.'

'But it'll take ages.'

'Time doesn't matter,' he says. 'Everything has to be right. Every rank has to be straight.' He hands me the tape measure. 'Now you go and do the same at the other end.'

'But, Granddad, pleeease.'

'What? Would you really prefer to do something else?'

'Yes!'

'Something less physical ... perhaps ... che—'

'Nope!'

12

Rebecca's a Genius ☺

*Measure sixty centimetres, move the stick, tie the string, pull the
throttle, mind the cable, push and mow the file. Release the throttle.
Stop. Where are we now?*

a8.

Granddad's voice goes on and on, over and over, like it's stuck
on repeat:

Measure sixty centimetres.

Move the stick.

Tie the string.

Pull the throttle.

Mind the cable.

'Stop. Stop!'

I lean forward and rest my head on the table.

'Felix, what's wrong with you?' Jake rubs my arm like he's trying
to keep me awake.

'It's my granddad,' I mumble. 'He's tiring me out.'

'But he's an old man.'

'I know, Jake, but that's got nothing to do with it.' I lift my head and see Jake munching on his sandwich and Rebecca talking to a girl in Year Nine about *Incredibles 2*, which she saw with her sister at the weekend. It sounds way more fun than Granddad's list. The rest of the canteen is full of the clatter and hiss of boys and girls eating and talking, but I'm so tired that everything and everyone is blurred. I hold out my hands. 'Look,' I say. 'He's been making me do chores all weekend – I've cut stacks of cabbages, scrubbed the garden patio, polished the brass and mowed the lawn.'

Jake laughs.

'It's not funny,' I whine. 'My fingers have turned green and stink of farts! Smell them.'

'Get them away from me!' Jake scrunches his nose.

'But it went on for ever. That's why I'm so tired. I nearly fell asleep all the way through geography and science.'

'I thought you were just daydreaming as usual,' Jake says, munching on his sandwich. 'But why did you do those things anyway?'

'Because they were on his list.'

'What list?'

I sigh. 'The ten things he wants to teach me. And one of them is chess!'

'Chess?' Jake chokes on his sandwich. 'Chess! Only swots play that.'

'I know – that's what I said.'

'Oi, I heard that,' Rebecca says, glancing over her shoulder. 'You know I play.'

'My point exactly,' Jake says and grins.

Rebecca glowers at him. I think of saying I didn't mean her, but she's already turned back to her conversation.

'So.' Jake leans across the table. 'Basically he's getting you to do all the housework now your gran's dead.'

'Well, I wouldn't say—'

'Yeah, that sucks,' Jake cuts in. 'I'd come and help if he wasn't so scary.'

'He's not scary ...' I say. 'Is he?'

Jake holds his hand out and waves it like a balancing scale. 'Well ... Yeah, a little bit. My dad thinks he's ...'

'He's what?'

Jake shrugs.

'What does he think he is?'

'Oh, nothing. He just thinks he's weird because of his curtains and he never speaks to anyone when he goes out ... But my mum said your gran was nice!' Jake says brightly, like he realizes he's upset me. 'Yeah. She really liked your gran.'

'I know.' I rest my head on my arms. Everyone liked my gran. People stopped and talked to my gran. It took her all morning to get to the shops and back because she talked so much. Granddad used to say she was gone so long the bread had turned stale. He'd pretend he was mad with her, but then he'd turn the TV over for her to watch *The Chase*, then I'd put the kettle on for tea. My granddad can be nice too. I wish Jake hadn't said anything about him. It's okay for me to think he's grumpy and it's boring staying with him, but it hurts when your best friend says it. You don't say things that might hurt your friends, like I've never told

Jake that my mum saw his dad kissing another woman behind the little Tesco last Christmas. I wasn't supposed to hear that, but it's not my fault Mum talks so loudly on the phone.

'Felix! *Woo-woo!*' Jake spins his hands around my head like a police siren is going off. 'Come back to Planet Earth!'

I shake myself awake.

'Blimey, Felix, you really are whacked.'

'I think he was trying to teach me algebra. He kept getting me to mow and repeat random letters and numbers, over and over again – a1, b8, d4, h6 . . .'

'Oh,' says Jake. 'That's a weird way to teach algebra.'

'I know, but it must have worked because I can see them all the time – b6, f4, h6 . . . It's like I'm sinking battleships in my head.'

'Well, I guess it's better than sitting in the classroom with Mr Andrews . . . and at least you didn't have to play chess.'

Rebecca turns around, smiling.

'What's wrong with you, Brains?' asks Jake.

'You two,' Rebecca says with a grin. 'Are you really that dopey?'

'No!' me and Jake say at the same time.

'Well, you must be. Did he get you to mow ranks and files?'

'Yes, how did you—'

'And you made squares and gave them letters and numbers?'

'Yes. I just said that.'

Rebecca puts her hand over her mouth. 'Oh, Felix,' she laughs. 'Can't you see what he did? Those letters and numbers are the names of the squares on a chessboard.'

'What?' I narrow my brow. 'They can't be.'

'If you are playing the white pieces, a1 is the square in the bottom left corner. h8 is the—'

'. . . Top right.' My jaw drops open.

Jake facepalms. 'Oh my god, Felix, you idiot!'

'Don't call me that!'

'But it's obvious,' says Jake. 'It wasn't algebra. He was teaching you chess all along.'

'You didn't know either,' says Rebecca, sticking up for me, but I'm not sure she should. How could I have been so dopey to fall for it? My granddad has got me playing chess. Chess. Chess!

'Ah, god!' I screw up my face. 'What am I going to do?'

The table shakes as Jake tries to stop himself laughing.

'It's not funny, Jake.'

'Sorry.' He puts his hand over his mouth.

'There's nothing wrong with chess,' says Rebecca.

'There's nothing right with it either,' says Jake with tears in his eyes. 'Oh god, Felix, look at you. You look like you've seen a ghost!'

'Leave him alone,' says Rebecca. 'You wouldn't have guessed either.'

'I would,' Jake replies. 'But that doesn't matter – look at him, he looks like he's seen a ghost.' Jake puts his arm around my shoulders. 'It's okay, Felix.' He grips me tightly. 'We'll get you out of this.'

'How? This is a nightmare. I saw squares all night. He's brainwashing me. Mum was trying to tell me about her yucky romantic weekend away, but then gave me a weird look when I asked for h2 for breakfast.'

Rebecca tries to stop her laugh spilling out. Jake stares into space.

'We've got to do something,' he mutters. 'We've got . . . I've got it!' His face suddenly lights up like someone has given him ten doughnuts. 'It's easy! Just tell him you'll play chess, but only if he does something you want to do in exchange.'

'But I don't want to play chess!'

'You don't have to. You pick something he'll never be able to do, and he'll say no, and then you won't have to play chess.'

A smile creeps across my face.

'That's brilliant.'

'I know.' Jake beams.

'But what shall I choose?'

'Easy,' says Jake. 'Let's make a list.' He reaches into his bag and pulls out his maths book. 'We'll use this.' He grins. 'Now all we need is . . .'

Rebecca hands him a pen.

'Thanks.'

'Don't mention it.'

'Right,' says Jake, 'just shout stuff. Things you want to do that he'll hate.'

'Zip wire,' I say.

'Good one.' Jake scribbles on his book. 'No way would he be able to climb up a ladder or a tree. What else?'

'Go-karts.'

'Ha, yeah, go-karts. Imagine him going round in his pink car! Anything else?'

I shrug.

'Don't look at me,' says Rebecca. 'I think it's a bit mean.'

I start to think she might be right, but before I can say anything Jake jumps up and shouts, 'Scuba diving!'

'What?' Rebecca stares at me.

'What?' I turn to Jake.

'Scuba diving! I've only ever seen young people do it and you have to be really fit like Bear Grylls.'

'What's Bear Grylls got to do with it? He's a survival expert.'

'Exactly.' Jake puts his hand on my shoulder. 'And Felix, my friend, this is survival!'

13

Guilty ☹

'Scuba diving? Mmm . . . scuba diving?' Granddad's so shocked he's repeating everything like my talking Action Man did after I dropped him in the bath. 'Scuba diving?'

'Yes, Granddad.' I lean against the mantelpiece.

Granddad reads my 'Ten things I'd like to do with Granddad' list for the tenth time. 'Scuba diving?'

'Well, it doesn't have to be scuba diving,' I say. 'It could be a zip wire, or skateboarding, or you take me to Thorpe Park . . .'

'Yes.' Granddad nods. 'I see all these things are here on your list.' He squints at my piece of paper. 'But you have specifically circled scuba diving.'

'I know, Granddad,' I say, staring at Jake's scrawled circle. 'I just thought it might be fun, and maybe after you've done one of these things then we could play . . . chess?'

'Mmm.' Granddad looks at me suspiciously. 'It is a good idea, but scuba diving ...' Granddad puts his cup of tea down on the dining table. 'I'm thinking this is a bit of a strange one.'

'It is, Granddad. But you don't have to do it. Not if you really don't want to. It's dangerous, and it's miles for us to get to the sea ... and of course, it's *really, really* expensive.'

Granddad runs his hand through his hair. 'Yes, and of course I only have my pension ... But I'll think about it. Perhaps I could cancel my subscription for German TV.'

'No, Granddad,' I say. 'Don't do that. You watch it all the time.'

Suddenly I feel guilty. I walk towards the coffee table for the TV remote.

'Would you like me to watch *Wer wird Millionär* with you?' I ask.

'No, I don't want to watch people become millionaires, I am still thinking about scuba diving.'

'But I said you don't have to.'

'I know, but we should find out about it. Look it up on your phone.'

I reluctantly pull my phone out of my pocket. Granddad puts his glasses on and peers over my shoulder.

'Type in "Bristol scuba diving",' Granddad tells me. 'What does it say?'

'Umm ...' I look at the screen. 'Umm ... I think I typed it wrong. It says, "Did you mean: Brickpit Scooba?"'

'Oh,' says Granddad. 'Try it again. B, R, I—'

'It's okay, Granddad,' I say. 'I know how to spell it.' I type 'Bristol scuba'. But it doesn't really matter, because once Granddad sees they don't do scuba diving at the leisure centre and we'll have to travel miles, there's no way he'll—

'There!' Granddad points at the screen. 'Scuba diving.'

'What? No way!' I turn the screen towards me. 'It's at the docks, Granddad!' My voice goes high in panic. 'We can't go in the docks. It's full of boats, and fish . . . and crabs!'

'No . . . No . . . Underneath that one!' Granddad says excitedly, like when Grandma gave him socks for his birthday. 'At Speedwell Baths . . . "Bubble Makers – learn to dive and have fun with all the family." We don't have to take our family, but it will be good fun with just me and you. I don't think we've done anything like that together since Grandma and I took you Cadbury World.'

'I don't know, Granddad,' I say, wishing my phone would die. 'It might be dangerous.'

'Dangerous? No, not in a swimming pool – and they will have qualified instructors, see here. Do that thing with your finger.'

'Scroll down?'

'Yes, scroll down.'

I flick my finger up the screen.

'See, "All lessons are with our master scuba instructor, Mark Slade,"' Granddad reads.

'No, Granddad,' I say. 'I really don't think you should do it.'

I look at my phone in disbelief. There must be some way out of this. I search for something that says the lessons are at five o'clock in the morning or late at night. Or you can't only have one; it's a course of ten and costs five hundred pounds. I'd make something up if Granddad wasn't still looking over my shoulder. *Come on, there must be—*

'Oh look.' Granddad points at the screen and reads, '"Come along on Fridays at the friendly time of seven in the evening. There's a special concession rate for old-age pensioners and children." See.' He smiles at me. 'This is perfect.'

I scan the rest of the website. There has to be something. I have to get out of this. There!

'Ah, no, Granddad!' I show him the screen. 'All health problems must be declared.'

'That is okay. We don't have to tell them about your problem. Besides, it doesn't matter if you can't sit still with scuba diving.'

'No, Granddad,' I say. 'I meant you.'

'Pwah.' Granddad waves his hand in the air. 'They don't need to know about that.'

'But wouldn't that be lying, Granddad? What if you had a giddy spell like you did in Halfords last year?'

'Mmm . . .' Granddad's smile disappears. 'That's true,' he sighs. 'I don't want your dad to stop work to pick me up again . . . Let me think about it, but maybe you are right.'

'Okay, Granddad.' I click off the screen.

He's still not discounting it! I have to do something to take his mind off scuba diving. 'Granddad,' I say brightly, 'is there anything else you want to do now?'

'Well, not really . . .' he says like he's still thinking. 'Perhaps we should just make tea.'

14

Jake's a Genius

(I think)

'So that's it,' whispers Jake. 'We're going to sleep in our tree on Saturday night. Bring a sleeping bag and torch.'

'I'll try,' I say. 'But I might be playing chess if Granddad goes through with the scuba diving.'

'He won't,' says Jake. 'We both know that when adults say they're thinking about it, they actually mean no.'

'I hope so. He had me out on the lawn naming the squares with letters and numbers after tea last night.'

'How did you get into this, Felix?' Jake shakes his head. 'Chess … Chess? My Auntie Laura got me a set ages ago and told me off because I coloured in the white squares with red crayon.'

We both laugh.

'Lads, the film is about to start,' says Mr Keytes.

Me and Jake stop talking. We're in history getting ready to watch a film about the First World War. I try my hardest to behave in history because I like learning about the war, but also because Mr Keytes is cool. He's not like some of the other teachers, who just tell me off or send me to isolation. He actually talks to me. I think it might be because he understands, as he never sits down in class.

The classroom turns dark as Harry Giles closes the blinds. The film starts with a black and white picture of soldiers standing in trenches. I try to concentrate, but it's hard with Jake whispering in my ear.

'He doesn't know we've figured him out.' Jake nudges me. 'Your granddad – he's just letting it drag on until you give in.'

'I hope you're right, if not I could be playing chess for a lifetime!'

'A lifetime!' Jake puffs out his cheeks.

'Yes. That's how long he says it takes to learn it.'

'A lifetime? That's like more than a week, a month, a year!'

'Lads, come on,' Mr Keytes whispers as he crouches down between us. 'You can't be messing around all the time. We need to improve your grades and this should be really interesting for you both, so just try to watch.'

'*I* am,' I say, glancing at Jake.

Mr Keytes moves away.

On the screen, soldiers dig trenches and set their guns on top of sandbags. The classroom booms with the sound of gunfire.

'It might not be so bad,' Jake whispers. 'It might only be a few years if he means his lifetime, not yours.'

'Shush!' I elbow him in the ribs.

On the screen, soldier medics run with first-aid satchels and billycans.

'Felix.' Jake holds his side. 'You need to calm down. It's not going to happen. There's no way he'll go scuba diving.'

'I can't. I really can't.' My chest cramps. I can't tell Jake I hate swimming, that I hate just putting my head underwater. I definitely can't tell him I even wore a raincoat when Grandma took me on the Pirate Falls Log Flume at Legoland.

'Look at me, Felix.'

'What?' I turn to Jake and see his eyes lit up bright in the dark. 'What are you staring at me like that for? It's weird!'

'It's not. I saw a magician do this on TV. He hypnotized a woman and made her rob a bank.'

'But I don't want to rob a bank.'

'I know.' Jake waves his hand. 'Forget I said that, just repeat after me: "My granddad will not go scuba diving."'

'But . . .'

'Repeat, Felix. "My granddad will not go scuba diving."'

I take a deep breath.

'Okay. *My granddad will not go scuba diving. My granddad will not go scuba diving.*'

Jake smiles. 'Feel better?' he asks.

'Sort of.' I let out my breath. 'Thanks.'

'No probs.' Jake smiles then nods at the screen. 'Now all we've got to do is work out how we're going to get one of those Howitzer cannons up our tree!'

I smile and sit back in my chair. Thanks to Jake, it now feels like an elephant has stepped off my chest.

15

SCUBAAAAAAAAAAAAAAAARGH!

'Have you brought a towel?'

'Yes, I brought a towel.'

'And flip-flops?'

'Umm ... No, Granddad, I didn't bring flip-flops. But we don't need them. We're going in the swimming pool, not walking along the beach.'

'No!' Granddad's voice echoes in the changing cubicle next to me. 'In Germany I always used flip-flops, or sandals, just so I didn't catch anything when I was walking around. But here, I brought these ...' A pair of sandals drops like magic into my cubicle. I bend down and pick them up.

'But these are my jelly shoes, Granddad ... Where did you get them?'

'Your grandma kept them after we took you on the caravan holiday in Wales.'

I lean back against the cubicle wall and close my eyes. How did I let this happen? Granddad didn't mention scuba diving for three whole days and I'd thought he'd forgotten about it, but he must have told Mum and Dad last night because it was the first thing Mum mentioned this morning. I told her that I didn't want to go, but she just said she and Dad thought it was great that Granddad was getting out and doing things with me.

I jump as someone knocks on my cubicle door.

'Are you ready?' shouts Granddad.

'I'm coming.' I stand up and try to put my swimming trunks on, but I'm shaking so much my feet won't fit through the holes. The last time I was here, some boys from Year Eight laughed at me because I was clinging onto the side in the shallow end.

Granddad picked me up from school as usual, but my heart dropped into my stomach when I saw his towel and swimming trunks on the passenger seat. I tried everything to get out of it.

I told him I'd only just eaten and might get stomach cramps.

I told him I feel sick.

I've got earache.

I've got a verruca!

I tried all the excuses I used to say at primary school to get me out of swimming, but Granddad ignored them all.

'Felix!' Granddad knocks on the door again. 'You need to hurry,' he says.

'Okay,' I shout. I try to put my foot into my trunks. I can hear the instructor's voice echoing through the changing room, something about being nearly ready, just waiting for two more. That's me and

Granddad. This is going to be so embarrassing. What person signs up for scuba diving when he can't even put his head under water? Everyone is going to laugh at me.

'Granddad,' I shout. 'I don't ...'

'I will go on in,' says Granddad. 'Here is the key for the locker.'

'No, Granddad ...'

The locker key slides under the door.

'Granddad, wait. I don't want ...' I pull my trunks up and flick the latch. It's not too late to catch Granddad; he's bound to want to go to the toilet. I look up and down the changing room for him, but the only person I see is an attendant wearing a red and yellow trackie, mopping the floor. I put my clothes in the locker and run.

'Oi!' the attendant shouts and points at a yellow triangle on the floor. 'Can't you read? No running. Slippery surface.'

'I'm sorry,' I gasp. 'But I'm looking for my granddad.'

The attendant nods at the footbath.

'He couldn't wait.'

'For the toilet?'

'No, for the pool. He went through here quicker than Usain Bolt!'

'What?!' I turn and splash through the footbath and out into the pool.

Granddad smiles at me as I walk towards him. He's standing in a line by the pool next to six other people. They all look at me, but I just look at Granddad. He's wearing a blue polo shirt and trunks that make his legs look as skinny as a chicken's. He's way older than anyone else here. They must be thinking that's a bit weird, but not as weird as his grandson walking along the edge of the pool in red jelly shoes.

'Ah,' says the instructor. 'So this is your grandson, Felix?'

'Yes.' Granddad puts his arm around my shoulders. 'This was all his idea.'

Well, it was Jake's actually.

'Great,' says the instructor. 'Well, I'm Steve, as most of you know, so would everyone else just like to introduce themselves?'

I lean forward and look along the line. A man about Dad's age says his name is Andy, a girl a bit older than me says her name is Isobel, and then there are Jon, Karen, Mark, Josh, then ...

'Francke!' barks Granddad, so loudly it echoes around the pool area.

'Excellent,' says Steve. 'We'll get you all in the water soon, but I just need to run through some important points first.' He turns towards a flip chart where there's a picture of a diver with his hands flapping around and bubbles coming out of his mouth. 'First and most important rule of diving,' says Steve. 'Don't panic!'

Don't panic! I shiver and Granddad glances down at me.

'Are you okay?' he whispers.

I nod.

I never thought we'd actually be here.

Steve tells us how panicking can be dangerous, that if anything goes wrong the most important thing is to remain calm. Then he tells us not to worry, because once we get used to it, breathing under water will become second nature, just like when we breathe fresh air.

I wrap my arms around my body and try to stop myself shaking.

Jake, why did you think of this?

'Okay,' says Steve. 'I'm just going to show you the equipment and some simple tips. This is the mask.' He holds a blue mask up to his face. 'It covers your nose and your eyes, as you'd expect. Now when you first get in the water it may fog up, but all you have to do is let some water in – I'll show you how in a minute ... The next thing to tell you about is the regulator – now contrary to what many people think, the worst thing you can do when scuba diving is hold your breath.'

Let water into your mask? Don't hold your breath? He's teaching us how to drown, not dive. I can't do it. I can't. I look up at Granddad and hope that he's feeling the same, but he's got his fingers over his nose.

'That's it,' says Steve. 'Just blow – that's how you clear your eustachian tube, which is important otherwise the pressure will build and it'll feel like your head is going to explode.'

Everyone laughs except me.

'Felix, did you understand that?' asks Steve.

No. I shake my head.

'Like this,' says Granddad. He clamps his fingers over his nostrils. I do the same. 'Now just blow inside your head. Like when you blow your nose.'

'Okay,' says Steve. 'I'm sure you can't wait to get on with it.'

Oh we can.

'Right, let's have you all in the water. Just walk forward until your toes are gripping the edge.'

I stand still as everyone else edges forward.

'Granddad.' I grab his elbow just as the others splash into the pool. 'We don't have to do this.'

'Don't worry,' he replies. 'I'll be fine.'

You might be, but I'm not.

'Felix, Francke. Are you joining us?' Steve is in the water with a

79

mask pushed up on his forehead and everyone else is treading water while looking at me.

'Of course we will join you!' says Granddad as he edges forward.

I want to pee.

I want to run.

Water splashes over my legs as Granddad jumps into the water.

'Come on, Felix,' says Steve. 'Just you now.'

'Yes,' says Granddad, wiping water out of his eyes.

'Just you now. In you jump.'

'Yes. Just jump.'

'Granddad!' I whisper. 'I never wanted to do this. I thought you'd never do it. All I wanted to do was get out of playing boring chess!'

Granddad smiles down at me. 'You think I did not know?'

'What? You knew!'

Granddad holds out his hand like I'm a toddler. 'Come on,' he says, grinning.

He knew all along and this is getting more embarrassing by the second.

There's nothing for it.

I hold onto my nose and jump.

16

The Army in the Box

The pink shower curtain sticks to my body as the water pours down. I'm at Granddad's trying to wash the smell of the swimming pool away, and the panic of what just happened. Granddad didn't say much in the car, just played music and whistled, but I was too drained of energy to talk anyway. I think Granddad thought I was upset because for the first time ever he stopped at McDonald's and let me get a McFlurry.

I turn the taps off and pick up a pink towel. Even in the bathroom, bits of Grandma are everywhere – pink flannel, pink soap, pink shower cap hanging on the back of the door. If she was here now she'd be telling Granddad off for teasing me and hugging me and telling me to take no notice. But I have to take notice. Mine and Jake's plan was pretty rubbish if my granddad knew about it all along.

I pull on my shorts and T-shirt and walk out onto the landing. I hear the rumble of the TV coming up the stairs as I hang my towel over the banister to dry. It's Friday evening. All my school friends will be on their Xboxes or watching DVDs or going to football or rugby matches or the cinema, and now I've got to stay here and play chess all weekend. But a deal is a deal and Mum and Dad were right, even though I hate swimming, it was good to spend time with Granddad. Especially as he seemed to be enjoying himself.

There's a wooden box on the dining table when I get downstairs. It's shiny and dark brown, with gold lines around the edges and gold hinges and latches.

Granddad sits down and smiles like he's got the thing he most wanted for Christmas.

'I have not seen this for a long time,' he says. 'Your grandma always told me to play, but I have not since . . .' His smile suddenly disappears.

'Since when, Granddad?' I ask.

He flips up the latches and looks at me.

'Since a long time.'

I think of asking why, but from the sad look in his eyes, I don't think I should.

He opens the box and turns it towards me. Inside are brown and white chess pieces, lying on their backs, surrounded by green velvet.

'Aren't they beautiful,' he says, grinning. 'It's a Selenus set, made of bone in the early nineteenth century.'

'Bone?' I squirm. 'Like a skeleton!'

'Ha!' He chuckles. 'These are animal bones, not human.'

'But I'm—'

'Shush.' Granddad puts his finger up to his lips like the chess pieces are sleeping.

'I will show you one,' he whispers. 'This one.' He picks up a white chess piece and lays it gently in his palm like he's holding a butterfly.

'This is a pawn,' he says softly. 'It is a soldier, one of the infantry – sometimes they were peasants, the poorest part of the army. There are eight of them on each side. Do you remember the letters and numbers I gave the squares on the lawn?'

'Just about, Granddad,' I say. 'I think I repeated them enough.'

Granddad smiles. 'Well, all the white pawns start here, on the second rank, from a2 to h2.' He lifts the rest of the white pawns out and places them in a line across the chessboard. 'Most times the pieces are black and white. I will tell you the names of all the other pieces and how they move. Here.' He holds out another chess piece. 'Take it,' he says. 'Feel how heavy it is, and feel the jagged edges on its head.'

I hold the chess piece gently in my palm, and touch the jagged edge with the tips of my fingers.

'It's like a castle,' I say.

'Exactly.' Granddad grins. 'That's what it is, a castle. Except players today call it a rook. It's used to ward off the enemy. There are two of them on each side, and on the chessboard they can only move in straight lines.'

I turn the rook in my palm.

'It's beautiful, Granddad,' I say.

'Really?' says Granddad, surprised.

'Yes, really.' I smile.

'I am glad you think so,' he says. 'It starts here,' he says, taking the rook from me, 'on a1 and the other on a8.' He places the rooks in the corners of the chessboard behind the line of pawns. 'Here,' Granddad smiles, 'let me show you the others.'

Then he picks up a horse and tells me it is actually called a knight because it represents the knights that rode into battle in the cavalry. It can move forward and sideways but only three squares at a time. He tells me there are supposed to be two on each side, but one of them is missing so we will use an old plastic one for a while. I look at the horse. I thought chess was just a boring game where people sat quietly and moved counters, not a game of war with real castles and knights, parts of a medieval army. I think of telling Granddad this, but he's already picked up another piece that looks like BB-8 from *Star Wars*. He tells me it's the bishop. It used to be called the runner and can only move in diagonal lines. Granddad places the white knights on b1 and g1, the bishops on c1 and f1.

'And this is the king,' he says, putting the king on e1 . 'And this . . . this is his queen, the most powerful piece on the board. She can move everywhere. Here, hold her too.'

I hold the queen in my palm. She's got a staff in her hand and a crown on her head. And she has green velvet on the bottom like all the others, which must be to stop them scratching the board.

'Look after her,' says Granddad. 'And she'll look after you.' He takes her from me and places her on d1.

I look at the board. All the pieces actually look like what they are: a real army that I can hold in my hand.

'See,' says Granddad. 'Chess is not so boring. Isn't that better than firing guns on your computer games?'

'But at least I know how to play my games. I'll never be able to play something as complicated as chess.'

'Of course you can.' Granddad nudges a pawn onto the middle of its square.

'No, Granddad,' I say. 'You don't understand. I can't do it even if I wanted to. I can't remember the dates of battles or the names of kings and queens in history, so there's no chance I'll remember the moves that they make on a chessboard.'

'But that is the point,' says Granddad. 'I will teach you.'

'How?'

'Ah.' Granddad's face lights up. 'It's up to me to work out the how. Besides, you already know more about chess than you think.'

'Do I?'

'Of course. You know why I got you to cut the grass, but I got you to do all the other chores for a reason too. When you cleaned the patio you learned how to be prepared and do things in the right order, and when you cleaned the brass you learned how to have patience and pay attention to detail, and when you played the glockenspiel you learned the letters and numbers of the keys and how to play them in the right order.'

'That's crafty, Granddad,' I say.

Granddad touches the end of his nose. 'No point in getting old if you do not get crafty,' he says, grinning.

'So what did I learn when I made the Rouladen? How to follow instructions?'

'Yes, that.' Granddad nods. 'But also I got you to do it because I hate chopping cabbage!' A smile creeps across his face as he reaches out and places all the black pieces on the board. I turn and peer through the tiny slit in the curtains. Jake's bike is propped up against the tree. He'll be up there waiting for me to draw a map of the enemy positions so we can plan an infantry attack over the weekend. Last week—

'Felix!' Granddad raps an envelope against my arm.

'Sorry, Granddad,' I say. 'I was just—'

'I know what you were doing. But you need to concentrate.'

'I'll try.'

'Good, so take this envelope. For now, everything you need to know about chess is in here. Don't read it now. Take it home and put it on your bedroom wall.'

'Great.' I take the envelope. 'So can I go now?'

'No, we've only just started.'

I glance at the clock. 'But we've been here half an hour. I thought that would be enough.'

'Enough?' says Granddad. 'Chess can't be taught in half an hour. What would you rather – me teach you or you read every one of the six hundred pages in that book?' He nods at his giant chess book on the side table.

'Well, when you put it like that.' I grimace. 'Maybe I could stay a while.'

'Wonderful.' He beams. 'Because for some, learning chess can take a lifetime.'

'A lifetime.' My voice cracks as I speak. 'I'm only eleven. If I live until I'm eighty I could be here for like ... sixty-nine years.'

'All the more reason we should get started then. Besides, this is not just about chess – perhaps having the discipline to learn it will help you concentrate more at school, improve your grades.'

'I don't think so, Granddad.' I smile, but I'm not sure Granddad sees me because he's busy turning the board round.

Now I'm sitting behind the white pieces and he's behind the black. 'Come on,' he says. 'This is the first rule you will learn.'

'What's that?'

Granddad nods at the board. 'That it is your move. White always goes first.'

I look down at the board. I know the names of the squares and the chess pieces, but I've already forgotten what they do.

'Granddad,' I sigh. 'This isn't going to work. I'm never going to be able to remember all this – there are too many pieces and too many squares.' I push back my chair and stand up. 'I'm going outside. Mum told me not to stay indoors all weekend because it's good for me to get fresh air.'

'Well, we could always play on the patio,' says Granddad.

'No, Granddad!' I snap. 'You don't get it. I can't sit still all the time. I need to get out. I can't concentrate in here.' I walk towards the door. I feel bad for snapping. Granddad is so excited about me playing chess but I'm scared I won't be able to do it, that my 'problem' will get in the way and I'll let him down.

'Felix.' Granddad puts his hand on my shoulder. 'You cannot just leave when you can't do something. How will you learn? If you do this when you get a job they will dismiss you on the first day.'

'I don't care, Granddad,' I say, walking towards the door. 'I just need to get out of this room.'

The phone rings in the hall.

'Don't answer it,' Granddad says sharply.

'I won't,' I say. 'I never do.'

I don't know why he doesn't just answer it, but he never did even when Grandma was here. She told me it's because he doesn't trust phones, but Dad told me it's not that Granddad doesn't trust phones, it's that he doesn't trust the people on the other end.

The ringing stops.

'Okay,' says Granddad. 'Now where were we?'

'We were just saying goodbye.'

'Yes, we were.' Granddad pauses. I wait for him to say something else, but all I hear is the ticks of the clocks. I look around the room. Not only is it dark but suddenly it feels empty – no picture or sound from the TV, just me and Granddad standing in silence, with Samson curled up on the sofa and Grandma smiling at us from her picture on the mantelpiece.

I want to go outside, but I don't want to leave Granddad alone.

I sit down by the chessboard.

'What are you doing?' asks Granddad. 'I thought you were going out.'

'I was, Granddad,' I say. 'I just thought I might stay a while.'

'Wonderful,' says Granddad, sitting next to me. 'So this one?'

'Granddad,' I say, 'can't we just sit here and have a break?'

'Of course. Of course. We can have a break ... Just for a while.' His eyes sparkle.

I don't think we're going to break for long.

17

Dad, Help!

One board, sixty-four squares, sixteen pieces each – eight pawns,
two rooks, two knights, two bishops, one king and one queen. a1, b1,
c1, d1 ... eight pawns, two rooks, two knights, two bishops, one king
and one queen. a2, b2, c2 ...

'All right, Felix!' Dad makes me jump as pokes his head around
the side of my bedroom door. 'How's it going?'

'I'm okay, Dad,' I say wearily.

'Doesn't sound like it.' He walks in wearing his work overalls with
black oil stains on the front. 'What's up, mate? Did the scuba diving
wear you out?'

'Yeah, just a bit.'

'Well, I think your granddad must have loved it. I just popped in
on him on the way home and he's full of beans. How did you get him
to do it?'

I sigh. 'It's complicated, Dad.'

'Try me. Just don't tell Mum I sat on your bed in these.'

Dad sits down and I tell him how Granddad made a list of chores when all he really wanted was for me to play chess. And then I tell him how I made a list of my own to do in exchange, things I thought Granddad would never do.

'Like scuba diving.' Dad smiles.

'Yeah,' I say, 'but he did it and it's all gone wrong because I've been playing chess all afternoon.'

'What? With Granddad? But he hasn't played since ... since ... Well, he certainly never played it with me.'

'You were lucky then,' I say. 'He's going on about chess so much that I've got black and white squares in my head. I can see them everywhere ...'

Dad laughs.

'It's not funny,' I say. 'Look at all the stuff I've got to learn.' I point at the back of my bedroom door.

'What's this?' Dad turns and looks at the list from Granddad that I've put next to Astro Boy on my door. 'Ten things for Felix to learn about chess.' He scans down the list. 'Blimey,' he says. 'This should keep you quiet for a while.'

I get up off my bed and read the list with Dad.

1. *Do not eat prior to a game. Your blood will go to your stomach to digest food and not to help your brain.*

2. *Never take the easiest path. If you don't play you don't lose and that's wrong. You lose to get better.*

3. *Do not trust the clocks. There may be a power cut and they stop, or they will be slow because of flat batteries, or your opponent may be a cheat. The best clock is the one in your head.*

4. *Do not smile or stare at your opponent (especially if they are wearing glasses). They will think you are not concentrating on your game. Which you will not be.*

5. *Do not fidget or pick your nose or cough or sniff. This is not about chess; it's about good manners.*

6. *It is okay to yawn, but only when it is your opponent's turn.*

7. *Always shake your opponent's hand before and after the game, win, lose or draw. Again, this is good manners.*

8. *Never storm off or let your opponent see you are upset. This is a weakness and anyone who sees it will know what to do when they play you.*

9. *Trust me!*

Dad turns the piece of paper over. 'What's the tenth thing?'

'I don't know,' I say, 'but I'm tired of Granddad's lists. Can't you get me out of it? Maybe tell him the black and white squares hurt my eyes and give me headaches, and it'll affect my schoolwork?'

'I can't, matey,' says Dad. 'You made a deal with him.'

'But ...'

'But nothing,' says Dad. 'To be honest, you should feel honoured

91

that Granddad is talking and doing these things. He never did with me – he always kept it to himself, like he was a closed book. But I will give you one piece of advice.'

'What's that, Dad?' I say hopefully.

'The next time you try to bargain with your granddad, don't.'

'Dad!' I facepalm. 'You could have told me before!'

Dad laughs. 'Maybe you should get some sleep,' he says. 'Sounds like you've got a busy weekend.'

'But can't we do something together, you, me and Mum?'

'No,' he says. 'I'm on call and Mum's taking a double shift.'

'But we never go anywhere.'

'I know.' Dad shrugs. 'I wish it was different, mate. But I don't get to choose my hours any more, now I'm not my own boss.'

'But Jake's dad is taking him to play golf tomorrow.'

'Didn't he ask you?'

'Yes, but I don't have any money.'

'How much is it?'

'Ten pounds, I think.'

Dad winces. 'I'd love to, matey,' he says. 'But Mum would go mad if I gave you money for that when you need other things, like new shoes.' He nods at my scuffed-up shoes by the door.

'It's okay,' I sigh. 'I didn't want to go with his dad anyway.'

'Yeah, maybe not, but at least you've got Granddad.'

'Yeah.'

Dad looks at me, concerned. 'Felix, is this about chess or something else?'

'Or something else,' I mumble as Dad leaves my room.

I wait for Dad to ask again, but he just turns and goes out of the door.

I rest my head back on my pillow. We don't go anywhere as a family any more. Every time I ask it's, 'We haven't got the time ... Mum is working ... Dad is working ... we're both working ... we haven't got the money.' I think the last time we went anywhere was when we went to see *Guardians of the Galaxy Vol. 2* for my tenth birthday and that was only because Grandma paid. I didn't notice how little Mum and Dad were around when she was alive, but now it's like there's a gaping hole every evening and every weekend and the only person trying to fill it is Granddad, which might be okay if he didn't want to fill it with chess.

I roll over and close my eyes ...

18

Our Square Is a Battlefield

*The sun has gone down and the fighting is over. Me and Jake are in our
tree, drinking Coke and surrounded by smoke from the fires around us.*

'That was close,' he says. 'I thought we'd had it.'

'Me too,' I say. 'Lucky you brought the Howitzer.'

*Jake laughs and opens a tube of Pringles. We lean back against
the trunk, Jake stuffs four Pringles in his mouth and tells me he thinks
his family are getting a new car, a brand new white Lamborghini. It's
only got two seats so we won't be able to go in it together, but if I'm
lucky his dad might let me sit in it on the drive.*

*I straighten up and look around the square. Everything is quiet
and still. All the windows are black and all the fires have gone out.
But in the distance I can hear the sound of guns, and the ground is
rumbling under my feet.*

*'Something has happened, Jake,' I say. 'Something has changed.'
I stand up and look around the square.*

'What is it?' asks Jake.

'Shush.' I listen again. More shouting, more people, more footsteps, like a commander and their army marching towards us.

'Come on,' says Jake. 'If we're quick we can escape in my dad's Lamborghini.'

We pick up our bags and scramble down the tree.

'Hurry,' shouts Jake.

'I'm co—'

A light flashes on above us, like a huge spotlight shining from a helicopter.

I stop still. Jake does the same. The shouting gets closer, so close it's like the commander is shouting in my ear. I turn towards the square entrance. An army is marching down the road towards me. I try to run, but my feet are stuck fast. The ground starts to shake and the grass roots pull apart. Underneath is black. Underneath is white. Huge square concrete slabs are pushing through the earth.

'Felix!' Jake shouts above the roar. 'What's happening?'

'I . . . I . . . I don't know!'

'You load the cannons,' yells Jake. 'And I'll get the guns.'

'No! I don't think they'll work. Not against this army!' I point ahead as the army marches on – a row of eight black pawns with two rooks, two knights and two bishops behind them. In the middle, riding on horseback, are a queen and a king.

'Run, Jake,' I shout. 'Run!'

Me and Jake pick up our rifles and run into the dark.

19

Weakness

'So how come you're in here again, Felix?'

I stare at the wall.

'Well, you must have done something?'

'Mr Groves said I hadn't done any of the science work.'

Mrs Ewens leans forward.

'And is Mr Groves wrong?'

'No, but he is an idiot.'

'James, did anyone ask for your opinion?'

'No, but you got it anyway.' James King rocks back on his chair.

'I think maybe you should move,' says Mrs Ewens. 'Over here.' She stands up and walks over to the corner of the room near the door. James King gets up. His bag bumps my shoulder *accidentally* as he passes me. 'Sorry 'bout that,' he smirks.

I stare at the wall. I've been trying to do better in class, but improving my marks and playing chess at the same time is making me tired, especially when I'm having weird dreams about chess like I did last night. I hardly did any work in science and I was even worse when I was in the reading group with Mrs Hudson. Michael was reading and she got annoyed with me when I lost the place on the page. I told her about my dream, but she thought I was trying to get out of reading. I wasn't. I just wanted to get the dream out of my head. It feels like I've been studying chess non-stop for three days, but me and Granddad still haven't played a game. He just gets me to repeat chess information over and over again while he sits in a chair tearing letters and bills into tiny pieces. I love my granddad, but the more time I spend with him the weirder he seems to get – not answering the phone, only watching German TV, even ripping up the wrappers from Samson's cat food.

'So,' says Mrs Ewens, as she sits beside me. 'Tell me what's going on?'

'Nothing,' I say. 'I don't mean to get into trouble. I just do.'

'I know,' she says, leaning closer. 'I know you're not a real troublemaker, but you have to keep trying – you can't keep disrupting lessons by talking about cannons and Lamborghinis.'

I smile.

'Yes,' Mrs Ewens says, smiling back. 'We teachers do talk to each other, you know ... So, is there anything you want to tell me?'

'Not really.'

'Would you like me to chat to your mum and dad?'

'No.' I look at the desk. I don't want Mum and Dad down here. They are way too busy. 'I'll try harder,' I say, looking at Mrs Ewens. 'I'll really try.'

'Good,' she says. 'Because I know you can do this, Felix. We've just got to get you concentrating and, if you do, I think your marks will improve by themselves.'

The bell rings.

'See ya!' James King picks up his bag and walks out of the door.

Mrs Ewens sighs as I stand up.

'Please try, Felix,' she says. 'I don't want you in here all the time like James.'

'I will,' I say. 'So can I go now?'

'Yes.'

I pick up my bag and head for the door.

Jake's waiting for me when I get outside.

'What were you in there for?' he asks.

As we walk down the corridor I tell him about my weird dream. He thinks it was really cool, especially the bit about his dad having a Lamborghini. He says I look really tired, like a walking zombie, and I think that's exactly how I feel.

We walk past the noticeboard, the school office and then turn towards the library. All the time Jake's in my ear talking about the things he did at the weekend. That his dad hit the golf ball so far at pitch and putt that they had to look for it on the road and afterwards they went to Laser Land, which makes me annoyed because we promised that we would wait until we could both go together.

I stop walking.

'What's wrong?' says Jake. 'I told my dad I wanted to go with you, but they had a special offer, kid and parent half price.'

'It's not that.' I nod at the sign on the library door.

CHESS CLUB

ARE YOU INTERESTED IN CHESS?

WE ARE LOOKING FOR NEW MEMBERS

COME ALONG – TUESDAY AND THURSDAY LUNCHTIMES

CONTACT MR KEYTES OR RICHARD PANELL

'Oh, this is a good idea,' says Granddad's voice in my head.

'Felix.' Jake's standing in front of me and follows my eyes to the poster. 'Chess club? You can't be serious.'

I look past Jake into the library. Some boys and girls are writing at the tables in the study area. I lean against the glass and peer down past the book loan desk. Right at the end is Mr Keytes and Rebecca sitting with Chris Price and Leah Gibbs from my year. There are also two boys from Year Eleven, who I've only ever seen when they've been line monitors in the canteen. They're all sitting around a chessboard.

I put my hand on the door handle.

'Felix,' Jake says urgently. 'What are you doing?'

'Rebecca's in there,' I say. 'And Mr Keytes is okay. I was just going to take a closer look.'

'But we agreed, chess is for swots!'

'I know, but . . .' I pause as Chris Price reaches out and moves a chess piece. The others start talking like they're discussing if he made the right move. Then one of the Year Eleven boys says something and they all laugh.

'They don't look like swots,' I say. 'They just look like you and me, except they've got more brains.'

'Exactly,' says Jake, trying to guide me away. 'What would you talk to them about? Who's got the best calculator, or who got the highest mark in science? Come on, let's go.'

I look back through the window. All the players have gone quiet and are staring intently at the board like they're watching an ant crawl across it. Rebecca glances up. I don't know if she's seen me or not because she just looks for a while, like she's thinking, then turns back to the board. I could never sit still and be quiet like that. Maybe Jake is right. I wouldn't have anything in common with them. Sometimes I think Rebecca only hangs out with me because we were friends when we were younger, before she got super brainy. I take my hand slowly off the door.

'Phew,' says Jake. 'You had me worried.'

'I know,' I say, trying to shake the fog out of my head. 'They're all dweebs! I don't know what I was thinking.'

'You were thinking it was a good idea.'

'No, Granddad. I wasn't.'

Jake gives me a strange look.

'What?' I say. 'I'm not going in there.'

'No,' says Jake. 'It's what you just did. You were talking to your granddad.'

'Did I? Was I?'

'Yeah. It's like he's getting inside your head, brainwashing you. Maybe he's a spy. My dad always says he's a bit strange.'

'My granddad's not strange,' I snap. 'And he's not a spy. What does your dad know? He's never even spoken to him.'

'Sorry, didn't mean to upset you.' Jake puts his arm around my shoulder. 'He's not strange. Not really . . . Now let's get some dinner and then we'll go and shoot some hoops.'

'Hoops? What is hoops?'

Granddad, I say in my head. *You're going to have to stop this.*

20

Me, the Knight and the Wardrobe

'So, tell me what you've been doing at school today?' Granddad shouts in from the kitchen.

'Umm ... Not much, Granddad,' I yell back. 'Just the usual things.'

'But what about your marks?'

'Granddad.' I look up from my books. 'Why do you keep asking about my marks? We don't have a test every day.'

'I know, but I like to see if you are improving.'

'To be honest, Granddad,' I sigh, 'you know you said that chess might help my schoolwork?'

'Yes.'

'Well, I wasn't going to tell you, but I think the chess is making my work worse.'

'Worse!' says Granddad. I hear the clink of crockery. 'This should not be. Perhaps we need to make some tweaks.' He puts his tea and my juice down on the table.

'I think it needs more than tweaks, Granddad,' I say. 'I nearly fell asleep in a lesson today because of the dream I had last night. It's making me really irritable. I snapped at Rebecca because she said I should have gone to che—'

'To where?' says Granddad. 'Did you say chess?'

'What? No, Granddad,' I say, trying to cover my mistake. 'Cello, I should have gone to cello lessons.'

'Cello?' says Granddad. 'I did not know you were learning a musical instrument.'

'Um, I'm not Granddad . . . I was going to listen to her.'

'I see,' says Granddad suspiciously. Then he slurps on his tea, all the time looking at me. I stare down at my books.

I don't tell him how I nearly went to chess club, and that Rebecca snapped at me because she *had* seen me at the door and thought maybe I was too embarrassed to go in because I was with Jake. I told her it was nothing to do with being embarrassed; it was just that I didn't want to play chess with brainy people like her. She looked hurt when I said that so I apologized, but I'm not sure she forgave me.

Granddad keeps slurping. I put my drink down and turn the page of one of my books.

'No,' says Granddad, putting his hand on my book. 'Have a break, because I've got a surprise for you.'

'Have you?'

'Yes.' Granddad's face lights up. 'I went into town today and got you a present.'

'You went to town, Granddad? You haven't been to town since Grandma—'

'I know,' Granddad interrupts before I can say the D word, 'but stop talking and open it.' He slides a plastic bag across the table. 'It's a DVD.'

'What?' I say excitedly. '*Spider-Man: Homecoming*? Did Mum tell you I wanted it?'

'No. It is not *Spider Coming*. Just open it and see.'

I reach in and pull the DVD case out. On the front is a picture of the actor who played Spider-Man in the first film I've got, but the writing says something totally different.

'*Prawn Sacrifice*?'

'Pawn *Sacrifice*,' Granddad jumps in. 'I hope you like it. I told the man in the shop that you are only just starting to like chess but you love watching TV.'

'I do, Granddad,' I say, flipping the case over. 'But what's it about?'

'A game of chess,' he says.

'Oh.' I can't help but feel disappointed.

'It's not just any game of chess,' Granddad says brightly like he's trying to lift my spirits. 'It is about perhaps the best match ever, between two of the greatest Grandmasters – Bobby Fischer and Boris Spassky. I thought it would be good for you because you learn visually.'

'Do I?'

'Of course, you learn from that video game you play at home.'

'What, Fortnite?'

'Yes, and in your tree you learn how to be prepared, get resources, head to the higher ground.'

'I didn't think you took any notice,' I say, surprised.

'I do not go round with my eyes shut, you know,' says Granddad. 'And neither should you. Now let's watch the DVD.'

I unwrap the DVD and bend down in front of the TV. I insert the disc and pick up the remote. I'm not sure the film will be as interesting as Granddad says, but it's better than watching German TV. Granddad must be thinking the same because when I turn round he's sitting on the edge of his seat, rubbing his hands.

'Come and sit here,' he says, tapping the sofa seat cushion. I smile to myself. It's like he bought the present for himself, not me, because the last time I saw him this excited and happy watching TV was the last time Germany won the World Cup. In fact it's been ages since I saw him happy full stop.

I sit down next to him and the film starts to play. A news reporter is standing outside a library-like building, and he puts his microphone up to his mouth and says, 'This is the World Championship and Bobby Fischer chose to stay in bed today.'

'Ha,' says Granddad. 'Maybe this is not the best example of a chess player to show you after all!'

I laugh and keep watching. The film switches back to when Bobby Fischer was a young boy. He's sitting in a room playing chess against a man. He beats the man after eleven moves and then the picture changes to Bobby Fischer walking around a smoky dark hall, playing chess with ten men, all at the same time. Each time he pauses to make a move he hits his hand down and stops a clock. As the film keeps playing the narrator says Bobby Fischer was the American chess champion at the age of fourteen and was followed around by reporters and cameras like a film star. I think that maybe being good at chess isn't boring after all. I go to tell Granddad this, but he's too engrossed in the film as a news reporter says something about the match being part of the Cold War between communist Russia and free America.

I lean forward.

'What's the Cold War, Granddad?'

Granddad keeps watching.

I tap him on the leg.

'Granddad, what's the Cold War? Is it a war fought in the winter?'

Granddad pauses the DVD.

'No, the Cold War was when the politicians in the East and West stopped talking to each other. Instead, the Russians in the East and the Americans in the West made their armies and their navies bigger and designed weapons that were larger and more powerful.'

'Like Stark Industries versus Wayne Enterprises?'

'I do not know what that is, but this was a time when everybody thought there was going to be a huge war, with weapons more destructive and powerful than ever before. And they built a wall too: the Berlin Wall. They constructed it overnight.'

'What, an actual wall?'

'Yes, it split my city in half, to stop people in the east of Germany from going to the west.'

'Couldn't people just climb over or walk around it?'

'No,' Granddad shakes his head slowly. 'No, it was far too big for that.'

'What like massive, Granddad?' I hold my arms out wide. 'Like the Great Wall of China?'

'Not quite, but it was one hundred and forty kilometres long with barbed wire on top, so no, you could not climb over. They destroyed all the houses near it and created a wasteland, no-mans-land, where nobody could go. I was on the eastern side, where the authorities, the police, watched everyone like hawks in case they did or said anything against the government. People were scared to go out and even scared to stay in because they thought they were being watched. There were government spies everywhere.'

'Spies? Like in films!'

'Yes,' says Granddad. 'There were lots of ...'

I think of saying 'spies' again because it sounds exciting, but suddenly Granddad's eyes are so watery the TV reflects in them.

'Granddad.' I lean forward. 'Are you okay?'

Granddad looks down at the DVD remote. 'I think ... I think maybe we should just watch the film.' He presses play and the DVD starts again. A reporter talks into a camera. 'And so the 1972 World Chess Championship begins – the battle between Boris Spassky and Bobby Fischer, the battle of defence and attack, but perhaps most of all, the battle between East and West.'

Out of the corner of my eye I see Granddad take off his glasses and wipe his eyes. I want to know more about the Wall, but I don't want to upset him any more.

I lean forward again.

'Who did you want to win, Granddad?' I ask, trying to cheer him up. 'Boris or Bobby? Whose side were you on?'

Granddad picks up the remote and turns the TV off.

'I'm sorry,' he says. 'I think I made a mistake.' But from the look on

107

Granddad's face, I think it was my fault for asking too many questions about the past.

Granddad reaches over the arm of the chair and turns the king on its square.

'Did you want to teach me some more, Granddad?' I say.

'Yes,' he says. 'That would be good.'

'Okay,' I say, standing up. 'But I need to go to toilet first.'

Granddad smiles wearily as I walk out into the hall. 'Oh, Felix,' he suddenly shouts. 'While you are up there, can you bring down the knight? I found it yesterday. It's on the dressing table.'

I stop on the stairs.

'But it's in your room, Granddad.'

'Yes,' says Granddad. 'On the dressing table.'

I walk to the top of the stairs. I've not been in Granddad's bedroom since Grandma was ill. I've never wanted to.

On the landing, I turn the handle and open the door. The room is dark like the sitting room. I reach for the wall and turn on the light. It illuminates Granddad's bed, his flowery duvet and pillows, and the machine that Grandma used to make tea to save her getting out of bed in the morning. I take a step, but it feels like I shouldn't be here. I look across the room and see the knight on the edge of the dressing table in front of the window.

I walk towards it. A floorboard creaks and Granddad's wardrobe door slowly opens. It smells old, like little bits of Granddad's aftershave mixed with Grandma's scent. I peer inside. All I can see is Granddad's shirts and jackets and his long coats, then a flash of something pink. I reach inside and gently pull the hangers apart. Between Granddad's suits are three of Grandma's flowery pink dresses. I thought Mum had taken them all to the charity shop. I remember Grandma was wearing one of them the last time I went with her to town. I kept on at her to take me to McDonald's for a Creme Egg McFlurry and she gave in and had one too. We sat at a table by a window and watched people walking by for ages. She said she would always remember it, and I will too, because my McFlurry tasted of her rose perfume.

As I go to close the door, I spot a box file peeking out between Granddad's shiny shoes. On top of it is *The Little Prince*, the book Grandma was reading when Granddad first met her, and the book she used to read to me. I pick it up and flick through it, see the picture of the little prince standing on a mountain. As I turn each page I can hear Grandma's soft voice reading to me, and the pages seem to smell of her. I swallow hard. I miss my grandma loads. If I read any more I think I'll cry and Granddad will wonder what's wrong.

I go to put the book back but then notice the lid of the box file has slid off. I lift it up. Inside are old photographs of Granddad and Grandma. I pick up a bundle of them and flick through – Granddad and Grandma on a bridge. Granddad and Grandma sitting together on a tram. Granddad and Grandma standing by a huge wall covered in graffiti with soldiers guarding it. Someone who looks like a young version of Granddad, standing next to a small boy in a hall, surrounded by lots of chessboards on tables.

I drop them back in the box and pick up some yellow cards. There's a lot of German writing and even if I could read German I still don't think I could understand it because it looks like it's written in code: 'Vorgart-MFX 8628/76'. In the middle of it is Granddad's name:

'Francke Schopp' and then his birthday: '21/12/1943'. On another card someone has written 'Ministerium für Staatssicherheit' and there's a picture of a red hand holding a rifle. All the cards have the same name at the bottom: 'Commander Steiner'.

'Have you found it?' Granddad shouts up the stairs and makes me jump. 'I'm sure I put it on the dressing table.'

I quickly drop the cards back in the box.

'You did, Granddad,' I yell back. 'I got it, now I'm just going to the toilet.'

I close the wardrobe door slowly and pick up the knight.

21

X + Y = Spy!

The enemy are retreating. Our machine-gun fire has scared them away – we can hear the rumble of tanks as they flee back to base.

It's Friday evening and I'm sitting on the platform. Jake's leaning against the tree trunk, chewing gum.

'So say it again?' he says. 'You found cards . . .'

'Yes. They were a bit like his appointment cards for hospital, only in German.'

'And you found pictures of soldiers.'

'Yes, standing by a wall. I don't know if it was the same one but he told me about a massive wall in Berlin with barbed wire on top and people on one side of it watched the other side like spies. I wanted to know more, but that's all he'd tell me.'

'Mmm . . . weird.' Jake looks across the grass towards Granddad's house. 'It's strange that he never talks about his past, and how he keeps his curtains closed all the time.'

'Jake,' I sigh. 'Please don't go on about my granddad again.'

'I'm not.' He gives me his *I'm innocent* look. 'I'm just saying it's weird. Like the way he doesn't talk to anyone and how he's got into your head so all you talk about is chess. It's like he's brainwashing you.'

'Don't be daft,' I say. 'He's just teaching me.'

'But, Felix, you almost went to chess club today. And that's serious. We can't let that happen again.'

'I won't.'

Jake looks at Granddad's house, like he's thinking of another plan. He'd be thinking even harder if he knew I was seeing chessboards in shop windows and on the back of buses.

'What if he's a spy?' Jake suddenly blurts out.

'What?' I say disbelievingly.

Jake kneels up. 'Your granddad. What if he's a spy?'

'But he's not!'

'But he might be. It's weird that his curtains are always closed. Maybe it's not to stop people looking in, but so he can hide behind them and spy on us.'

'You're being stupid,' I say. 'He's just my granddad.'

'But that's the point,' says Jake. 'He's just a granddad. No one would suspect a granddad. It's a trick – that's how they don't get caught. They are careful and meticulous like your granddad, and they never leave evidence. I saw it on a film once – they shred every piece of paper after they've read it.'

'Well, my granddad does tear paper into tiny pieces,' I joke.

'There! See! Your granddad could be the head of a Russian spy network!'

'Jake,' I laugh. 'For a start he's German, plus I don't think the head of Russian spies would live in Bristol. And who'd want to know what happens at the diabetes clinic or at Lidl?'

'But that would be a brilliant alibi; no one would even think it.' Jake crawls to the edge of the platform. 'We should follow him,' he says. 'Track his every manoeuvre.'

'Jake.' I roll my eyes. 'Not now!'

'I'm not doing it now. I'm going home for tea. We'll spy on him after.'

'I think it's stupid,' I say. 'Anyway I can't, because I'm playing chess with Granddad again.'

'Of course!' Jake huffs. 'How could I ever forget ... We'll do it tomorrow then ... Be here early, and bring your binoculars, because there's only one way to catch a spy.' Jake slides down the rope.

'And what's that?'

'It's obvious,' he says, looking up at me. 'Tomorrow we've got to do some spying of our own.'

22

Pass the Sauce

'So what were you and your friend talking about in your tree?' asks Granddad when I get back to his house.

'What, Granddad?'

'You and your friend. I saw you talking earlier.'

'Oh, nothing,' I say, cutting a piece of meat. 'We were just talking about school,' I add, thinking quickly. 'We're doing a project together in science.' I feel bad for telling Jake about Granddad's past, and from the way Granddad skipped the subject earlier I think he may have had enough of talking about it for one day. 'What are we doing tonight?' I ask brightly, trying to change the topic.

'Learning about chess, of course.' Granddad puts a piece of bread in his mouth.

'Still learning, Granddad,' I say. 'When are we actually going to play a game?'

'I am thinking this will be soon.' Granddad picks up his glass. For a moment I think he might be smiling, but it could just be his lips looking wonky through the water.

'But it's been ages, Granddad,' I say.

I wait for him to reply, but all he does is chew food and drink water. Practising all the time is so frustrating. It's like driving a thousand practice laps in Forza without actually being able to race.

I cut another piece of meat and put it in my mouth. Granddad suddenly puts his knife and fork down and asks, 'Can you see the board?'

'What, Granddad?'

'Can you see the board?'

'Yes.' I nod at the cheeseboard. 'Why? Do you want it?'

'No, not that one! The *chess*board in here.' He taps the side of my head with his finger.

'What?' My jaw drops. 'How did you know I see chessboards?'

'Because I put them there, just like my father did to me. Now, can you see it?'

'But we're eating.'

Granddad raises his eyebrows.

'All right,' I say. I stare ahead at the wall and concentrate. 'Okay,' I say. 'I can see it.'

'And if you look at the table, you can still see it?'

'Yes.'

'Okay. So where is your fork?'

'It's here.' I pick up my fork.

'No. What square is it on?'

'Umm . . . c1?'

115

'Ah. One moment, I am thinking I need to recalibrate my board.' Granddad closes his eyes then opens them again like a shutter on a camera. 'That is better,' he says. 'It's like synchronizing watches – we have to start in the same place. We have to see the same thing. But yes, I see your fork is at c1 . . . And your knife?'

'f1?'

'Yes. This is good. They are your bishops. Now take your plate out of the way.'

I move my plate to the end of the table. Granddad does the same, then hands me the jars of pickle and mustard.

'Put them between your bishops,' he says. 'The pickle is your queen and the mustard is your king.'

I laugh.

'Right.' Granddad hands me a bread roll. 'Rip it into eight little pieces and roll them between your palms, like this.' He shows me a piece of bread that he's now rolled into a ball the same size as a marble. 'These are your pawns! We have eight each.'

I break my roll into eight pieces. This is weird, but I can't stop myself smiling as I place the balls of bread in a line in front of my mustard and pickle.

Granddad does the same on his side of the table, except his king is a jar of strawberry jam, his queen is blackcurrant jam and his bishops are his knife and fork, too. Then he says we should have two sauce bottles each for rooks and two gherkins for our knights.

'Okay,' he says. 'Are you ready?'

'Yes.'

'Wonderful, now I will pick up a piece of bread and move it to e4.'

He moves the bread.

'And what do I do?' I ask.

'You . . . You move your bread to c5.'

I pick up a ball of bread and move it as Granddad said.

'Wonderful,' says Granddad. 'Now I move my gherkin to f3.'

Granddad moves his gherkin. I don't know exactly what we are doing, but Granddad's smile is as wide as mine feels.

'Right,' he says tapping another piece of my bread. 'Now you move this to d6.'

'This is weird, Granddad,' I say.

'I know. This is how my father taught me. With food like this and this exact cutlery, but we didn't waste bread for our pawns. We used coins – Schillings and Marks.'

'Was your dad really good at chess too?' I ask.

'Yes.' Granddad moves his other gherkin to c3. 'My father was one of the best . . . '

'So if he taught you, does that mean you are better than he was?'

Granddad tilts his head like he's thinking about it.

'I do not like to say. But possibly. I won the German youth championship when I was twelve.'

'Wow! You must have been really good! Could you have beaten Bobby Fischer?'

'Perhaps not, but I was okay.' Granddad ignores my question and tells me to move my bread to d6. 'I played all through school,' he continues. 'At first I was rubbish like you.'

'Ha, thanks!'

'Sorry, but it is true. I was very much like you. I couldn't sit still

117

or concentrate. But chess helped me at school and I got quite good at it. Now cut your sausage.'

I cut my sausage.

'Where do I move it, Granddad?'

'Nowhere,' he says, grinning. 'Just eat it!'

I laugh and put the sausage in my mouth. It's so good to be back in the house with Granddad talking about growing up. He's been my granddad all my life, but now it's like I'm really getting to know him for the first time.

I cut another piece of sausage and we keep eating while we move our mustard, bread and gherkins all over the invisible board.

'So why did you stop playing?' I ask as we play.

Granddad stares at the board like he's made a wrong move. I wonder if he's ignoring me, or just didn't hear me.

'Granddad,' I say, leaning across the table. 'If you loved chess so much and you were so good, why did you stop playing?'

Granddad looks up. His face is serious and his eyes are shining. I've said something wrong, but I don't know what. I look down and push the meat around with my fork. I don't like it when he gets upset. Then I hear his voice, so quiet it's almost a whisper.

'What's that, Granddad?'

'I said, can you pass the sauce?' he asks.

I look up. He can reach the sauce. It's on h3, right in front of him. Maybe he can't see it.

'Are you okay, Granddad?' I ask.

'Yes. Why do you ask?'

'Because you're . . . Because the sauce is right there.'

'I know this,' he says. 'But I don't want it. I just want you to move it.'

'To where?'

'hl.'

I pick up the sauce and go to move it, but Granddad suddenly reaches out and holds my hand. I try to move it away, but his grip is so tight my hand is trapped and I can feel him shaking.

'Granddad,' I say. 'What are you—?'

'Shush.' He holds a finger up to his lips. 'Look around.'

I look around the room, at the clock on the sideboard, the picture of Berlin on the wall, Grandma on the mantelpiece, the TV in the corner.

'No.' Granddad shakes his head. 'Not around you, around the table.'

I look at all the pieces on the board. What am I supposed to be seeing? I know the pickle is my queen, the mustard is my king. They are still on their squares – they haven't moved. But my knife and fork have advanced up the board, and so have my breads. What does Granddad want me to see? His balls of bread are scattered in the middle of the table. His sauce bottles are isolated in the corners and his strawberry jam, his king ...

'Do you see it now?' Granddad releases his grip slowly and the blood rushes back to my fingers.

'Have I just won my first game?' My face cracks into a grin.

'Yes.' Granddad smiles. 'You have won your first game.'

23

Astroboy2008

I'm sitting in my room, looking across at Granddad's house. After I won my first game, he told me I'd just learned the Sicilian Defence. It's one of the post popular moves in chess. He told me it is the black chess pieces' response to when a white pawn moves to e4, as well as lots of other things that I can't remember. It was great to finally play and win a game (even if he did make my moves for me), but now I can't stop thinking about the weird things I found in his wardrobe. They might just be something simple. Maybe he collects appointment cards like some of the boys in my class collect Top Trumps. But Jake obviously doesn't think that, because he just messaged to ask if I've still got the walkie-talkies to help us spy on Granddad tomorrow. He's totally forgotten that they got smashed last summer when we put them on our bikes, pretending they were police radios.

My phone buzzes again. *What does he want now?* I pick it up and see a message from Rebecca.

Hey, me and my mum saw yours in town today.

Oops. How did that go?

No. It was okay. Think they might be friends again.

Cool.

Means I can come to yours.

Yeah.

☺

I smile. It would be good if Rebecca could come over more and hang out like we used to. But I'm pretty sure Jake wouldn't like it. He'd say she was in the way, that there weren't any girls in our army or the cavalry. It would be embarrassing if she knew I was still playing 'armies', so I'd just have to make it that she comes over when Jake's doing stuff with his dad.

My phone lights up again.

What are you doing?

Nothing much.

Playing chess?

Done that. Granddad just taught me the Sicilian Defence.

Wow!

Really?

Yes. Means he knows a lot about chess.

Cool.

Now you've had a game, you can play online now.

What?

You can play online. Just like any other computer game. It makes you a better player. Here: https://www.chess.com/play-chess-online

I'm not that interested in playing.

I think you are ☺ Got to go now. Watching Mamma Mia, AGAIN! with Mum.

Okay.

I look at the link. Would it hurt just to click on it once and play a game? Granddad showed me the Sicilian Defence, but I'm not sure I remember every move. Still, I could play another game, and if I lose no one would know. But what would Granddad say? He doesn't trust the telephone – there's no way he would trust a computer. Maybe I'll just go on Fortnite instead.

I reach for my PS4 controller.

My phone lights up again.

Do it, Felix!

?

I know what you're like. You'll go and play Fortnite or something instead.

I laugh. She really does know what I'm like.

I click on the link.

Play Chess Online
Play real players or the computer
There are 53,716 players online now

Fifty-three thousand, seven hundred and sixteen players online! Granddad definitely wouldn't like this. He's so suspicious of people that he wouldn't trust playing with one of them.

I stare at the screen. It's the same as any of my computer games, except instead of Angry Birds jumping around an island it's chess pieces on a board.

I click on a white pawn, move it to f4. The computer moves a black pawn to d5. I move another to g3. The computer moves one to h6. Then a box suddenly flashes up in the middle of the screen.

Glad you visited?
Sign up right now.
It's FREE!

Dad always tells me to check with him if I want to sign up for anything, but this is free – it's not asking for any credit card details. It wouldn't hurt to play just once, just to see if I'm any good.

I click on the box. It asks me for a password username, usually your name and a significant date.

I type in a password, then think of a username . . .

FelixS2019?

No.

Schopp2019

No. They're both too obvious. Jake said chess is for swots. I don't want to be identified.

I type in 'Bobbyfischer1972'.

Sorry, this username has been taken. Try something else.

I look around my room, see the old poster Dad gave me. That's it!

I type in 'Astroboy2008'.

Congratulations, you are now a member!

Select a level.

I press 1.

Computer or find a member?

Computer.

Great. Let's begin!

24

We Spy

'Astroboy2008!' Jake laughs. 'What were the others, Nerdforever? Geek-till-I-die?'

'I knew I shouldn't have told you.'

'Too late now. But did you win?'

'No,' I say sheepishly.

'What? You got beaten by a computer. Which level did you play?'

'How do you know there are levels?'

'There must be levels,' he says. 'It's like any computer game.'

'Oh . . . yeah.'

'So which level was it?'

'Umm . . . one.'

'Ha!' Jake laughs. 'I told you chess was a bad idea. You best give up right now.'

I think maybe Jake is right. I should never have played. Granddad said I wasn't ready, but maybe I'll never be ready.

'I might ask Granddad if we can switch to draughts,' I say.

'Shush . . .' Jake waves his hand in the air. 'One second.' He trains his binoculars on Granddad's house. 'I thought I saw someone come out, but it's just Mrs Flower nosing again.'

'Jake,' I sigh, 'can't we just stick to playing pretend war with our armies?'

'No, this is much more fun . . . And keep watching, you know what spies are like; they can disappear into thin air.'

It's Saturday morning. I didn't want to go to Tesco with Mum and Dad. There was nothing else to do, so I reluctantly joined Jake to scope Granddad through our binoculars. I'm cold and my arms are beginning to ache. We watched the postman deliver letters around the square. And we watched Mrs Flower take her dog for a walk. And we watched a white van drive around the square, deliver a huge parcel to number forty-eight and then drive out again. That's all that's happened in over an hour. Jake made spying sound so exciting, but it's more boring than watching the news on TV.

'Jake, this is pointless,' I say. 'Let's go and play Fortnite at mine.'

'No, we have to be patient – something will happen soon. Spies don't stay in all day. Now tell me what the cards in his wardrobe were like again.'

I take my binoculars down, but Jake's are still trained on Granddad's house.

'I told you, they had a symbol like a hand holding a rifle, and I remember seeing the name Commander Steiner.'

'Commander Steiner. Who has a name like that?' asks Jake. 'Hang on! Felix! Felix!' He waves his arm at me. 'Pick up your binoculars. Your granddad's just come out!'

I lift my binoculars and scan across to Granddad's house. The front door is open and Granddad's walking around the garden in his dark suit, which he hardly ever wears.

'He's checking no one's watching. Now he's bending down,' Jake whispers like a snooker commentator. 'What's he doing? Wait. He's picking something up.'

'Yeah, it's just dog poo, Jake.' I sigh. 'He checks every morning.'

'But we don't know that. It might just be an excuse to get outside and see what we're all doing, or check the wires to his surveillance cameras.'

'He hasn't got any surveillance cameras.'

'No, then what's that? Check the lamppost outside his house.'

I scan left until I see the concrete pole sticking out of the ground.

'It's just a lamppost,' I say.

'No, it's not the lamppost,' Jake says urgently. 'It's what's attached to it.'

I track up the lamppost and see the grey camera that got put up there while we were at school last week.

'See,' says Jake. 'Told you.'

'But that's just the camera the council put in to stop people spraying graffiti on people's fences and breaking into cars!'

'That's what they want us to think.'

I take the binoculars down. Jake's looking at me bug-eyed.

'Spies get everywhere,' he says. 'I looked up on the internet what your granddad told you. There really was a wall.'

'I know,' I say. 'He wouldn't lie to me.'

'Okay, he wouldn't, but then I looked up the spies. There was a secret police in Germany, where your granddad comes from. They were called the Stasi and they went through people's bins, looking for evidence that people were working against the police or the government. They got everywhere, bugged people's phones and TVs, and they tortured people and put them in prison.'

'What's that got to do with my granddad? He'd never torture people.'

'Maybe not, but didn't you say he hates using the phone and rips up every single piece of paper?'

'Yes, but . . .'

Jake kneels up. 'Look, he's going out. He's been and got his hat and coat and now he's locking his door. Come on!'

'Where are you going?'

Jake grins back at me as he crawls across the platform. 'To follow him of course!'

'But he'll only be going to the shop to get some bread or to meet his friends at the GFG.'

'Then we'll follow him there.'

Granddad puts his hat straight then closes his garden gate. Jake slides down the rope.

'Come on,' he whispers urgently. 'We don't want to lose him.'

'Jake, this is ridiculous.'

'So? It's better than sitting up there all day.'

I laugh as I grab the rope. Jake's taking this way too seriously, but I can't stop myself from following him.

At the bottom we hide behind the tree and watch Granddad turn down the alley that leads out to the main road.

'On the count of three.' Jake holds up three fingers. 'ONE, TWO, THREE!'

We scuttle across the grass like we've seen marines do in films.

When we reach the fence by the alley, we crouch down. Granddad is now at the other end, wearing his long grey coat. He looks left then right.

'He's looking for his accomplices,' whispers Jake.

'No, Jake,' I say. 'He really isn't. I think he's just crossing the road.'

A bus passes in front of Granddad. He looks left and right again, and then crosses to the other side. Me and Jake run down the alley. At the end we stop and crouch behind the green box that contains all the wires and fuses to the telephones on our estate. We peer over the top and see Granddad walking towards the row of shops.

Jake points to a white van parked outside them.

'We'll hide behind that,' he whispers. 'I'll go first, you follow.'

Before I have chance to nod he's already gone without even checking to see if the road was clear first. This is mad.

Jake reaches the white van. I look along the row of shops and spot Granddad going into the florist's. The road is clear, so I run across and join Jake behind the van.

'This is so cool,' he grins.

'Jake,' I say. 'This is stupid. He's only come out to buy flowers.'

'Yeah, but that's what spies do. It's like a secret code so they know who each other are – some wear hats or carry newspapers, or . . .'

'Flowers.'

'Exactly.'

Granddad comes out of the shop carrying a bunch of pink flowers.

'And they can hide stuff in there too, like tiny cameras in the petals, and even poison in the stems.'

'Jake. You're making it up.'

'I'm not! There was a Russian man who got poisoned by the tip of an umbrella. I found it on the internet when I was looking up stuff about your granddad ... Anyway, he's getting away from us. Come on.'

Granddad crosses the road by the kebab shop. Me and Jake sneak past the newsagent and the florist until Jake suddenly stops and holds up his hand. Granddad is talking to a man outside the chip shop – one of his friends from the GFG. They walk together. Me and Jake track them to the bus stop and crouch down behind a car.

'Jake,' I say. 'This is pointless; they're just talking like everyone does.'

'That's what spies do,' Jake whispers urgently. 'They look like everyone else so they blend in.'

Me and Jake move onto the pavement as a bus hisses by. The man gets on but Granddad doesn't, he just glances back down the road towards me and Jake.

We jump into the estate agent's doorway.

'Do you think he saw us?' asks Jake.

'I don't think so,' I reply. 'He can't see us in our tree and it's about the same distance.'

'Cool.'

Me and Jake poke our heads around the doorway. Granddad is walking away from us and he's waving at his friend on the bus as it passes him by. Then he turns down the road that leads to the park.

Granddad hasn't been to the park for ages. We used to go all the time when I was little. He'd carry my bike and Grandma would come too and I'd cycle around the botanical gardens. But why's he going there now?

We run down the pavement and into the park until the path forks. We look left and right but all I can see is a man jogging and a woman bending down and talking to her child in a pushchair. Jake holds his arms out wide.

'Where did he go?'

I shrug.

'See, Felix,' says Jake. 'I told you that spies can vanish into thin air.'

We both spin around but I can't see Granddad anywhere.

'We can't have lost him,' I say. 'He can't run quicker than us when he's seventy-two. Maybe we should just go home.'

'Home?' says Jake. 'You're joking. It's just getting interesting. Come on. Let's split up. You go that way towards the pond; I'll take the path to the play area. Okay?'

'Okay,' I sigh and hope that Jake will lose interest soon.

'Text me if you find him.' Jake holds up his phone. 'And if we don't, meet me on the other side.'

I nod as Jake turns away towards the play area. For a moment I watch him as he crouches down and creeps along the path. Every once in a while he stops and hides behind a bush, peers out, then moves on. It's like he thinks he's in the special forces.

I turn along the path towards the pond, but I don't bother hiding because it's getting silly now.

My phone vibrates in my pocket.

Anything?

132

I look around the pond.

Nothing. Just ducks.

Keep looking. Gotta be here somewhere.

I walk on around the pond, and then over the bridge that leads to the exit. A man in a dark coat enters the park. For a moment I think that it's Granddad, but this man is taller and is smoking a cigarette.

Jake emerges from a bush in front of me.

'Don't know where he got to. He could be anywhere.'

'Maybe he just went back home like we should,' I say.

'Or the toilets,' says Jake. 'I didn't check them.'

'He does go to the toilet a lot,' I say, 'but he doesn't go for twenty minutes.'

'Unless he is thinking that someone is following him, Felix!'

I jump at the voice. Jake looks at me, bug-eyed.

We turn around slowly.

'Granddad,' I say. 'Where did you come from?' My heart beats like he's caught me at the biscuit tin.

'I am thinking the same thing.' Granddad looks at me sternly.

'We were just ... We were just ...' I glance at Jake, thinking, *Help me out!*

'We were just walking,' says Jake.

'Yeah, we were just walking.'

'And watching you, because we think you might be a spy.'

What? No, Jake!

'A spy?' asks Granddad.

'Jake.' I glower at him. 'Stop!'

'But you think it as well, Felix. It was you who said he might have a microphone and a camera hidden in those flowers.' Jake points at the bunch in Granddad's hands.

Granddad frowns at me. 'Is this what you are thinking, Felix? That I am a spy?'

'It's just pretend, Granddad,' I say. 'A joke.'

'A joke?' Granddad steps towards me. 'You think this is funny? You do not know how bad what you're saying is. Especially today.' His eyes sparkle as tears gather in his eyes. I glance at Jake, but he's looking at the ground, like he's been told off by Mr Mclugash.

'Granddad—'

'No.' Granddad shakes his head. 'I am thinking that we should not talk for a while.'

'But, Granddad.' I walk after him. 'Granddad, please stop ... Jake didn't mean it. I didn't mean it. Please let me explain. It was just a game.'

Granddad ignores me. He's so upset that it's useless me saying anything. I stop walking and watch as he reaches the end of the path and turns out of the park exit.

Jake arrives by my side. 'Don't worry about him, Felix, He's just upset because we've blown his cover. Now he's off to—'

'Jake, don't!' I snap.

'What? I was only saying—'

'And I said, don't!'

25

What Have I Done?

'I don't know. He just said he couldn't pick Felix up tomorrow, and didn't think he could for the rest of the week.'

'Has he got doctor's appointments?'

'No, not that he said. He just didn't seem himself. It's like he's too upset to see anyone. Maybe I should have tried harder to get him over for dinner. Felix,' Mum adds, looking across the dining table at me. 'Have you noticed anything wrong with your granddad?'

'No, Mum,' I say, nearly choking on my runner beans. 'He was okay the last time I saw him.'

'Only you never went over to play chess with him this afternoon,' says Dad.

I shrug, then push my food around my plate. It's been an hour since I upset Granddad and my stomach is so chewed up with guilt that looking at food makes me feel sick. I sense Dad looking at me like he does when he's trying to figure out if I've done something wrong at school. I cut a tiny piece of Yorkshire pudding. Out of the corner of my eye I spot Dad slowly putting his knife and fork down.

Ah no. Here it comes.

'Felix,' he says, leaning forward. 'Are you sure you don't know what is wrong with your granddad?'

Me and Jake told him he was a spy.

'No, I don't.'

'Only you seem pretty quiet, and you're not eating much.'

Neither would you if you'd done what I just did.

'You know you can tell us if you do,' Mum chips in.

'I said, I don't!' I push my plate away. I feel so guilty about Granddad that my throat aches like the Yorkshire pudding is jammed in it.

'Felix,' says Mum. 'Where did that come from? We're only concerned about your granddad.'

'Well, so am I! And I said I don't know what's wrong with him. Okay!' My chair screeches across the floor as I stand up.

'That's right,' says Dad. 'Kick off, like you always do.'

'Mark!'

'Well, it's true.'

'Felix,' says Mum. 'Just sit down. We can't afford to waste food.'

'Yes,' says Dad. 'You can't keep running off when things get tough.'

'Shut up!' I shout. 'Both of you, shut up! Shouldn't you be at work or something?' I storm out of the kitchen into the hall. I hate what I did to Granddad, and seeing him upset. If Mum and Dad find out they'll go mad. I swing round the banister and run up the stairs. Dad's feet thud behind me.

136

'Leave him, Mark,' shouts Mum. 'I'll talk to him after he's calmed down.'

I run across the landing to my bedroom. I wish I'd not listened to Jake. I wish I'd never gone into Granddad's bedroom and looked in the box. Why did I look in the box? I slam my bedroom door behind me. I've shut Mum and Dad out, but I can't shut Granddad's hurt look out of my head.

It must be ten minutes later that the front door clicks open. I walk over to my bedroom window. Dad's striding across the square towards Granddad's house. He didn't get an answer out of me, so he's going to ask him. Granddad's curtains are closed like they always are. I hope that he's gone to bed early, that he won't be able to hear Dad knocking on his door. That way Dad won't be able to talk to him until tomorrow and by then everyone might have calmed down. Maybe I could do something really good at school, try to concentrate and come top in a maths test, or read a really long passage out loud in English. But I have more chance of scoring the winning goal for Bristol Rovers at Wembley than doing any of that.

Dad pushes Granddad's gate open and walks up the garden path.

I pick up my binoculars and watch Dad knock on Granddad's front door.

Please don't answer.

Please let the TV be up too loud.

Dad steps back onto the grass and looks up at Granddad's bedroom window.

Yes, he's in bed. We can all go to bed. And when we wake up in the morning this day will be a dream, have never happened.

Granddad's sitting room curtains twitch.

It's the wind.

It's Samson trying to catch a fly.

The curtains close. Dad steps onto the garden path as the front door slowly opens. I try to focus in on Granddad's face, but he's standing too far back from the door. Dad steps inside and they start talking.

My phone buzzes on the table. I glance across. Jake's name flashes up on my screen.

Why's your dad gone over there?

I look across to Jake's house. All the windows are lit up except for the one in his room.

I pick up my binoculars and see him looking through his right back at me. I message him.

Jake, don't you ever just watch TV?

Not when there's a spy in our square.

He's not a spy. Didn't you see how upset he was?

I throw my phone onto my bed and scan across the square. Dad closes Granddad's gate, then waves to him. Granddad waves back and closes his door. Dad's got a confused look on his face like when he was trying to work out how to fix our washing machine. I walk over to my bedroom door and press my ear against it.

I hear the front door open, then the mumble of my parents talking in the kitchen, but I can't make out what they are saying. I gently twist my door handle and creep out onto the landing.

'He looks awful,' says my dad. 'I've not seen him look so upset. Not since Mum died.'

He looks awful. Never seen him so upset.

My heart thuds in my chest.

'But he's been doing so well ever since we suggested he saw more of Felix. He's been going out more. He loved the diving,' says Mum.

They suggested he saw more of me? What about them going away last weekend for a break? Was that just a plan to get me and Granddad together? But why?

I creep closer.

'Thing is, I think it was working,' says Dad. 'Like you said, he's been getting out more and Felix has actually been interested in something for once, although I'm not sure he really likes chess.'

'It doesn't matter, at least he's been doing something other than sit in that tree, but now your dad's not eating and Felix is up crying in his room. Something must have happened.'

'I know, but Dad wouldn't say. He's just looks so depressed again, sitting in that dark room staring at the TV. I hope he doesn't go back to how he was after Mum died.'

My heart beats so fast that my pulse beats against the banister. Granddad has been depressed since Grandma died? I knew he was missing her, but I thought he was just being tired and grumpy.

When I reach the bottom stair I turn and see Mum with her back to me, talking to Dad.

I edge down the hallway.

Dad, I'm sorry. I told Granddad he was a spy.

I spot Dad sitting at the kitchen table with his head in his hands.

'Dad . . .'

Mum spins round. 'Not now, Felix,' she says, shaking her head. 'We're worried about your granddad.'

'Yes, I know, that's who I want to talk—'

'Felix!' Dad snaps. 'Like Mum said, for once this isn't about you. It's your grandma.'

'But she's gone.'

'Yes, exactly, and we all forgot – it was a year ago today!'

'What? So that's why Granddad was at the florist. He was going to . . .'

Mum gives me a weirded-out look. 'Felix, what *are* you talking about?'

'Nothing . . . Nothing . . .' I say, backing away into the hall. 'Nothing.'

I think of running out of the front door and across to Granddad to explain. But Mum says he's too upset to see anyone, and that would especially mean me.

I run up the stairs into my bedroom.

I've been so stupid.

I try to get my breath back and look out of the window. Outside it's now so dark that all I can see is the silhouette of our tree and the lights shining from the neighbours' windows, except for Granddad's. He's probably sitting in his chair in the dark like Dad said.

My phone buzzes on my bedside table. I pick it up and try to read the message, but the writing is blurry. I wipe my tears on my sleeve.

Did your granddad tell them what we did?

He was taking the flowers to Grandma's grave!

Oh . . .

Now go away!

I drop the phone and fall face down on my bed.

26

Tipping Point

I'm in geography sitting next to Liam because Jake's in a different set, but I wouldn't want to sit next to him even if he was here. He sent me another ten texts last night, asking me what was wrong, why was I taking things so seriously because he thought it was just a bit of fun. But it wasn't fun. It was one of the worst days of my life.

'So,' says Mr Fields, pointing at a diagram on the board. 'This is longshore drift; this is ...' My mind zones out. He says something about the sea bashing the rocks on the coastline, breaking them into pebbles and depositing them somewhere else along the coast, but the only thing being eroded is my mind. I can't stop thinking about Granddad sitting at home on his own.

I look out of the window as the traffic passes by. I wish Granddad would drive by right now in his pink car. I'd run through the gates after him and apologize properly for what I did. Why was I so stupid to go along with Jake's idea? How could I have ever thought Granddad was a spy? He was just taking Grandma flowers. And what makes it even worse was that I didn't even realize it was a year ago she died. How could I forget the day I lost the most important person in my life? I rest my head on my arm.

Mr Fields says something about a good example of longshore drift is a place called Slapton Sands in Devon and behind me I hear Sarah Fox say she went there on holiday.

I stare at the board. Everything is getting jumbled up in my mind. Last week all I was thinking about was chess and the whiteboard was full of black and white squares, and now it's just blank. Last week I could hear Granddad's voice in my head, and now all I hear is fuzz.

I close my eyes and wish they would come back. I wish I was sitting at the table playing chess with the bread again. I never thought I'd wish that. It was sneaky that Mum and Dad planned for me to spend more time with Granddad, but I have to admit I was enjoying it and I think he was too. He'd actually started to smile, and he went to town for the first time since Grandma died. I might be missing seeing the black and white squares, but I think I'm missing Granddad way more.

I stare at the whiteboard until it goes blurry at the edges. I can't cry in school. I can't.

'Felix!'

I jump.

'I asked if you are listening?' Mr Fields is standing right in front of me.

'Yes,' I say, trying to scramble back to the room.

'So what's the process called when the rocks are moved along the coastline?'

I shrug.

'Come on, Felix. No?'

I shake my head.

'Anyone else?'

'Transportation, sir.'

'Yes, Liam. Transportation.' Mr Fields glances at me. 'Got that, Felix?'

I nod and look at my desk. I wish I could get transported out of here.

My body is moving but I don't know who's moving it as I walk down the corridor. My head is full of noise as the boys' and girls' shouts echo off the walls, but above them I hear someone yelling my name.

'Felix! Felix!' Rebecca taps me on my shoulder. 'Felix, what's wrong?'

I open my mouth, but all that comes out is air. I look up and down the corridor, anywhere but at Rebecca. I swallow hard.

'Felix.' Rebecca rubs my arm. 'Tell me what's wrong. You were so quiet in class.'

I shake my head. I feel bad not answering her, but I've got a lump in my throat. I've already lost Grandma. I don't want to lose Granddad too.

I turn and walk away.

'Felix, just tell me what it is.' Rebecca walks alongside me. 'You've been acting weird all morning and Jake says you didn't wait for him to walk to school. Felix!'

'I'm sorry,' I say. 'I don't want to talk about it … It's just my granddad …'

'Oh, god.' Rebecca puts her hand up to her mouth. 'Is he dead?'

'No, but he might as well be. He doesn't want to see me again.'

'Why?'

I take a deep breath and tell Rebecca everything – how me and Jake followed Granddad through the park, how Jake told him he was a spy when all he was doing was putting flowers on Grandma's grave, and how now he won't talk to me any more. I pause and wonder what Rebecca is thinking, that maybe she thinks I was silly to follow Jake's plan, or she's even mad with me. But she just smiles kindly and says she thinks it'll be okay because her mum and her nan didn't talk for two years, but they get on like best friends now. I tell her that I know she's only trying to help, but to me two years without talking to my granddad feels like a really long time. I tell her it's not just that, that I'm missing Grandma, that I'm missing Mum and I'm even missing chess. Then she smiles and I look at the ground until she says, 'Felix, it's okay to be upset. Sometimes you don't miss things until they are gone.'

'But then it's too late,' I say.

'No, it's not.'

'I think it is.'

'Look.' Rebecca puts her hand on my arm. 'Why don't you come to chess club with me? You might not be talking to your granddad, but at least you can play chess.'

'No,' I sigh. 'I don't think so.'

'Chess club isn't as bad as you think.' Rebecca smiles. 'There's Richard – he's the club leader and is a bit of a twerp – but Chris, Tom and Leah are okay. We're all at different levels, but we still have good games. And Mr Keytes helps run it. You like him.'

Playing chess is the last thing I want to do, but I need to go somewhere to calm down. I start walking with her. Maybe the next best thing to being with Granddad is to play chess.

We turn at the end of the corridor and stop. Jake's running towards me with a huge grin on his face.

'Hey, Felix,' he shouts. 'Where were you this morning? And why aren't you replying to my texts?'

'I'm not talking to you,' I say.

'What? Because I said your granddad was a spy? It was just a bit of fun.'

'But it wasn't,' I say. 'Not for me, and definitely not for my granddad.'

'Oooooh,' says Jake. 'Somebody's stroppy.'

I stare at Jake. Feel my fist ball. My heart is jumping, even though I don't know what will happen next.

'We need to go, Felix.' Rebecca tugs my arm, like she senses my anger. 'Or they'll start without us.'

'What? Where are you going?' Jake asks.

'Chess club,' says Rebecca.

Jake laughs. 'Felix, are you serious?'

'If it means getting away from you.'

'What?' Jake holds out his arms. 'Felix, I told you, the spy thing with your granddad was a joke.'

'A joke!' My anger snaps inside me. I push Jake up against the wall.

'Wow, Felix!' He laughs like he thinks I'm messing around. 'I surrender. I surrender.' He holds his hands up in the air.

'Fight.'

146

'Fight.'

'Fight.'

A group of Year Eight boys have suddenly surrounded us.

'Ha!' says Jake. 'We're not going to fight. We're best—'

'Punch him.'

'Knee him.'

'Fight.'

'Fight.'

'Fight.'

'Ha!' Jake laughs. 'Tell them, Felix, we're best friends.'

'Were!' I say.

'Fight!'

'Fight.'

Jake stops laughing. My head is so close to his, our noses are nearly touching. Someone pushes me in the back. I fall forward. My head bashes into Jake's face.

'Fight.'

'Fight.'

'Fight.'

Jake puts his hand up to his nose. For a moment I think he's going to punch me. I wrap my arm around his neck and we fall to the ground.

'Fight. Fight!' We're scrapping on the floor. My heart thuds as blurred faces look down on me.

'Fight. Fight!' Jake's by my side. I kick my legs, flail my arms . . .

'Get off. Get off me!' I roll over. Everything is blurry and I'm moving in slow motion. 'Get off me!'

'Fight. Fight!'

I can't breathe. I can't breathe.

'Okay, that's enough. That's enough!'

A pair of brown shoes. Mr Keytes's voice. He grabs me by the arm and pulls me up.

'It was . . .'

'It was . . .'

Me and Jake stare at each other, trying to catch our breaths.

'Okay, Year Eights, get on your way, there's nothing to see here.'

Jake's nose is bleeding and his eyes are watering.

I gulp for air.

Mr Keytes puts his hand on my shoulder, the other hand on Jake.

He looks at me.

Then looks at Jake.

'You two! What on earth's going on? You're friends!'

'I know.'

'I know. I . . . I . . .' That's me starting to cry.

27

That Kid

The cars and buses are hissing by me as I walk home from school in the rain. Out of the corner of my eye I can see boys and girls glancing at me, talking about me, snatches of conversation about me . . .

'Is that the kid who had the fight at lunchtime?'

'Is that the kid who ran out of school crying?'

'Is that the kid whose Granddad picks him up in a pink car?'

Yes, I'm that kid. I'm that kid who had a fight with his best friend and is now walking home on his own.

Because Jake ran off as soon as we were let out of the Isolation Room. We were in there all afternoon, staring at the wall. I was hoping I'd see the chessboard squares and hear Granddad in my head, but the wall was blank and the only voice I could hear was Jake's as he put his head around the side of the cubicle and said, 'I was just wiping blood from my nose. Felix, I wasn't going to hit you!'

Mrs Ewens told him to be quiet, that we were both in enough trouble as it was. That's when James King said, 'What were you fighting about? Who got to ride shotgun in your granddad's pink car?' He laughed when he said that and Jake told him to shut up. Mrs Ewens said we should all be quiet. Me and Jake have got to see Mr Hunt, the Head of Year, tomorrow.

As I turn the corner I look towards the petrol station. For a moment I think I see a flash of pink car, but it's just a delivery truck with pictures of puppies and pink toilet roll on the side. Granddad still hasn't forgiven me. Why would he come and pick me up when he doesn't even want to see me?

I stare down at the pavement and don't look up until I get home.

There's a note from Mum on the kitchen table when I get in.

> Felix There's a pizza in the freezer. Put oven on number 8
> and cook for 15 minutes. Don't forget to turn it off.
>   I'll be home around 7.
>   Love Mum
>   PS We'll sit down and talk soon ☺

I push the note away. It's too late to talk now. She's going to be so mad with me; the last thing she needs after finishing work is to come home and find out I've had a fight.

When the pizza is done I carry half of it up to my room. My duvet is all scrunched up like I left it when I rushed out this morning, my PS4 is humming where I left it on and there are little Post-it notes with some of the chess moves Granddad taught me stuck on the poster of my times tables.

I sit down on my bed and see Granddad's chess rules on the back of my door:

Do not eat prior to a game ... Never take the easiest path ... Do not trust the clocks ... Do not smile or stare at your opponent ... Never storm off or let your opponent see you are upset ... Trust me!

I turn and look over at Granddad's house. *Trust me.* Granddad said trust is a two-way thing, but will he ever trust me again?

I stare at his sitting room window; remember cleaning the brass, scrubbing the patio, cutting the lawn.

I'd even cut the cabbage again if it meant I could hear Granddad's voice. I try to imagine it now.

'Pick up the stick.'

'Measure sixty centimetres.'

'Pull the string.'

'Put the stick back in.'

I imagine the sun burning down on my head.

'This is a1. This is h8. This is b1. This is g8.'

'This is ... This is ...'

Granddad, I miss you.

I wipe my eyes on my sleeve.

My phone buzzes on the table. I pick it up.

Hey, Felix, are you okay?

We're not supposed to talk.

This is text. Ha!

Are you still mad at me, Felix?

Are you?

I'll see you tomorrow, yeah?

Felix, I'll see you tomorrow?

I glance up out of the window, see Jake at his bedroom window with his binoculars trained on me. I wish I hadn't hit him. You shouldn't hit your best friend. But I wish he'd never got me to play his stupid game.

I blow out my cheeks and try to breathe calmly, but the square feels like it's closing in on me, getting smaller and smaller until it's crushing my ribs. I want to go out in the tree. I want to watch annoying German quiz shows on TV. I want to sit in a dark room and play chess. I'd even eat sausages.

Felix, you going to reply?

I wipe my tears again.

Out of the corner of my eye, I spot something moving. I stand up and look out of the window. Granddad's standing at his front door, staring across the square.

I wave to him.

He looks down, lets Samson in, then closes the door.

28

Loser!

'We're considering a suspension.' That was Mr Hunt.

'Suspension?!' That was my mum. 'But he's been much better lately – you must have noticed.'

'Yes.' That was Mr Hunt nodding.

'That's right, blame it on my Jake. As always.' That was Jake's dad. 'It was just two kids pushing each other. You want to see what I had in the army. They were real fights.'

'Dad, it's okay.' That was Jake, glancing across Mr Hunt's office at me.

'Felix, have you got anything to say?' That was Mr Hunt again.

'Not really.' That was me looking at Jake, then looking down at my shoes.

'Well, the school can't be seen to tolerate violence,' said Mr Hunt, 'but given they were . . . *are* best friends, let's just say they don't come in tomorrow, to give them both time to think and maybe calm down.'

'Ridiculous!' *Slam!* That was Jake's dad walking out.

*

'I just don't get it,' Mum said in the car on the way home. 'Jake. Jake! You had a fight with Jake. Why would you do that with your best friend?'

I couldn't tell her it was about me and Jake following Granddad in the park. I couldn't tell her anything when she was that upset.

'How do you think it makes me look? Getting called into school like that? I had to take time off work, and you know I can't afford to.'

I thought about saying that if she was around more it might not have happened, but she'd have gone totally mad if I had. So I just stared into the footwell, or out of the window, or fiddled with the zip on my bag – anything but look at her. The last thing she said to me was that she was really upset, and when we got home I'd have to go to my room. 'No TV. No phone. No Fortnightly, or whatever it is, just sit and wait till Dad gets home.'

That was yesterday. Luckily for me, Dad got back too late, but unluckily for me, Mum had to take the day off to stay at home with me today. And I can tell she's not happy because she's downstairs slamming doors like she's lost something. I already feel bad about Granddad, and her banging around is making me feel even worse.

I sit down at my desk and reach for my history book.

Write an account of what it felt like to be in the trenches in the First World War. In particular, think about the conditions they were living in.

I look out of the window. I should be able to do this. All I have to do is imagine I'm out in the tree with Jake, firing our cannons, sharpening our bayonets. I pick up my pen and start to write . . .

If I was a soldier in the trenches, I would be tired, and my feet would be wet

154

And ... and ... and what's next? Think about the conditions; think about what it'd be like to watch other people die. It'd be cold and wet ... I've already got that ... And men would be shouting and screaming like me and Jake when we run for cover. But how do I write that?

I tap my pen on my desk. I tap my pen against my head. I look over our tree to Granddad's house. I wish he'd come out. I hope he's okay. I hope he eats tonight. I thought he just didn't want to talk to anyone.

I look down at my book, tap my pen on the page.

What next?

What next?

It's all in my head, but it won't come out. *What next?*

I look out at the square. It's almost empty of cars because everyone has gone to work. James King makes being suspended sound fun. He says he walks around town or hangs out by the boats in the docks. But this isn't fun. I glance across at Jake's house. I bet he's as bored as I am. This is when I'd normally text him, but we've been told to keep away from each other and after what he did I don't want to talk to him anyway. Besides, Mum's got my phone. She'd have taken my laptop too if I didn't need it for schoolwork.

I slide it across the desk towards me. I type in my password.

Welcome back, Astroboy2008 appears on the screen.

I'm supposed to research the First World War ... but maybe just one game wouldn't hurt. I jump and go to my door. Mum's downstairs talking to someone on her phone. I close the door and go back to my desk.

A message is now flashing across my screen.

Tired of playing me? Why not play real people at the same
level as you?

I click on the members' board. Hundreds of players are split into
leagues according to their levels, just like on any video game. I think
of selecting someone from level three, but I've only played one proper
game with Granddad and I don't want to get beaten straight away. I
scroll down. There's a green icon telling me who is online. I select a
player from level two: Dynamo2011. A profile loads up – picture of a
knight in full body armour, and underneath it says *Dynamo2011 has
been a member for a month.*

Only a month and on level two – he or she sounds as new to the
game as me.

A message lights up – Dynamo2011 has seen I'm looking at
the profile.

Want a game?

Yes, I type, even though I know I shouldn't.

Cool.

But it's not cool, not really. I shouldn't be at home playing chess, I
should be in school learning with the rest of my class.

I move a pawn to e4.

Dynamo2011 moves a pawn to d5.

I pause as Mum's voice gets louder. I overhear her say something about Granddad not touching his food again last night, didn't even take the cellophane off the plate. She thinks there's definitely something wrong with him. Everything is going wrong, Granddad is still upset with me and I've fallen out big time with Jake.

I move a pawn to f4.

Dynamo2011 moves his knight to a6.

I rest my head on my hand and look at the screen.

I should never have let this happen – all I had to do was play chess with Granddad for a few days, but now I've upset him and his depression has come back.

I stare across the square. Still no movement at Granddad's. Just Sampson sitting on the step. I look across at Jake's. His bedroom curtains are still closed, like he hasn't got a care in the world and is going to sleep all day.

I move a pawn to g3.

Dynamo2011 moves a pawn to h5.

I sigh. I wish I was out in the tree, before chess, before falling out with Jake. Everything was so much simpler when all we had to do was load our rifles and cannons. Sometimes the enemy would overrun us, but at the end of each day me and Jake always won.

Everything is going wrong. I've lost my granddad, and my best friend, and I know this is nowhere as near important, but I also just lost to Dynamo2011 in fourteen moves!

29

Desperation

'Felix . . . Felix!' Rebecca leans across the school dining table. 'You've got to speak to him sometime. It's been three days.'

'I know this.' I pause. 'I mean, I know. But I can't if he doesn't want to speak to me.'

'But he does,' Rebecca says urgently.

'How do you know?'

'Because he told me. He said he was sorry.'

'He told you he was sorry? When did you speak to him?'

Rebecca gives me a confused look. 'Yesterday in maths, and today in English.'

I frown. 'Rebecca, who are you talking about?'

'Jake, of course.'

'Oh . . . I was talking about my granddad.'

'No, sorry. Would be a bit weird though if I had been speaking to him in maths and English.'

I smile as I picture Granddad sitting in a classroom being taught by Mr Andrews or Mr Dapre.

'Well, at least I cheered you up,' says Rebecca.

'Yeah.' I put my hand up to my mouth. It's been like forever since I laughed and it feels like my face just cracked.

Rebecca packs her pencil case into her bag and stands up.

'So are you going to speak to him?'

'No,' I say. 'He's an idiot.'

'But he's your best friend.'

'Was.'

'And he's sorry for what he did.'

'So what?'

'So are you going to speak to him?'

'No.'

'But you look so miserable.'

I shrug.

'I know,' says Rebecca. 'How about I come over and we practise chess, now our mums are talking again.'

'I don't think that's a good idea.'

'Why not?'

'Because Jake might see us.'

'So you do care about him, then!' Rebecca smiles.

'No, but I don't want to make things worse than they are. I'll just play online again, but I'm even rubbish at that. Last night Dynamo2011 beat me in fourteen moves.'

Rebecca puts her hand over her mouth.

'What's so funny?' I ask.

'Think about it, Felix – my username is Rubic2008. What's yours?'

'Astroboy2008?'

'Exactly . . . 2008, the year we were born. So Dynamo2011 is how old . . . ?'

'Ah, god!' I put my hands on my head. This is getting worse. I got beaten by an eight-year-old!

30

Gunfight

'Felix, are you going to stay in bed all weekend?'

'What? No. Go away!' I shout from under my pillow.

'Don't be so rude,' says Mum. 'I'm just saying it's a nice day.' I hear the swishing sound of her pulling back my curtains. 'Look. There's not a cloud in the sky.'

I peer out from under my pillow. Sunlight flashes across my room. I bury my head again. It might be sunny outside, but it feels like it's raining in my bedroom. It's Saturday morning and I've got nothing to do and even if I did I've got no one to do it with. Granddad still isn't talking or eating, because I heard Mum and Dad discussing it last night. Mum was worried; she'd made a roast especially for him, but he didn't even let her in the house. I'm still not talking to Jake, even though he has sent me four texts this morning and my phone just buzzed again. I reach over to my table.

Felix, come on. It's going to be a boring weekend.

I scroll back through the rest of the messages.

Mr Keytes said not to talk but that was days ago.

Felix?

?

Are you awake? ☺

I sigh and push my phone away.

I do miss him and it's a brilliant day to go in our tree because we'd see the enemy coming for miles. But even if I could forgive him, we couldn't go in the tree, because Granddad will see us and he'll think I've sided with Jake.

My phone buzzes again.

Jake's not giving up. I reach out and read the message.

Hey, Felix, come on. Meet me at our tree at 2.

Just send a ☹ so I know you got this message.

I press the off button and lie back on my bed. My granddad won't talk to me and my best friend – my ex-best friend – won't leave me alone. I roll over on my side and stare at the wall.

$4 \times 7 = 28$
$5 \times 7 = 35$
$6 \times 7 = 42$

I look at Granddad's chess rules on my door:

2. *Never take the easiest path. If you don't play you don't lose and that's wrong. You lose to get better.*
3. *Do not trust the clocks. There may be a power cut and they stop, or they will be slow because of flat batteries, or your opponent may be a cheat. The best clock is the one in your head.*

No path is easy and I've got too much in my head to worry about clocks.

I bury my head in the pillow again.

The house is empty when I eventually go downstairs. Mum has left a note for me on the table.

Popped over to see Fiona. We're out of bread and toilet roll. Here's some money to get some.

For once Mum isn't working, but instead of staying with me she's gone to see a friend. It's like she doesn't even notice anything is wrong. I push the note aside and pour myself some cornflakes, then go into the sitting room and turn on the TV. After a week of being with Granddad, there are loads of things I could watch on catch-up, but as I flick through the programmes I don't feel like watching anything at all. I put the remote down and start to eat my cornflakes, but Mum forgot to say we are out of milk too.

I blow out my cheeks. This is useless. It's Saturday and I can't think of anything to do.

I glance at the time on the TV. It's just gone twelve. What did I do before chess? What did I do when I wasn't meeting Jake? I take my bowl into the kitchen and go back up to my room.

I pick up my PS4 controller and start playing Red Dead Redemption. John Marston is on the run from the Bureau of Investigation. I guide him into a bar where three men are sitting in the corner talking. One of them pulls a gun from his holster. I shoot him and the other two men stand with their hands up.

My phone buzzes on my desk. It'll probably only be Jake again, but it might be Mum or Dad telling me what time they will be home.

I crawl across to the desk.

Felix, I know you're there. I can see your TV flashing.

I sigh, then type:

You're a weirdo. Are you always watching me?

Only when I'm bored.

Idiot.

You are.

164

Argh!

What?

You just made me get shot.

Ha-ha. So will you meet me at the tree? Better to fight our
enemy than help Marston run from the Bureau.

Thinking about it.

Cool.

I said I was thinking about it.

See you in an hour ☺

I put my phone down. Maybe it will be okay if I meet him. Perhaps he
wants to apologize. But if Granddad peers out between the curtains
and sees us he'll think me a traitor for talking to the enemy and that
will make things even worse.

I pick up the controller and lead John Marston out of the bar where
he jumps on a horse that will take him over the border into Mexico.
The land is flat and bare like the desert, but there are bound to be
people hiding behind the rocks in the distance. I search up the ammo
and prep his guns, but I can't stop thinking about what Jake said. He's
right: it is more fun fighting the enemy from our tree.

I put the controller down and change out of my pyjamas into my clothes. The time on my phone says 13.50. I check out of the window to see if Jake's already there, but our tree is empty and the only person outside is Mrs Parfitt walking her dog around the square. Maybe he's changed his mind.

I walk downstairs and put my trainers on in the hall. What if Jake's at his window waiting for me to go out? Then he'll start laughing because I made the first move and he didn't really want to be friends at all.

I sit on the bottom stair. The clock on my phone says 13.55. It doesn't normally take me five minutes to tie my trainers, but I'm not normally scared to go and meet Jake. Up to now we've gone everywhere together, but now I don't even know if he'll come to the tree.

13.56. If I was John Marston I wouldn't go out yet. He would never reveal his position. But then he'd probably have arrived an hour early and set up an ambush. What if Jake does that? He's probably out there now, hiding behind the cars with his hands loaded with eggs to throw at me.

13.57. I walk into the kitchen and open the fridge. We've got no eggs, but in the bottom drawer I find four tomatoes.

13.58. I'm back on the stair. It's still too early. Jake will be out there with his binoculars trained on my door. It only takes thirty seconds to run to the tree. I'll wait a little longer. I need to play it cool. I don't want him to think I'm desperate to be friends again.

13.59. I open the door slowly and peer out. The sun shines across the grass. I shoot a look up at Jake's window to see if the sun is reflecting off his lenses. Nothing. He's too clever for that.

I creep out onto the path, and crouch down. I can't see Jake's trainers behind any of the cars, but he could be clinging to the side of one like Spider-Man. I inch on, checking behind the wheelie bins. No ambush. No sign of Jake.

My phone vibrates in my pocket.

I reach in slowly, all the time keeping lookout.

Felix, you look such an idiot!

Where are you?

The other side of the tree.

I can't see you. I'll kill you if this is a trick.

It's not. I'm hiding from the enemy. Ha. Keep going.

I slide my phone back into my pocket then take a tomato out of the bag. He's bound to be here somewhere.

I walk between the parked cars and cross the road onto the square. Jake's dad is working on his car, but I can't see Jake. I walk towards our tree, expecting him to leap out any minute and pelt me with c—

'Wha—?' I stop dead in my tracks.

Ahead of me, Granddad is standing by his gate with a plate in his hand.

My heart beats like a drum. He takes two steps across the pavement and stops at the kerb. I look around to see if he's come out to feed

Samson or check on the gnomes, but he doesn't even look at the lawn and I can't see Samson anywhere.

Granddad crosses the road onto the grass. For a moment I see him smile, or it might just be the sun shining in his eyes. He walks slowly towards me. I take a step forward, then another, pausing in between like I'm a pawn on a chessboard. Granddad is moving like a grandmaster and is now halfway to the tree. Did he see me come out of the house and decide it's time to talk? What if Jake's going to ambush me, but ambushes Granddad by mistake?

I keep walking and Granddad does the same. Slowly we get closer until we stop in front of each other under the tree. I still feel so bad that I don't know what to say or do. I look down at my feet. Then Granddad says, 'I think someone has been missing me . . . Or maybe they are just missing playing chess.'

'Yes,' I say quietly and look up.

Granddad nods at the base of the tree. A chessboard has been set up on the grass.

'When did you put that there?' I ask.

Granddad gives me a confused look like he does when he's lost the remote.

'I didn't,' he says. 'I would not have a chessboard with the squares coloured in.'

I look down at the chessboard and see the white squares coloured by red crayon.

'But . . .' I narrow my brow.

Granddad pulls a piece of paper out of his pocket. 'And I suppose you didn't write this, either?'

I read the scrawly writing:

Granddad, meet me at the tree at 2 p.m.
Love Felix
PS That's on Saturday.

'But I was meant to be meeting—' I shake my head slowly. I'd recognize that handwriting anywhere. It's the same handwriting as on the school toilet door, the same as the handwriting on the Isolation Room wall, and the same writing that's scrawled all across the front of my maths book. I look back at the crayoned-in squares on the chessboard.

'Jake!'

I look across at Jake's bedroom window to see if he's watching, but all I can see is the sun reflecting on the glass. I feel my face crack into a smile.

I look back at Granddad and see him smiling right back at me.

'I'm sorry, Granddad,' I say. 'I didn't mean … I didn't …' My voice cracks.

Granddad puts his finger up to his lips. 'It is okay,' he whispers. 'It is okay. The most important thing is that we are here.' He glances down at the ground. 'And the second most important thing is that we get to play chess.'

He picks up the white and black kings and puts them behind his back. His face cracks into a grin.

'You choose,' he says.

31

No Chance

I'm in history between Jake and Rebecca. All the class are talking while Mr Keytes is trying to sort a problem with the projector. I've been thinking what to say to Jake about him getting Granddad and me back together, but if I say the wrong thing he'll say I'm soppy. I'm just glad he did because I played chess again all day and Mum and Dad were so pleased that they let us play another hour in the evening while they watched *Dragon's Den*. We played so long that the chessboards were back on my bedroom walls when I got home, and on the insides of my eyelids when I went to sleep.

Mr Keytes tells us the projector problem should be sorted in a couple of minutes. Jake scuffs his shoes on the floor. Rebecca opens her eyes wide at me. *Go on*, she mouths. *Tell him now!*

I take a deep breath and lean towards Jake.

'Thanks for getting me and Granddad back together,' I mumble.

'It's okay,' Jake mumbles back. 'We're cool ... Even if you did break my nose in a zillion places.'

'I did not.'

Jake looks up and grins. 'Maybe not, but it did bleed a bit.'

'That was a zit!' says Rebecca, leaning across.

We all laugh.

'Well, I'm glad you two got that sorted,' Rebecca says, beaming. She seems as happy that we are friends once more as she is with her joke. 'Maybe you can concentrate on chess again now.'

'I already am,' I say. 'I've started seeing chessboards everywhere.'

'What?' says Rebecca.

'I see chessboards everywhere.'

'So, can you see them now?'

'Yes.'

'Amazing!'

'No, not amazing. When I woke up this morning they were on my bedroom walls and when I went downstairs they were on the fridge, the kitchen table, the front door, the road and the pavement, and they were on the backs of buses as I walked to school. My granddad was supposed to make a few tweaks to help my work, but the boards are getting in the way.' I nod at Mr Keytes, who is talking about how the First World War started. 'Tell me, what do you see on the whiteboard?' I ask Rebecca.

'A picture of the Archduke Ferdinand,' she whispers.

'See – I can see a rook sliding from h2 to h6 to take a knight.'

Rebecca puts her hand over her mouth. 'Well, I'd love to have that,' she says. 'But it must be annoying if you're trying to watch TV.'

'I don't know,' I say. 'I've been playing so much chess I don't get time for TV.'

'You should tell Mr Keytes. He'd love to have—'

'What should you tell me?' Mr Keytes is standing right in front of us.

'Nothing, sir,' I say, glancing at Rebecca like, *Don't say anything.*

'He's turning into a chess nerd!' Jake jumps in.

'What?' Mr Keytes looks at me.

I nudge Jake under the table, but all that does is nudge more words out of his mouth. 'Yeah,' he says. 'Some people see ghosts, Felix sees chessboards. Nowhere near as exciting, just weird.'

'I knew I shouldn't have told you!'

'What?' Jake grins. 'I'm just saying.'

Mr Keytes smiles. 'Well, it's good to see you two are friends again, but let's get on with some work.'

I pick up my pen and glare at Jake. Then Mr Keytes leans between me and Rebecca and says, 'If he's really seeing chessboards, take him to chess club at lunchtime.'

'Ha!' says Jake. 'There's no chance of that.'

'Felix, don't do it! Don't! I beg you. It'll be like getting on an alien spaceship and they'll fly off and turn you into one of them . . . You'll be like Dr Banner turning into the Incredible Hulk, only you won't turn back into a normal person, you'll be stuck as a monster! It'll be like a step to nerd-dom!'

'Jake!' I say. 'This is for real. I'm not turning back this time.'

I'm standing outside the library with my hand on the door. Jake puts his hand on my shoulder.

'Please, Felix! No! I'm begging you.'

Rebecca pushes the door open and looks back at me.

'Coming?' she asks.

I nod then step into the library.

'Felix, pleeeeease . . .'

Jake's voice fades away to another planet.

My heart is beating fast while my feet feel like they're moving in slow motion. But I'm ready for this. Jake and Rebecca are walking beside me, but somehow I feel like I'm on my own.

In silence I pass the loan desk. Chris, Tom and Leah, the members Rebecca told me about, have got their heads turned to the table as they take all the chess pieces out of wooden boxes and place them on the boards.

It's so quiet all I can hear is my breath and my feet skimming over the carpet.

Jake says it's a step to nerd-dom, but it's not. It's a step to doing something I want to do, something I love doing with Granddad, something that will make us both proud.

'If you want a book, you'll have to come back later.'

I stop dead. A boy with dark hair and glasses gets up and looks at me like I'm an alien.

'I don't want a book,' I say. 'Are you Rich?'

'Yes,' he replies. 'But what do you want?'

I nod at the other kids with their heads down. 'I-I want to play chess,' I stammer.

'He doesn't really.' Jake's followed me in and now has hold of my arm. 'He's joking . . . Aren't you, Felix?'

'No,' I say. 'I want to play.'

Rich glances behind him at all the others who are now looking right at me. Rebecca nods at me like she's willing me on, but I suddenly feel so small like I've walked out at Wembley Stadium on my own. Part of me wants to turn away, but a bigger part keeps my feet superglued to the floor.

Rich turns back to me.

'We don't have any spaces left,' he says.

'You do,' I say. 'You need new members. I read it on the noticeboard.'

'That's an old message,' says Rich, 'and besides, we don't want troublemakers anyway.'

'I'm not a troublemaker!' I protest.

'You are. I've seen you go into the Isolation Room loads of times.'

'I don't get sent there because I cause trouble.'

'Well, you don't get sent there to play chess either. Does he?' Rich smirks at Tom as he returns to his seat.

He thinks I can't play. They think I can't play. They think just because I get sent out of class, I'm dumb.

Rebecca says something, but I'm too annoyed to hear.

I step towards Rich and stop right by his table.

'I said, I *want* to play.'

'Ha, are you still here?' Rich leans back in his chair with his hands on his head like he owns the library. 'Okay,' he suddenly says. 'You can play me.' He nods at his friend to get up.

'Felix, I am thinking this is not a good idea. It is very early.'

It's okay, Granddad, I think to myself. *I've got this.*

I sit down opposite Rich, who's already lined the chess pieces up

174

on their squares. I didn't think I'd have to play the captain of the chess club, but I have to start somewhere. I glance up at Rich. It feels weird having someone other than my granddad sitting opposite me, telling me what to do. Suddenly it's like there's no one else in the room, it's just me and Rich. My heart beats quickly and my hands start to sweat. I wipe them on my trousers.

Rich picks up two pawns – one white, one black – and hides them behind his back.

I choose his right.

'You're white,' he says. 'You're first move.'

'I know,' I reply.

'Well, that's a start,' Rich says with a smirk.

I take the white pawn and put it on its square.

Rich touches the top of each of his chess pieces, like he's doing it for luck, but then I see he's moving them a millimetre so that each piece is sitting exactly in the middle of its square. When he's finished he looks at his watch.

'Thirty-five minutes,' he says, and then reaches across the table. For a moment I think he's going to punch me, but his hand stops over the board. I look at it, then realize he wants me to shake it. It's like he thinks he's playing in the World Championships. I've never shaken anyone's hand – well, just Jake's, but that was ages ago in the tree when we pretended to cut them and be blood brothers. Rich will never be my blood brother, but one of Granddad's rules was to always shake your opponent's hand. I reach out and do it. There was something else I should remember now, but I can't think what.

Rich stares at me.

I stare back.

Argh! That's it, rule four. Don't stare at your opponent!

Rich's face breaks into a grin like he's won before we've started.

He thinks I'm useless, just like everyone at school. What if he's right? What if I'm about to embarrass myself in front of everyone? I stare at the board, try to remember what all the pieces are, all the things that Granddad wrote on the list. But after days of seeing squares and numbers, my mind is suddenly blank. I take a deep breath. Then another.

'It's your move,' says Rich.

'I know,' I say. 'I know.'

I can feel Rich staring at me, waiting. Out of the corner of my eye I see Jake standing by the door and Rebecca and the others have stopped playing. They're all watching and waiting for me to make my first move like a multi-eyed monster. I pick up a pawn and move it to e4, then sit back.

Rich moves a pawn to c5.

I stare at the board. My heart is beating fast, but my brain feels like it's stuck in syrup.

I move a knight to f3.

Rich moves a pawn to d6.

He's moving too fast. We make four more moves. Each time it takes me two minutes, but he only takes two seconds.

The squares on the table start to throb every time my heart beats.

I shouldn't have done this. I shouldn't be here. I close my eyes, hoping I can see a chessboard and the numbers, but all I see is black. It's like someone has locked me in a cupboard and turned off the lights.

'It's your move!' Rich folds his arms.

My blood thumps through my body. My mind has gone blank, like someone has picked up a whiteboard cloth and wiped away the chessboard and pieces. I have to do it. I have to do it for Granddad. I reach for a chess piece, but I can't remember its name or how it moves. My face begins to burn. I thought I could do this, but I'm going to fail like I always do.

My throat is closing over and my body is shaking.

'You want to see my move?' I hear a voice. My voice, trembling.

'That's the idea,' Rich says, grinning.

I stand up and lean over the board. The others are still watching, but their uniforms are a blue blur.

'Well, this is my next move!' I say, gulping for breath. 'This is my move!' I lift my arm and smash all the chess pieces off the board.

Rich sits open-mouthed. 'You idiot,' he says. 'I was going to beat you.'

'Well, you won't now!'

'Oh no!' Rebecca holds her hand up to her mouth as I storm off.

'Oh my god! Brilliant, Felix.' Jake's beside me laughing. 'Amazing, Felix. Totally amazing!' He grabs my arm. 'Now run!'

32

Postmortem

'It was a nightmare, Granddad. He just sat there laughing at me.'

Granddad tuts as we drive past the chip shop.

'I'm sorry,' I say. 'I can tell you're mad with me for losing.'

'Losing? No. I'm not mad at you for losing. We all lose, we all have to play, that's how we get better. No, I'm annoyed that you stormed out. That you are going back to your old ways!'

'I couldn't help it, Granddad,' I say. 'He was so irritating.'

'Then we will address this,' says Granddad. 'Just give me time to think.'

I blow out my cheeks. Granddad stares ahead. He's annoyed with me, but I'm glad that he's back to picking me up from school again, although after losing my temper I feel like the walk home might have helped calm me down. I've been thinking about it all afternoon – Rich's huge grin, my hot head. I didn't even notice I'd run past Mr Keytes on the way out. That afternoon, our class were learning about

Archimedes' principle in science. Mr Groves filled a bucket with water and put something in it, but I was too busy watching the classroom door thinking Rich would have snitched to Mr Keytes and I'd get sent to the Isolation Room. I hoped not because I was tired of getting sent there. Jake thought smashing all the pieces over the board was funny, but after Mum and Dad were so pleased I was back with Granddad, I didn't want to disappoint them by getting into trouble at school again.

The car stops at a traffic light. Granddad turns to me. 'Look,' he says. 'I can tell you are upset, but this is a good thing.'

'Is it?' I say, still disappointed with myself.

'Of course. It shows you care, but unfortunately it shows you also forgot one of my rules.'

'To be honest, Granddad, I was so mad I think I forgot them all!'

'Yes.' Granddad chuckles. 'I am thinking you did.' He lifts his hand. I screw my eyes and wait for the rap of his knuckles, but all I feel is his hand ruffling my hair.

I smile. 'I forgot number eight, didn't I, Granddad. Never let your opponent see you are upset.'

'Yes.' Granddad nods as we pull away from the lights. 'But we can remedy that. For now we should concentrate on number two, that you lose to get better. So tell me about the game, the moves you both made.'

'I can't remember much, all I know is that I was white, so I couldn't use the Sicilian Defence, even if I could have remembered it.'

'Just try,' says Granddad. 'Start with the first move. That is always the best place.'

I rest my head against the seat and try to remember the start of the game. I tell Granddad the moves Rich made and the moves I made too. Granddad makes an 'umm' sound and stares at the road, like he's moving the chess pieces around in his head. I tell him the next ten moves and then pause. Granddad looks across at me.

'And what happened next?' he asks.

'That's when I got up and did it. That's when I swiped the pieces off the board.'

'No, before that. You've missed lots out. Go back to the beginning . . . You moved a pawn to e4. Did he move a pawn to c5 . . . Then a pawn to d6?'

'Umm . . . I'm not sure . . . But yes, I think so.'

'Just think,' he says. 'It's important . . . did he take your pawn at d4, and then you took his pawn?'

'Umm, y-e-s.'

'Ah! Then he is playing the same game as your friend!'

'Jake? He doesn't—'

'No, not him. Your friend Bobby Fischer. The game was called, *Night off from Najdorf.* He played it in Santa Monica in 1966.'

'Granddad,' I say, shaking my head. 'You're really confusing me. All I know is that I lost and the game hardly lasted ten minutes.'

'Ten minutes!' Granddad says as we turn into the square. 'Ten minutes is good against the Najdorf Variation.'

'No, it's not good against anything, Granddad,' I say, turning to him. 'I heard Rich tell the others that I should stick to snakes and ladders!'

'It is okay,' says Granddad. 'Doesn't worry, I told you, we all have to lose to get better.' He stops the car outside his house. 'When I was your age I lost my first game to an eight-year-old boy from Pankow, a suburb of East Berlin where I lived. He didn't even seem to look at the board and his hands moved as quickly as a Venus flytrap, just like this Rich. So we all lose.' Granddad gives me a kind smile, the same type of smile Grandma gave me when I dropped an ice cream in the park.

'It's okay, Granddad,' I say dejectedly, looking into the footwell. 'I know you're only trying to make me feel better. But I'm as rubbish at chess as I am at everything else.' I pick up my bag.

'No, this isn't the case,' says Granddad. 'I would not just say things for no reason. And, Felix, one more thing.' He puts his hand on my bag. I wait for him to say something, but he just looks at me for a long time.

'What is it, Granddad?' I ask.

'We all learn from our mistakes,' he says slowly.

'I know, Granddad, you just said.'

'Yes, but not just chess. I mean what happened that Sunday. When you thought I was a spy.'

'I know, Granddad,' I repeat. 'And it was a mistake and I did say I was sorry.'

'Yes, you did, but I think I should say sorry too.'

'It's okay, Granddad. You don't have to. I'm just glad we're playing chess again.'

'Me too, but I need to tell you something if we're going to keep playing. We cannot have suspicions about each other. We must have trust if we are to continue.'

'But I do trust you, Granddad.'

I wait for Granddad to say something else, but he just stares ahead like he's a world away.

I reach for the door handle.

'Just sit still a while,' says Granddad, glancing round the square. 'It is best I tell you here.'

Granddad watches Mrs Hardy cleaning her windows, then turns his head and watches a man outside number twenty-five strap a little girl into a pushchair.

'What's wrong, Granddad?' I ask. 'What do you need to tell me?'

'Why I keep the curtains closed. Why I don't like the phone.'

'And why you tear up pieces of paper?'

'Yes, that too.' Granddad takes one more look around the square, then leans closer to me. 'Felix,' he whispers. 'It is true – my country was full of spies.'

'So you are . . . !' Granddad's words take my breath away.

'No, no . . . I was not one of them, but there were so many that no one in my country trusted each other during the Cold War, after they built the Wall. When the East was split from the West like I told you. My country had a secret police, a police that watched everyone, all the time. It was called . . .'

'The Stasi,' I whisper.

'Yes.' Granddad nods. 'How did you know?'

'Jake told me. He looked it up.'

Granddad makes an 'mmm' sound like he might have forgiven me but not Jake.

'As I was saying, my country was full of spies. You could not trust your neighbour, you could not trust the owner of the corner shop, sometimes you could not trust your own family. Every shop, every office, every room could have a listening device.'

182

'So it really was like in *Pawn Sacrifice*,' I say. 'When Bobby Fischer thought his room and the telephone were bugged.'

Granddad waits for the man with the girl in the pushchair to pass us.

'Yes.' Granddad checks his rear-view mirror. 'It was just like that.' His voice is so low, I can hardly hear him. 'They had listening devices everywhere; your great-grandfather, great-grandmother and I, we could not even talk in our own home, and when we went out we would be followed. Guards stood in towers and aimed guns down onto the street. So we stayed in all the time. If we wanted to say something important we would write it down on a piece of paper and after we'd read it we tore the paper into tiny pieces so the spies would never know what we had written. And we kept our curtains closed all the time, just in case they were watching from across the street. It was always dark, but at least if we couldn't see out, then they couldn't see in. And of course we couldn't escape because they had built the Berlin Wall. The Wall that split the East from the West that I told you about.'

I try to think of something to say, but Granddad's life sounds so bad it's like a film. I wonder if it can really all be true, but from the serious look on his face I can tell there's no way he has made the story up.

I stare out of the window. Sometimes I feel like the square is closing in on me, that everyone knows what I'm doing, but that's really only Mrs Flower when she snitches on me for going into her garden to get tennis balls. Mum says she knows everyone's business. But what must it be like to have thousands of Mrs Flowers – going through your rubbish, listening to every word that you say? Even that doesn't feel anything like as bad as what Granddad had when he was growing up. They had uniforms. They had guns.

I look across at Granddad. He stares ahead. I've said I'm sorry twice, but now I want to say it a million times.

'Granddad . . .'

'It is okay.' He takes the keys out of the ignition. 'It was a long time ago. We do not have to talk about it any more.'

'But . . .'

'But nothing,' says Granddad. 'We have said all we need. I think we should go inside now. And besides, I have a plan. I will show you after tea.'

'For the Stasi? Are they still around? Are they still in the towers, pointing their guns down at the Wall, at all the people scrambling over the barbed wire?'

'No, thankfully not.'

'So what's the plan for?'

A smile creeps across Granddad's face. 'To beat this Rich, of course!'

33

I Can Keep a Secret . . .

(for thirteen hours, twenty-three minutes
and twenty-five seconds)

'Okay, everyone. Just draw the x and y axes first. Are we getting there? Who are we waiting on? Liam . . . Jake . . . Felix?' A shadow creeps across my desk. I look up. I'm in maths with Mr Andrews and he's standing right in front of me and Jake.

'Come on, you two,' he says. 'Jake, at least Felix is trying but you've not even got your pen or ruler out.'

'Sorry, sir,' says Jake.

I put my hand over my mouth and try to stifle a yawn.

Mr Andrews tuts. 'You need to stop playing Fizzer Motorsport all night, Felix.'

Jake laughs.

'What's so funny?' asks Mr Andrews.

'It's Forza, sir,' says Jake, 'not Fizzer.'

'I don't care what it's called; all I know is that something is stopping both of you drawing a simple graph ... Now come on!' He stares at me and Jake, then slowly moves away.

I pick up my pencil and ruler.

I am getting on with my work, but I'm so excited about the new move Granddad taught me after tea last night. We set the knives and forks, salt and pepper and all the other condiments out on the table again and he taught me the Maróczy Bind. It's named after a Hungarian grandmaster and it's used by lots of chess players to combat the Sicilian Defence. So now I've got two really good moves – one if I'm playing black, and the other when I'm playing white. I can't wait to use it on Rich, but Granddad told me not to tell anyone about the move because one of the best tactics of chess is the element of surprise.

I draw the x axis.

'Oi.'

I move my ruler vertically on the page.

'Oi.' Jake nudges me.

'What?' I say. 'I'm trying to work and you just made my y axis go wonky.'

'Oh well, never mind.' Jake grins. 'But where were you last night? I thought we'd agreed we were going up the tree.'

'Sorry, I totally forgot. I was playing chess.'

'Again?!'

'I know.'

I draw the x and y axes again.

Jake knocks his knee against mine.

'Felix,' Jake says urgently. 'I said, you're playing all the time.'

I ignore him and look at my exercise book; it tells me to plot point (3,6) on the graph. I move my pencil along the x axis to three, then up the y axis to six, and put a dot.

'Felix,' says Jake. 'Are you actually *doing* work?'

'Yes,' I say, picking up my ruler.

'But why?'

I shrug.

Jake gives me a *you're weird* look, then leans over and says, 'Felix, you're not going all swotty, are you? You wrote a short story in English and didn't mess about in PSHE.'

I ignore him and keep plotting the points. Jake's right, I do seem to have started working – not lots, but Mum said I seem to be concentrating more. I don't know how she knows, because I've been at Granddad's all the time. But I am working better, because yesterday in science I put my hand up and answered a question about why magnesium burns so brightly.

Jake kicks me under the table.

'Felix!'

'What?'

'I said, if it's still raining after school, do you want to come over to mine and play Call of Duty?'

'You know I can't. I've—'

'Felix!'

'Sir?' I look up and see Mr Andrews staring right at me.

'I said, less talking and get on with your work.'

'But I am, sir,' I reply.

'Well, it doesn't sound like it. Now get on.'

I look back at my page.

Jake nudges me. 'But I am, sir,' he says in a girlie voice that sounds nothing like me.

I seem to be getting into trouble even when I'm trying to work.

I plot another three points and all the time Jake is jabbering, then I sense a shadow standing over me.

'So,' says Mr Andrew, 'given that all the noise is coming from this table, I'm assuming one of you has the answer. So . . . Felix, question three – tell me the shape you have after plotting the coordinates.'

I look down at my paper and see a hexagon, but I don't trust myself that it's right. If I was sitting next to Rebecca I could check my work with hers, but the only other page I can see is Jake's and all he's done is draw Terence from Angry Birds.

'Well, Felix?' says Mr Andrews.

'Uh . . . I don't think it's right, but I got a hexagon, sir.'

Jake sniggers.

'Yes,' says Mr Andrews, looking as surprised as I am. As surprised as the class, who always expect me to get the questions wrong.

'What?' whispers Jake. 'You never get anything right in maths!'

'I know.' I smile. I really don't, but it feels good that I have for once.

'And perhaps you could tell us the points you plotted,' says Mr Andrews. 'Just to remind us.'

'Yes,' I say, suddenly confident, but aware everyone in the class is looking at me.

'Felix?' says Mr Andrews. 'It's not a trick question. You've already done it.'

I look at my paper.

'Pawn to e4. Pawn to c5,' I blurt. 'Knight to f3. Knight to c6!'

'What?' Mr Andrews frowns.

'White's fifth move – pawn to c4!'

'Felix, what are you on about?'

'Uh ... Nothing!' I say, looking around. Some of the class are laughing and Jake's giving me a weird look like I've just arrived from Mars. Mr Andrews tells the class to shush, then turns back to me.

'Felix,' he says. 'You've got two choices – either sit and be sensible or go to the Isolation Room.'

I shake my head slowly. I can't risk speaking when my head is full of numbers – chess numbers.

'Well?'

'He'll be sensible,' says Jake. 'Won't you, Felix?'

I nod.

'Good,' says Mr Andrews. 'So, somebody else tell me ...'

His voice fades away. I sink back in my chair. It's like suddenly I've turned into a computer spouting code, but at least I did get the answer to the graph right. I glance around the class. Some of them have got their heads down to avoid answering Mr Andrews's next question, four have got their hands in the air. Simon Jones answers. Mr Andrews tells him well done and moves on to the next question. They're all carrying on like nothing has happened, except for Rebecca who's sitting right behind me, shaking her head and smiling at the same time.

*

'a3, b4, h5, m1.' Jake's talking in a robotic voice as we walk down the corridor. 'You had me worried, Felix.' He slaps me on the back. 'For a moment, I thought you'd gone all brainy.'

As usual he's got it totally wrong, there isn't even an m1 on a chessboard, but at least this way no one else will know I accidentally blurted the chess move Granddad taught me last night. I put my head down. Jake keeps speaking like a robot, but eventually I get some peace as he turns into the toilets.

I walk on a few more strides and wait for him by the noticeboard. Boys and girls rush past me on the way to the dining hall. I take a deep breath, try to shake the chess out of my head. *Granddad*, I think to myself. *I know I wanted to learn chess, but I don't want it to take over my life.* More students pass by, then I notice a pair of girl's shoes below blue tights has stopped next to me. I look up and see Rebecca giving me the same knowing smile that she had in class.

'It's okay,' she says quietly. 'I won't tell anyone what it was.'

'What what was?' I ask.

Rebecca checks up and down the corridor like she's going to tell me a secret.

'That was the Maróczy Bind, wasn't it? The letters and numbers you shouted out in maths.'

'No . . . No . . . they were just coordinates.'

Rebecca raises her eyebrows.

'Okay, okay.' I pull her to one side of the corridor. 'It was, but please don't tell anyone. My granddad said I have to keep it secret because chess moves are best—'

'When you have the element of surprise!'

'What?' I frown. 'My granddad is teaching you too?'

'No!' Rebecca laughs. 'I might be rubbish, but I am learning something from this.' She holds up her chess book. 'Anyway,' she says. 'Does this mean you'll be playing in this then?' She nods at the noticeboard.

I turn and look at the board. The notice for new chess club members has gone and there's a new one in its place.

SCHOOL CHESS CHAMPIONSHIP

WEDNESDAY 24TH APRIL

12–1 P.M. THEN AFTER SCHOOL UNTIL WE FIND A WINNER

SCHOOL LIBRARY

ALL COMERS WELCOME

BE SQUARE. BE THERE.

CONTACT RICH PANNELL (CLUB

PRESIDENT) OR MR KEYTES

Rebecca grins at me like she did when she got picked as Cinderella in our primary school play.

I step closer to the board. Under the writing is a picture of Rich with a trophy in his hands.

'What do you think?' says Rebecca. 'Would you like to get your own back on him?'

'What? After what happened last time?'

'Especially after last time!' says Rebecca. 'He deserves it.' She nods at the picture of Rich.

'What? I thought you liked him.'

'No way!' Rebecca screws up her face like she's just seen a cat being sick. 'He's so annoying.'

'Yes, he is . . .' I look at Rich with his cheesy grin on the poster and think how I'd like to wipe it off his face. 'Yeah.' I nod. 'He's really annoying.'

'So you'll play then?'

'What? No. I never said that. Besides, he'd never let me play.'

'It's not up to him,' says Rebecca. 'It's up to Mr Keytes, and it says all comers welcome.'

'All comers welcome? What does that mean?'

'It means anyone who turns up can play. So that's all you have to do – turn up.'

'I can't. It's tomorrow. I've got no time to practise.'

'That's why he does it. Chris said Rich only puts the notice up a day beforehand every year so no one has time to prepare.'

'That's sneaky,' I say. 'And not fair.'

'So you *will* play?' Rebecca jumps up and down like it's her birthday.

'Play what?' says Jake, wiping his hands on his sweatshirt. He follows my gaze to the board.

'What? No! Felix! You can't! It's bad enough being on my own when you play with your granddad, but not at school too.'

'I'm sorry,' I say. 'But I want to.'

'Brilliant.' Rebecca almost squeals with excitement. 'I'll tell Chris.' She runs off down the corridor, then turns around. 'It'll be great,' she shouts. 'Just make sure you practise with your granddad again tonight.'

Jake turns and looks at me.

'Felix,' he says. 'You don't know what you're doing. He'll embarrass you again.'

'But I've got to try.'

'But . . .'

Jake's voice fades away as I stare at the board. A weird feeling grows inside me and I don't know what it is. But I do know that I actually want to play. It's something I *want* to do, and not because a teacher, Mum or Dad, or Jake are telling me to. It's something I want to do on my own. I feel a smile creep across my face. I'm going to do it. I'm going to do it for Granddad, but also I'm going to do it for me.

34

The Mechanical Turk

'One moment.' Granddad holds up his hand.

The phone is ringing for the third time since we got home.

We look across the table at each other in silence, waiting for it to stop. It rings for ages, like someone wants to contact Granddad urgently. I think of telling him, but he'll just wave me away. I don't know why he just doesn't get the telephone company to disconnect it. But that would mean he'd have to use the phone to ask them to do it. He would never do that, so as usual we sit and wait with the curtains closed.

'So,' says Granddad eventually. 'A championship? You have a championship. I am so pleased.'

The phone has stopped, but my ears are still ringing.

'Yes, Granddad, a championship. I can't wait, but I've realized that chess is so complicated. You've shown me two moves, but this afternoon, in IT, me and Rebecca found loads of others – there are the Bird's Opening, the King's Indian Attack, the Queen's Knight Defence, the Hedgehog Defence – so many attacks and defences.'

'Tsk!' Granddad waves his hand across the table. 'I told you, don't worry about the names. You will be fine.'

'I hope so,' I say. 'Because all this information is turning my brain to spaghetti.'

'But you are learning quickly.' He takes a sip of tea. 'And maybe you know more than you think, because much of what I have taught you is subliminal.'

'What?'

'Subliminal – it's when you learn something without knowing.'

'Well, I think I've had a lot of subliminal, because I'm still seeing chessboards on the classroom walls.'

Granddad laughs. 'I promise that you will be fine, but it is only natural you are nervous. I was before my first championship.'

'When was that, Granddad?'

'Oh, a long time ago. We don't need to talk about that now.'

'But I'd like to, Granddad,' I say. 'Why don't you tell me anything about you growing up? Dad says you never tell him much either.'

'Mmm ... That is because it is not important ... But maybe in this instance it is. Come on, let's go and sit on the sofa, where we are more comfortable.'

Granddad pushes his chair back and stands up.

'Oh!' He puts his hands on the dining table.

'What's wrong, Granddad?' I ask.

'Nothing,' he says. 'I am just a little giddy.'

I walk around to his side.

'Do you need your insulin?'

'No.' Granddad shakes his head. 'I checked my sugar levels before tea. I am thinking maybe I just got up too quickly. I am fine now.'

He says he's fine, but his face is as white as the moon. I've never seen him look like this. I stand by his side as he walks to the sofa.

'There,' he sighs as he sits down. 'Hey, don't look so worried.'

'But I am, Granddad,' I say. 'Should I call Mum?'

'No. No,' he says. 'I am fine.'

I sit beside Granddad. He takes a deep breath, then lets out a massive burp.

'There,' he smiles. 'I thought it was just indigestion.'

I laugh nervously.

Granddad taps my hand.

'I am okay,' he says. 'Now, let's stop you worrying about tomorrow. What was I going to do? Ah yes. I will tell you about my first championship. I was in Leipzig in the evening, on my own. The roads were wet with rain and the street lights were shining bright yellow. And I was nervous. Very nervous, just like you are this evening.' He puts his hands on mine to stop me picking my nails. 'My opponent was much older than me, and bigger too. When he shook my hand, he squeezed so hard my knuckles cracked. And he stared at me like a boxer in the ring. But that was the last I saw of him. That was the last time I looked him in the eye. After that he was just a wall, a faceless machine. That was when I remembered my father's words: to play chess, not my opponent. He said that I had to block them out – pretend they are a brick wall, or a faceless computer, like the Mechanical Turk.'

'The Mechanical Turk?'

'Yes. It was the first chess-playing computer. A box with arms that moved chess pieces. A robot.'

'Like Iron Man?'

'I do not know Iron Man – does he play chess?'

'No, he just flies all over the place blowing up buildings and cars.'

'Oh . . . then the Mechanical Turk is not the same, but it won lots of games and people came from all over the world to play the machine.'

'Cool!'

'It was *cool*, but then they discovered that it was just a wooden box with a man inside.'

I laugh. 'What happened to it?'

'It got burnt in a warehouse fire.'

'With the man still inside?'

'Well, I hope not. It may have been a cheating machine, but the man inside was still a good chess player . . . Anyway, I am taking you away from the point,' Granddad continues. 'I am telling you not to worry about your opponent. Just imagine this Richard is a wooden box.'

'Well, that won't be hard.' I laugh. 'But did you beat the man in Leipzig?'

Granddad's face breaks into a grin. 'Well, of course! And tomorrow you will win too.'

'I hope so.'

'You will.'

The grandfather clock chimes. Granddad looks at his watch, then at the clock on the mantelpiece, then the grandfather clock as it chimes for the seventh time.

'I think it is time for you to go home,' says Granddad.

'But I want to hear more,' I say.

'Ha,' says Granddad. 'I am thinking that I have told you enough about my past for one night.'

'But you haven't, Granddad,' I say. 'And we've not played chess yet.'

'Oh, you know more than you think after all your practice and hard work. We do not have to actually play chess all the time to learn.'

'You mean the subliminal,' I say.

'Yes. I prefer this to your friend saying I am brainwashing you.'

'Me too,' I say, feeling embarrassed.

I wait for Granddad to ruffle my hair or knock my skull with his knuckles, but he holds out his arms.

'Come here,' he says.

I lean towards him and he wraps his arms around me. I feel his chest rise and the bump of his heart. Grandma used to hug me lots, but Granddad would only ever put his arm around my shoulders. He's never hugged me like this.

'You will be fine,' he whispers. 'You have two good moves now – the Sicilian Defence I taught you with the condiments, and the Maróczy Bind. I think that will be enough.'

'I hope so, Granddad,' I say.

He squeezes me tighter, then lets go.

'You best be off,' he says.

I stand up and he follows me to the door. I don't want to leave, but if I don't sleep I will be useless in the championship.

I step outside. Samson jaunts up the path. I bend down and stroke him.

Granddad smiles.

'I will watch you so you get home safely,' he says.

'You don't have to, Granddad. I'm eleven!'

'Just read the rules I gave you before you go to sleep tonight, and everything will be fine.'

'Okay, Granddad,' I say. 'Goodnight.'

'Goodnight and good luck,' Granddad shouts as he picks Samson up.

I run across the square. I'm so excited about tomorrow that my legs seem to be moving twice as fast. I stop by the gate and turn round. Granddad waves and closes the door.

'Felix, is that you?' Mum shouts out to me as I walk through the hall. I stop and peer around the living room door.

'Everything okay?' She looks back from the TV.

'Yes,' I say. 'I'm fine.'

'And Granddad?'

'Yes. I think Granddad is fine too.'

Mum taps the seat beside her. 'Come and sit down for a bit,' she says. 'We don't get a chance to talk much.'

'I can't stop, Mum,' I sigh. 'I've got the school chess championship tomorrow. Sorry.'

Mum smiles. 'Don't apologize,' she says. 'I'm happy you're interested in something other than your computer games for once.'

'Yeah, right. I need to go.'

I close the door and walk up the stairs. Why did she have to say that? That I'm interested in something other than my computer games? Couldn't she just say 'well done' or 'good luck'? I am interested in other things, she just doesn't know it.

I walk into my room. I'm annoyed with her, but I can't let it affect my concentration. I lie down on my bed and look at Granddad's list on the wall.

Ten things for Felix to learn about chess.

Do not eat prior to a game ...
Never take the easiest path ...
Trust me!

I take a deep breath. Trust me, he says, but it's hard when the tenth thing is missing off his list. It might be really important, but what could it be? Maybe it's just making sure I get there on time, but that's obvious. Perhaps it's that I shouldn't pull my tie too tight to stop my blood from reaching my brain. I read that once, but can't remember where. Or maybe I just made it up when I was bored in maths.

I'm playing in a championship tomorrow. I might get knocked out first game, but at least I'm trying something for once. Maybe Mum was right; it is the first time I've really been interested in something other than computer games.

I roll over on my side and read the list again ... Trust me. Trust me. Trust me.

I do, Granddad ... I think.

35

Beginner's Luck?

I'm standing in the library and my stomach is grumbling like a bear in a cave. Granddad said not to eat, so all I had for breakfast was a bourbon biscuit.

'So these are our leagues,' says Rich, pointing at a flipchart. 'Two leagues of three. We all play each other once – one point for a win, half-point for a draw – and the top person from each league plays in the final after school.' Rich turns round from the whiteboard and smiles. 'Do we all understand that?' Everyone in the room nods. 'What, even you?' He looks right at me.

'Yes!' I say through gritted teeth. I can't remember if Granddad wrote 'Don't let your opponent wind you up,' but Rich just did.

'Okay, then let's play,' says Rich. 'Each game lasts for twenty minutes. Oh, and you all know how to work the clocks.'

Clocks? What clocks? Nobody said anything about clocks.

I look around the room. There are two chess sets on separate tables and beside each is a clock with two silver buttons on top. I saw them in *Pawn Sacrifice* and Granddad put them on his list, but he didn't tell me how to work them. I glance at Rebecca to ask her, but she's moving with everyone else towards the tables.

What do I do with the clocks? I'm going to look like an idiot and everyone will laugh. I don't mind people laughing when I mess around, but not when I'm trying to be serious. But what if they do? What if everything Granddad taught me flies right out of my head like my schoolwork?

I'm sorry, Granddad, I can't do this after all.

I take a step backwards towards the door.

'Where are you going?' asks Rich.

'I was just ...'

'He was just going to sit down and play. Weren't you?' Rebecca looks at me with her eyes wide open like she's trying to send me a message.

'Umm.'

'Yes,' she says. 'You're down this end.' My legs want to go backwards, but Rebecca comes over to me, grabs my arm and pulls me towards the end of the library. 'Come on,' she whispers. 'You're here now.'

'But the clocks,' I say urgently. 'I don't know how to work the clocks!'

'They're easy. Look.' She picks up a clock. 'As soon as one of you makes the first move, you bash this button on the top. That stops your clock and starts your opponent's at the same time. Then when he takes his move he bashes this button, which stops his clock and yours starts again. Got it?'

'No.'

'Think of it like a seesaw – when you're on the ground you make your move and you hang in the air while your opponent makes his.'

'But—'

'Okay,' says Rich. 'Is everyone ready?'

Rich is now sitting down, getting ready to play like everyone else. I search the room in panic. Tom, one of the boys from Year Eleven, nods at the seat opposite him.

'You're playing me,' he says.

But the clocks!

I glance at Rebecca. She lifts up her hand and brings it down like she's ringing a bell in a hotel.

Just bash it! she mouths, then smiles. I try to smile back but my jaw is clenched tight like I'm on the way to the dentist chair.

'Come on,' says Rich. 'We won't get the games in if you keep hanging around.'

I take a deep breath and pull out a chair.

'At last,' mutters Rich.

'Do not lose your temper.'

I know, Granddad. I won't. I won't.

A hand comes across the chessboard.

'Respect your opponent. Look him in the eye, but this is the only time.'

I reach out and shake Tom's hand and look him in the eye. He nods and wishes me a good game.

'Respect your opponent, but he is just that. Your opponent is not your friend.'

I nod but don't say anything.

Tom picks up pawns, one white and one black, then puts them behind his back. I nod at his left hand. He shows me the white pawn in his palm. I'm white. I start.

I stare at the clock.

I stare at the board.

I stare at the clock.

I stare at the board.

I see a hand lift in the air. I see a hand pick up a pawn. I see the pawn move two squares forward. Pawn to e4. The hand lifts away and comes back by my side. The hand is mine.

I breathe. I've made my first move. I sit back. Out of the corner of my eye I see a hand waving up and down. I glance up and see Rebecca mouthing, *HIT THE BUTTON! HIT THE BUTTON!*

'Oh.' I jump up and hit the button so hard it jabs into my palm like Lego. Rebecca puts her hand over her mouth to stop herself laughing. I want to laugh too, but I can't break my concentration. I look back at the board and wait for my opponent to make his first move.

He moves bread to e5. He hits the clock.

I stare at the board.

Make my move . . . Gherkin to f3 . . . Bash the clock.

My opponent moves his gherkin to c6.

I move knife to b5 . . . Bash the clock.

My opponent's move – he hits the clock. My move – I bash the clock.

Opponent's move.

My move.

His bread takes my bread on d4 and my pickle takes his bread. Bash the clock.

His bread to g3.

My bread to c4.

Brown sauce to … bash.

Red sauce … bash.

Fork … bash.

Knife … bash.

The clock ticking.

My chess pieces moving.

My head clear.

My hands a blur.

Honey to g6 … bash.

Knife to d6.

Mustard to …

Bash.

Bash.

Bash.

'Check.' My voice.

My voice?

Fork to h6.

'Check.' Still my voice! 'Check. Checkmate.'

My opponent lays down his vinegar.

I see a hand.

I shake it.

'Well played,' says Tom as he gets up.

'And you.' I sit back in my chair.

I won.

I just won!

36

Panic!

'I know, but what if I can't do it again?' I stare at my sausage roll.

'But you can,' says Rebecca. 'You've already done it twice.'

'But it's the final, and it's Rich! There's no way I'm ever going to beat him. Maybe I should stop while I'm ahead.'

'You can't. That's like a boxer giving up after the first round.'

'Two,' I say. 'I've won two games,' I say. 'Against Tom, then Chris. I could stop there.'

Rebecca sighs and takes a bite of her sandwich.

We're in the school canteen and I'm leaning over my lunchbox with my head in my hands and I can't think straight for the clatter of chairs and tables as they are packed away around us. We're supposed to be eating before we go back to lessons, but my stomach's tumbling over like a washing machine. I felt great after winning both games, but as soon as I left the library my confidence started to drain away. I won, but it didn't feel like it was me playing. It was like I wasn't in control, like

I was in a dream at the controls of a plane coming into land, only I was on autopilot with the computer overriding me and making every move.

I drop my sausage roll back into my lunchbox.

'I can't do it,' I say. 'Rich will beat me in ten moves and tomorrow it'll be all over the school.'

'He won't,' says Rebecca. 'It took him twenty moves to beat Leah.'

'And how does that help me?'

'Because you beat Chris and he usually beats Leah, so that means you've got a better chance. See?'

'No.' I roll my head in my hands.

'Ha! Did you lose?' Jake puts his drink on the table and sits down.

'Brilliant,' mumbles Rebecca. 'That's all we need.'

'Never mind, Felix.' Jake grins. 'Not like you wanted to be one of them anyway.'

'He didn't lose,' says Rebecca.

'Then why is he so grumpy?'

I lift my head. 'Because I've got to play Rich!'

'But I thought that's what you wanted. Revenge!'

'I did,' I say. 'I do, but I can't remember how ...'

'Can I have your sausage roll?'

'What?'

Jake nods at my lunchbox. 'Can I have your sausage roll? I didn't have any money on my account.'

I push my lunchbox across the table. I don't care about food. I don't care about chess. All I want to do is grab my bag and get out of here.

'Right,' says Rebecca. 'As I was saying, before *he* arrived, it's just a game and Rich is just another player.'

'And he just happens to be the school champion!' Bits of pastry fly from Jake's mouth.

'I know,' Rebecca sighs. 'But, Felix, you're not going to get anywhere like this.' She suddenly sounds serious like a teacher. 'You need to relax. Take deep breaths, like my mum does when my dad gets on her nerves.'

'Mine just screams and tells us to get out of the house.'

'Jake!'

'It's okay, I'm leaving if all you're going to do is talk about chess.' Jake pushes back his chair and stands up. 'Are you going to stay here with Brains or are you coming to shoot hoops?'

I shake my head. I'd love to just get out of this, but Rebecca is right. I can't just walk away because I don't like doing something. That's what I always do in science, in maths, at home with Mum and Dad. That's what I do with everything.

I look out of the window and watch Jake run into the quad. It would be easier to go and join him, but Granddad said I should never choose the easiest option, and after all the practise I've put in it would be silly to do that now.

'Felix ... Felix!' Rebecca waves her hand in front of my face. 'I said, we've not got long before we go back to lessons.'

'Sorry,' I say. 'I was just ...' Jake shoots a hoop and high-fives with Liam.

'You were just learning some deep breathing exercises. Look, it's like this. Just take a slow deep breath, count to five, then let it out again.'

'I can't,' I say. 'It reminds me of scuba diving.'

'Oh,' says Rebecca, 'then try something else. Something your granddad taught you. What about the rules he gave you?'

'They're on my bedroom wall, but my mind's so frazzled I can't remember them.'

'Try,' says Rebecca. 'Before the bell goes.'

'I am,' I say. 'I'm trying now, but all I can remember is the last one.'

'And what's that?'

'He just wrote "Trust me!"'

Rebecca rests back in her chair.

'Then that's it.' She smiles.

'What is?'

'He said to trust him.'

'Well, yeah.'

'Then maybe you should.'

37

Revenge?

The corridors seem twice as long when they're empty.

My footsteps echo as I walk and in the distance I can hear a teacher shouting to someone to be quiet and go home. Rebecca's walking beside me and I think she's as nervous as I am because we've hardly spoken since we left class. She didn't put her hand up to answer a single question in geography, and we both left Jake to mix the fruit cake in cookery.

I take a deep breath as I pause outside the library door. Rebecca looks at me.

'This is it,' she whispers.

'Yeah,' I sigh.

Rebecca pushes the door open and I follow her in. Chris, Leah and Tom are gathered in a group by the loan desk, but the only person I'm concentrated on is Rich. He's reading a book, at the far end of the room, under an 'It's polite to be silent' sign.

My fingers curl into my palms.

'Good luck,' Rebecca whispers.

I try to say thanks but all that comes out of my mouth is air.

I walk between the blue and red chairs, past the loan desk. Everyone has stopped talking and Rich keeps reading his book, pretending he doesn't know I'm here. But he must do now because my shadow is creeping across the table.

I pull the chair out opposite him. He slowly closes his book and looks up.

'Surprised you came back,' he says.

Not as surprised as me.

'I'm not,' I say. I'm trying to be cool even though my head is a blur. I sit down.

The chess pieces are already on their squares. Rich turns the board round.

'You can be white and I'll give you my queen.'

'What?'

'It's a handicap system.' He grins. 'Just to give you a chance. Means the game might go on for longer, but I'll still win.' He glances at the others who are now seated around us.

Handicap system! Who does he think he is?

My fingers dig into my palms.

'Number four. Do not smile or stare at your opponent.'

Smile? There's no chance of that, Granddad.

'Number eight. Never storm off.'

There's a big chance of that!

Rich reaches across the table with his queen in his hand.

My body tenses.

I glance at Rebecca. She shakes her head slowly, like, *Don't!*

'Trust me.'

Trust me.

I lift my head and look Rich in the eye.

'I don't need you to give me your queen,' I say. 'I'll take it fairly in the game.'

Rich chuckles.

'Okay,' he says. 'Was only trying to help.'

I pick up one white and one black pawn and put my hands behind my back.

'Which arm?' I ask.

Rich nods at my left.

I bring my arm round and open up my palm.

'Great,' Rich says. 'I'm white. Let's start.'

Yes, let's start.

38

Champion!

I'm the school chess champion. I AM the school chess champion. Yes, me. Felix Schopp, the kid who can't sit still, the kid who daydreams all day, the kid who got sent to the Isolation Room every week, the kid who's still got the times table poster on his wall, but all that doesn't matter because now I am the school chess champion. This is not a dream. This is NOT a dream. Is it?

Wake up, Felix, wake up! Pinch myself. Kick myself.

No, it's not a dream.

I really am.

I am the school chess champion.

It's Thursday morning and I'm walking down the corridor towards my history class and it feels like everyone is looking at me, like they knew what happened at chess club last night. I can't stop smiling as they pass by. I feel like poking myself in my chest and declaring loudly so everyone can hear, *Yes, it's me, the school chess champion, the dopey kid from 7H, the kid who can't concentrate for longer than a flea, the kid who beat the chess club captain Rich in sixteen moves.*

Granddad was pleased when I told him last night. He didn't whoop or do a jig around the sitting room, but he did smile and give me another hug. He told me he was proud of me, but most importantly I should be proud of myself. Mum and Dad were pleased too. Mum said the usual thing about me finally doing something, but at least she promised to take me to Nando's at the weekend, because I'm the school chess champion, yes I am. And I'm smiling at Mr Keytes, as he walks down the corridor towards me.

'Well done for last night, Felix,' he says. 'I had no idea you'd taken to the game so quickly. It took me two years before I won my first tournament and Richard tells me you used the Sicilian Defence in a couple of games. This is a very technical move.'

'Is it?' I ask proudly.

'Yes. And I've never seen you so focused.'

'Were you there?'

'See.' Mr Keytes smiles. 'You were concentrating so hard that you never saw me come in.'

'So this isn't a dream? I really did win.'

'No.' Mr Keytes laughs. 'If this were a dream, do you think I'd still be stuck in school teaching history?'

'Suppose not.' I smile.

'Anyway.' Mr Keytes rubs his hands together frantically. 'How about the Inter-Schools Championship. Are you up for it?'

'The what?'

'The Inter-Schools Championship. I wanted to tell you last night, but you were in such a daze. It's always the first Monday in May. That's why we have our championship the week before. You're the obvious person to go.'

'But what about Rich?'

'He'll be going too – it's a team event as well as individual.' Mr Keytes looks at his watch. 'Listen, the bell's about to go,' he says, moving off. 'Have a think. Talk to Rebecca or Rich – they'll tell you all about it. But it's your chance to represent the school.' He walks away towards the staffroom then turns round. 'And, Felix!' He holds up his thumbs. 'Well done. Really well done!'

My smile feels as wide as a gate. I never thought I'd be the school chess champion, let alone get selected by a teacher for a real-life tournament. He wants me, Felix Schopp, to represent the school!

I start walking again.

I smile at the caretaker as he unplugs the floor cleaner. I smile at Miss Lewes standing at the photocopier and I smile at Mrs Ewens as I walk past the Student Support Office.

'Good to see someone's happy.'

'I am.'

'Let's hope it lasts,' she says as she closes the Isolation Room door. I smile at James King, sitting inside.

I am the school champion. I'm the school chess champion. Nothing else matters. I'm the school chess champion and I love it – fist-bump me, high-five me, pat me on the back – I'm Felix Schopp, school chess champion.

I'm three metres tall.

My shoulders are a metre wide.

And I'm walking on air.

I'm—

'Felix, can you stop bouncing up and down like that? You look dopey.'

'Like what?'

'This!' Jake hitches his trousers up and takes giant loopy strides like he's walking on the moon. 'Going up on tiptoe makes you look like you're wearing ankle bashers!'

'I do not!'

'You do! You look like that skinny kid in Year Eight. But it's okay. You're the school chess champion!'

Yes, I'm the school chess champion. Jake wraps his arm around my shoulder as we walk into our form class. Mrs Drew looks up from her computer.

'As usual, the last ones in,' she sighs.

Jake bounces over to her like it's him who won.

'Jake, sit down. We've got a lot to get through.'

'But Felix is the school chess champion, miss.'

'Is this true, Felix?'

'Yes, miss,' I say. 'I won after school last night.'

'Well, well done if that's the case.'

'There were only six in it,' says Jake. 'But, still, he did win.'

I sit down at my desk and look across the room to Rebecca. We exchange smiles. I don't care that there were only six of us in it. I'm the school chess champion. This is one of the best days of my life and nothing is going to spoil it.

39

Tug of War

'You were brilliant.'

'What?'

'You heard. You were brilliant. I'll never forget Rich's face when you got him checkmate. It was like, *Oh!*' She opens her mouth and makes her eyes wide.

'Wish I'd seen it,' says Jake.

'It was amazing,' I say.

'Yeah, like he'd fallen down a drain,' says Rebecca.

We all burst out laughing. Miss Elliott tells us to be quiet, but we don't take any notice because we're in PSHE and no one listens in PSHE, not even Rebecca.

'So are you going to play in the Inter-Schools Championship?' she asks.

'I don't know.'

'But you've got to. It's great; me, Chris and Rich have been selected too, and we get to play schools from all over the county.'

'I know – that's what puts me off.' I've only been school chess champion for half a day but already my confidence is draining. I only won three games. What if they were all a fluke? I won with vinegar and sauce bottles – the Inter-Schools will be in a different league. And I don't want to let people down like Granddad and Rebecca – especially them – but also Mr Keytes and the school.

Miss Elliott hands out pieces of paper for us to write our thoughts down about why we think it's important to be nice to each other.

Rebecca leans close to me like she can tell I'm worried.

'You have to play, Felix,' she says. 'You'll be fine. You're better than the rest of us, and anyway, Chris said we get a day off and lunch at the sports centre where it's held.'

'I'm sorry,' I say. 'I'm not sure I can do it again.'

'You'll be fine.' Rebecca smiles. 'Meet me in the library at lunchtime.'

'What's that?' Jake's the other side of me. 'What did she say?'

'She wants me to practise chess at lunchtime.'

Jake shakes his head like one of our cannonballs just landed in the school canteen.

'He can't. We've got Film Club.'

'Yeah, I know, but maybe I should go to chess, just to—'

'No way, Felix. You said you were just going to play with your granddad, not go to chess club. Last week you said they were all dweebs!'

'Oi!' Rebecca nudges me.

'Sorry. I mean, you were ... they were.' I smile apologetically.

'Maybe your granddad could teach me too,' says Rebecca. 'Maybe get him to come to chess club. We're bound to win the tournament.'

'Umm, I don't know . . . I could—'

'What tournament?' Jake jumps in.

'The Inter-Schools Championship,' answers Rebecca.

'What? Another tournament?' Jake sighs.

'But I thought you were pleased I won the school championship.'

'I was . . . I mean, I am, but it's like you're going to be playing chess all summer.'

'I won't be, but I do want to play in this.'

'Okay,' says Jake. 'But your granddad can't teach her too.'

'Why not?' asks Rebecca.

'Because . . . because he likes to be on his own. He stays in all the time and keeps his curtains closed.'

'I know,' says Rebecca. 'It was like that when I used to go to Felix's.'

'Yeah, but he's way worse now, isn't he, Felix? He doesn't go out AT ALL. He's like a hermit.' Jake opens his eyes so wide they look like they're going to burst out of their sockets.

'Well, yes . . . I guess so.' I look at Jake and wonder what he's up to.

'Great,' says Jake. 'That's sorted. You're coming to Film Club.'

Rebecca smiles, like she knows I'm stuck about what to do. I suddenly want to meet her in the library but I did promise Jake. I give her a look that says, *Sorry!* I think she gives me one that says, *It's okay*. Then Jake grabs my arm.

'Come on, Felix,' he says. 'We're going to be late for woodwork.' He pulls me away and I leave Rebecca behind.

'Thanks for thinking of my granddad.'

'What?' asks Jake.

'Thanks for saying that my granddad doesn't like meeting people at the moment.'

Jake laughs. 'That's not why I did it!'

'Why did you then?'

'I did it because if your granddad can teach someone like you to win, think what he could do with a brainbox like her!'

40

The City and the Wall

Rebecca messaged me to say there were three good reasons why I should play in the Inter-Schools Championship:

1. She wants the school to win.
2. She thinks Leah likes Chris so they will sit together on the minibus and not talk to her.
3. She doesn't want to sit next to Rich on the minibus.

Granddad has been on at me to play too. It was the first thing he said to me when he picked me up from school and he's still going on about it during tea. But what he doesn't know is that I want to—

'Retire?' Granddad waves his fork across the dining table at me. 'Retire! You cannot retire. You are only eleven!'

'I know, but what if I get beaten really badly? Everyone will think I'm an idiot.'

'Ah. I see what is happening. You are losing confidence.'

'I know, Granddad,' I say. 'I felt amazing when I got up this morning. I was feeling amazing at Film Club. But in the afternoon, during maths, the amazing started to wear off.'

Granddad ruffles my hair. 'Come on,' he says. 'Remember Bobby Fischer. He didn't give up after three games! Now tell me the moves you made in the match yesterday with this Rich.'

I force a smile as I slide my notebook across the table. Granddad is listening to me but he's not understanding me. I thought the amazing feeling would last for ever. I don't want someone to pull the plug out and watch it all slowly drip away down the drain.

'Mmm ... This is interesting.' He nods. 'He was using the Ruy Lopez!'

'Roy who?'

'Not Roy, Ruy. This is the Spanish Game. Ruy Lopez was a bishop who wrote a book ... let me think ... yes.' Granddad's eyes light up. 'He wrote *The Book of the Liberal Invention and Art of the Game of Chess*. We could not get it in East Germany, not officially, but we smuggled copies of it in from the West. This boy is only eleven and using this move.'

'No, he's fifteen, Granddad,' I say. 'And he does read lots of books.'

'Umm, I see.' Granddad studies the moves. 'Pawn to e4. Pawn to e5. Knight to f3 ... c6 ... Bishop to b ... But look, you are playing it too.'

'I don't think so, Granddad. I really don't know what I was doing.'

'Then you were being intuitive.'

'Was I?'

'Yes, like it comes naturally to you. But this game, this game, it

222

is like a game that was used against me when I was a boy, before the Wall was built.'

'The huge wall with barbed wire on top that divided the city?'

'Yes.' Granddad pauses. 'You remembered.'

'It sounded horrible, Granddad,' I say. 'How could anyone forget that?'

'Indeed,' Granddad says, nodding slowly. 'Indeed.'

I want to tell him how huge I imagine the wall must be, but I don't want to interrupt because he's finally talking about the past again.

'The government of East Germany was friends with the Russians,' Granddad continues, 'so they built the Wall to separate Berlin from the rest of Germany and the countries in the West, like France and Great Britain.'

'Who built it, Granddad? The people that ran the secret police? The Stasi?'

'No, it wasn't the Stasi who built it, although they were a part of it. But it was the East German government, and some say it was the Russians that decided too. They gave the order and the Wall went up overnight,' he says. 'I know this because I was catching a tram across Berlin from Spreebogen to see my sister in Heinz Hoffmann-Straße. But the tram stopped in the middle of nowhere. Out of the windows I could see the army telling the driver to go back and in the distance I could see people working in the rain, building a wall and a fence, stretching barbed wire across the top. As they were building it I could see people from the west standing on the other side, not knowing what to do. But I had to get through – my sister was expecting me.'

I lean forward. Granddad's suddenly talking like he's there right now.

'I climbed down from the tram. I thought maybe there was a fault, and that the wall and barbed wire were protecting a new military building. So I walked along it, waiting for it to end, but it stretched on for kilometres, like electricity pylons disappearing into the distance. There was no way through. Everyone was walking around like me, like we were lost. We were lost . . .'

I lean closer.

'I thought of going back home, but my sister was there,' Granddad whispers. 'If I couldn't get through to her, how would she get through to me? There were too many soldiers . . . too much wire . . . But eventually it got dark and cold and I went home to my parents and told them. Early the next morning me and my father went back. He explained to the guards that he needed to see my sister, but they wouldn't let him through. People were shouting and screaming – they too had been split from their families and some . . . some never got to see each other again . . .' Granddad's voice trails off. I want to ask him more, like did he ever get to see his sister again, but from the tears in his eyes, I think it would upset him even more.

'I'm sorry I asked, Granddad,' I say quietly. 'I only wanted to know more about when you were younger.'

'I know. I know.' Granddad puts his hand on my knee. 'It's not your fault . . . Now, come on,' he says, trying to be cheery. 'Let's snap out of this – let us get back to this tournament. I was thinking that if you do well we could celebrate with doing another thing on your list, like zip wire.'

'It's okay, Granddad,' I say. 'I'm not really bothered about my list any more. I only put scuba on there to get out of playing chess.'

'But I enjoyed scuba diving – it was a wonderful challenge. We should do more things in the lead-up to the tournament.'

I haven't actually said I would play, but Granddad has a big smile on his face. I don't want to take it away, but the tournament is only a week off.

'I'd like to play, Granddad,' I say. 'But I've only got seven days to prepare.'

'Then there is only one thing for it,' says Granddad.

'What's that?'

'It's obvious,' he says, rubbing his hands together. 'We start practising right now.'

41

I'm Sorry, Jake

'But you've been playing all weekend.'

'I know. But I've got to. It's only two days until the Inter-Schools Championship.'

'But ALL the time, Felix? It's been so long since we were in our tree that the cannons have seized up.'

'They have not.' I step out of Granddad's front door and join Jake on the garden path.

'Great! So you're coming now!' he says.

'No, I'm just going back home.'

Jake sighs. 'Come on, Felix, this is boring!'

I take a deep breath and walk across the square. It's Sunday evening and this is the first time I've been out since I went to Granddad's this morning. In fact, I've not been out all weekend. All I've been doing is playing chess and learning new moves – the Stonewall Dutch Defence, the Chigorin Defence, the Cambridge

Springs Defence. The only time I haven't been learning is when Granddad stops to make tea and pee. He's been in my head at school too. His voice was there in woodwork when I was chiselling a mortise joint: *'Practise! Practise! Practise!'* It followed me to the gym: *'Practise! Practise! Practise!'*

I know, Granddad, I said to myself, *now go away,* but he was still chattering non-stop as I somersaulted over the horse. And in history when the British Army were landing in Normandy. *'Practise. Practise. Practise! At every opportunity. Because your opponents will be. They will be practising before they go to bed, dreaming of chess in their beds, making their first moves as soon as they get up.'*

Jake grabs my arm and we stop under our tree.

'Come on, Felix,' says Jake. 'You know you want to.'

I look at our tree. It wouldn't hurt just to go up there for an hour, would it? It was the last game today, and all me and Granddad are doing tomorrow is having a team talk. I could just talk to Jake for an hour, clean our guns and bayonets and blast a few cannonballs at the hills. I turn towards the tree.

'Yes!' says Jake.

'Practise. Practise. Practise. Think that your opponents will even play on Christmas Day. Would they even think about going up a tree?'

I stop still.

'I can't,' I say, moving towards my house. 'I need to practise.'

'Felix, you're turning into one of them.' Jake huffs as he walks alongside me.

'One of who?'

'The chess geeks.'

'I'm not.'

'You are.' Jake keeps walking, then turns round and says, 'You even put your hand up to answer a question in history.'

'Well, I did. But only because I knew the answer for once.'

'Ha!' says Jake. 'I bet it was Rebecca who told you.'

'It wasn't.'

'I don't see why you have to play chess with her every lunchtime.' He glares at me like he does to the teacher whenever he's sent to the Isolation Room.

'Jake,' I say. 'What's wrong?'

'Nothing's wrong with me,' he says. 'I've just been on my own all the time. All I want to do is go up in the tree for a few minutes and you can't even do that.'

'But it's only for two more days,' I say. 'Then I'll probably lose and won't play again.'

'Well, I hope you do lose.' Jake walks off as I reach my gate.

'Do you mean that?' I shout after him.

He turns and holds his hands out by his sides. 'I don't know, Felix,' he says. 'You've changed.'

I watch as he turns and walks across the square to his house. I feel bad that I haven't seen much of him this week, but he did the same to me when his cousin Kyle came and stayed at his house last summer. I had no one to hang out with all week. I got so bored that I ended up asking Dad to take me to work with him, but I soon found out that watching someone fiddle with a boiler for hours is even more boring than staying at home.

Jake walks past his dad's car. I wait for him to give me a thumbs up or pull a funny face like he sometimes does. But he just walks round the side of his house towards the back door.

I feel bad I didn't go in the tree, but chess is more important to me now. I never thought I'd ever think that, but it is, and I like being good at something for once. It's nice having people supporting me and believing in me and I don't want to let any of them down.

I open my front door, then close it behind me. The theme music from *Dragon's Den* plays in the sitting room. I slowly climb the stairs.

I hope Jake didn't mean it when he said he hoped I'd lose. I might be seeing Rebecca loads, but he's still my best friend.

42

Why Did Dad Do That?

It's the night before the championship and I'm in bed with the rumble of the TV coming up through the floorboards. But that's not what's keeping me awake. I can't sleep because my heart is racing like it's Christmas Eve. It's been like it for the last two days and it got worse today at school. Rebecca said it was okay, she was feeling like that too, which made me feel better for a while.

Mr Keytes called a meeting of chess club at lunchtime to give us a team talk. He told us we were exactly that, a team, and we should all support each other and work together. When one of us wins, we should all feel like we are winners. Rich puffed his chest out like Mr Keytes was talking about him specifically. Then Mr Keytes said the same applies when we lose, that we support each other. We are a team.

We're a team. I've never been part of a team before. I've never been good enough at anything to be in one. I was reserve goalkeeper for my primary school once, but that was only because George Drummond had a dentist appointment. But now I am in a team, I can't stop thinking about it, and the thought of letting the rest of them down is making me nervous.

After the others had left I stayed to speak to Mr Keytes on my own. I told him about my nerves, how I wasn't confident and didn't want to let the others down. He said everyone else would be feeling the same, but that actually nerves were a good thing and they would help me concentrate. All I had to do was remember how I played against Rich, and as soon as I made my first move the nerves would go away. But I was nervous when I went scuba diving with Granddad and jumping in the pool didn't make my nerves go away then.

I roll over onto my side. The red power light on my computer flashes in my eyes. I played and won two games online when I got home from Granddad's tonight. He told me not to. He said all I had to do was rest. 'Sometimes rest is the brain's best exercise,' he said. I wasn't sure what he meant by that.

I sigh and look at my computer. Maybe I should have one more game online, just to give me more confidence? But what if I lose? Then I really won't be able to get out of the door in the morning.

I pick up my phone and check my messages. Still nothing from Jake. We went to all our lessons together, but we didn't talk or mess around like we used to. I was so nervous about the tournament that I couldn't think of anything to say, and Jake still seemed a bit weird because I haven't been up the tree for ages. Rebecca told me that she thinks it's temporary, that me and Jake are such good friends that a game of chess won't get in the way. But I'm not so sure. I thought he'd be happy for me, now that I'm finally half-good at something, but he hasn't even been sitting with me at break.

The landing light shines under my bedroom door, then I hear Dad's heavy footsteps on the stairs. He'll be on his way to the bathroom for a shower.

His shadow stops outside the door. Then I hear two gentle knocks.

'Felix,' he whispers.

I put my phone back on the table.

'Felix, are you awake?'

The door opens slowly and Dad peers round.

'Yes,' I say.

He walks in and crouches down beside me. My laptop light flashes against his face.

'I've hardly seen you all week,' he whispers. 'I just wanted to wish you luck for tomorrow.'

'Thanks, Dad.' I smile. 'But I'm so nervous.'

'Of course you are. I would be too. But you'll be fine. Trust me.' He puts his hand on the side of my head. 'I bet that's what your granddad said too.'

'No . . . well, he did, but the last thing he said was that I should keep my mind as clear as the sky and my head as calm as the sea.'

Dad laughs. 'I'm not sure I've ever heard him say anything like that,' he says. 'But listen, you'll be fine. If you do well, me and your mum might eventually get you to Nando's!'

'Thanks, Dad,' I say.

He puts his hand on my bed and stands up. I wait for him to say goodnight and leave, but he just stands there looking at me.

232

'Are you all right, Dad?' I whisper.

'Yes.' He bends down and kisses me on the head. He never does that. 'Love you, mate,' he says.

'I love you too, Dad. But why did you do that?'

'Just felt like it,' he says.

43

Surprise!

'So, I just need to double-check everyone is present. Chris, me.' Rich points at himself. 'Leah . . .' We're standing outside the school minibus and Rich is counting us all for what seems like the tenth time, but all I want to do is get going because the waiting around is making me nervous. We're all wearing our school blazers which reminds me we are representing our school and that makes me feel even worse.

Rebecca nudges me and shows me a blue teddy bear.

'It's our mascot,' she whispers. 'To bring us luck.'

'Think we need a minibus full of them,' I say.

She laughs. I'm glad Rebecca is here, but part of me wishes that Jake was too.

I look across the car park towards the science block. This doesn't seem real. I'm used to being the kid in the classroom, watching the rugby or netball teams get on the minibus, not the one getting on it.

When the rugby team wins they announce it in assembly and Dan Wills, the captain, reads out a report of the match on stage.

Mr Keytes walks across the car park towards us, wearing a dark suit that I've only ever seen him wear at parents' evenings.

'Everyone here, Richard?' he asks.

'Yes,' says Rich.

'Then let's go.' Mr Keytes slides the door back. Rich gets in first and sits at the front. I get in line behind Tom, Chris and Leah, who smiles at me as we move forward. I force a smile back to be friendly, but from my reflection in the wing mirror I can see I look as nervous as I feel. If it wasn't for Rebecca, today would be like going on school camp without any friends. She texted me last night to ask what the Bobby Fischer film was called, but I know it was really an excuse for her to check I would turn up today. It's like she knows I've lost confidence, like I feel as if I don't belong here – on this bus, in this uniform.

Rebecca nudges me.

'Go on, Felix,' she says.

Part of me wants to stay at school, but the other part of me makes me step forward onto the bus.

'Felix! Felix!' I stop and turn around. Jake's running towards me, waving his arms in the air.

'Jake!' I shout. 'What are you doing here?'

'Yes.' Rich pokes his head out of the door. 'What are you doing here?'

'I'm ... I'm ...' Jake tries to catch his breath while looking at me like he wants me to think of an answer. 'I'm ... I'm Felix's coach!' Jake blurts. 'Yes, I'm Felix's coach. He said I could come.'

'What?' Rich looks at me.

Jake opens his eyes wider, like, *Back me up, Felix*. But I'm so happy to see him that I can't stop myself laughing.

'Yeah, he's my coach,' I say, smiling. I can't believe what Jake is saying, but I'm just glad he's here.

'Your coach?' Rich turns to me.

'Yeah.'

'Okay, so what does he do?' says Rich.

'Umm . . .'

'I carry his water.' Jake holds up his bottle of water. 'And I check that he doesn't get injured.'

'I don't think so,' says Rich. 'This is chess, not football, and besides, your name isn't on the list.'

Jake grabs Rich's pen. 'There,' he says as he scrawls on the paper, 'it is now.'

'Everything all right?' Mr Keytes shouts from the driver's seat.

'Yes, except *he's* here,' Rich snarls at Jake.

'Hi, sir!' Jake beams. 'Thought you'd like some support!'

'Well, it's appreciated, Jake, but did you get permission from your parents?'

'Course,' says Jake. 'My mum wrote you a note.'

I try hard to stop myself laughing as Jake holds up a piece of paper.

'Just get on, Jake,' says Mr Keytes, waving the note away. 'We've got a long journey ahead.'

'Great.' Jake heads to the back of the minibus. He isn't a real coach, but it is great to have someone in my corner.

I walk between the seats. Jake taps the one beside him. I glance at Rebecca.

'It's okay,' she says. 'I don't mind.'

It's not okay, because I promised I'd sit next to her, but I don't want to upset Jake.

'Do you mind if I sit with Rebecca?' I say cautiously. 'I'm really glad you're here, but I need to concentrate.'

Jake looks at Rebecca, then at me.

'Of course,' he says and smiles. 'You're the school champion!' he adds loudly enough for Rich to hear. He sits down behind me.

I take the seat next to Rebecca. She smiles but I can see she's shivering.

'Are you cold?' I ask.

'No.' She forces a smile. 'Just nervous. Aren't you?'

'Yeah ... Just a bit! My jaw has been aching ever since I got up.'

'It's adrenalin.' Jake pokes his head between the seats. 'I get it when I play football.'

'Jake, I'm sorry, but I said I need to concentrate.'

'Oops, sorry, Felix. Zip!' Jake pretends to seal his lips then sits back in his seat. Rebecca glances at me like she's about to say something and I do the same to her, but as the minibus pulls away I'm suddenly so nervous I want to pee. Mum and Dad tried to calm me as I left home. They wished me good luck and Mum gave me a comforting hug, but that hug is beginning to wear off. It's useless. I'm going to lose every game and let the team down. I don't care about Rich but I do about everyone else and now I know what it feels like to be good at something, I'm scared that someone or something will take that feeling away. *Granddad, why did we even start doing this? Couldn't you have taught me something else, like ludo, where all I have to do is pick up a counter and shake the dice?*

I look out of the window as the minibus stops at traffic lights. I could make a run for the door now – grab the handle, slide it back and jump out. I could do it. I could—

'Felix, I am thinking you need to stop this.'

'I know, Granddad, but I can't help it. I need to get out. I'm going to look like such an idiot.'

Rebecca gives me a weird look.

'Who are you talking to?'

'His granddad – he's always doing that.' Jake pokes his head between the seats again. 'It's a bit weird, but you get used to it.'

'Jake!' I yell.

'Sorry. Only saying.'

'Well, don't!'

'Shush!' Rich turns around. 'We need to focus.'

'See,' I whisper. 'I told you. If you're going to do anything, help. You're supposed to be my coach.'

'Okay ... Okay ... Keep your hair on, Felix. I'll think of something ... I know. Here ...' He reaches through the gap.

'Chewing gum?' I say.

'Well, I've got a bottle of Coke too ... I would have bought snacks, but they give us lunch!'

'Ha!' Rebecca turns around. 'So that's why you came!'

'Yes! And to support Felix, of course.'

'I think it's only the players and the teachers,' says Rebecca.

'That's okay,' says Jake. 'I'll just get crisps and chocolate from the machines. My dad knows how to rock them so you don't have to—'

'Jake,' I snap. 'Stop talking. I'm supposed to be concentrating.'

'We all are!' Rich glowers.

'Okay, okay!' Jake sits back. 'Keep your hair on.'

I lean back, bump my head against the seat rest. Dad told me it would take an hour to get to Cheltenham. That's how long I have to calm down. One hour to get ready for the most important event in my life. I wish Granddad was here to help. I close my eyes and think about what he would say to me if he was but all I can think about is what he told me when I left his house last night.

'Let your mind be as clear as the sky and your heart as calm as the ocean.'

Okay, clear mind, calm heart . . . Nope, it's no good. My heart's still racing and I need to pee!

'Take deep breaths. Nice deep breaths. Breathe out two seconds longer than you breathe in. I am thinking this will increase the air in your lungs, the oxygen in your blood, up into your brain. I am thinking this will help you stay calm. I am thinking this is best for you to concentrate.'

I take a deep breath, count to six. Let it out. Count to eight.

I take another.

'Oh my god! No way!'

'Not now, Jake.' I gulp.

'But, Felix—'

'No!'

'Argh! I can't look. This is the worst thing. Worse than dreaming of going to school with no clothes on.'

I sigh. He's not going to shut up until I look.

I open my eyes and turn around.

'What is it?'

Jake's slid down so far he's nearly on the floor.

'There,' he says, pointing over the back of his seat. 'He's there.'

'Who is?'

'Your granddad! He's following us in his pink car!'

44

First Round

'Granddad, what are you doing here?'

'I thought I would surprise you. I was at home watching TV, then I am thinking to myself, Felix must be getting nervous.'

'I am, Granddad, but you didn't have to follow us.'

'How am I supposed to know where you are going? I do not have this GPF.'

'It's GPS, Granddad.'

Jake sniggers behind me. I would normally laugh too and I would normally be embarrassed if Granddad was anywhere near my school, and if Mum and Dad were for that matter – but that's usually when they've been called in to see the head teacher. But I don't care about that now. I'm just glad Granddad's here to help.

I look across the sports centre car park to where about a hundred boys and girls and a few adults are funnelling through the main doors.

'Come on,' says Rebecca, 'they're going in now.'

I blow out my cheeks as we walk between cars.

'You will be fine,' says Granddad, trying to keep up with me. 'It is the waiting that is worst. Just remember what Bobby Fischer said.'

'He said lots of things, Granddad.'

'Yes, and they are all important, but today remember this one about what a great chess player needs: "A strong memory, concentration, imagination and a strong will."'

'I know, Granddad, but that's the point – I can't concentrate.'

'It's true,' Jake cuts in. 'He can't focus longer than a fly buzzing around a cowpat.'

Granddad stares at him. 'That's not how he is now.'

I feel a warm glow inside me as I realize that Granddad has noticed how much I've changed.

Jake shrugs, like he realizes this too. 'Okay,' he says. 'Maybe he doesn't mess around so much now, but it's fine, I can't hang around cowpats either.'

'Jake,' Rebecca jumps in. 'You're really not helping.'

'No, he's not.' Granddad glowers at Jake, then puts his arm around my shoulder. 'Come on, Felix,' he says, taking off his hat. 'Let's get inside.'

I follow the rest of the team through the doors. Mr Keytes shakes hands with a woman who must be another teacher and Rich stops and talks to a boy from another school.

Inside, the reception buzzes with the sound of voices. I feel myself shaking and when I smell the chlorine from the swimming pool I feel even worse. *But my granddad is here*, I tell myself. *What can go wrong?* I glance at Rebecca. She shrugs and gives me a nervous smile as we walk down a long corridor towards the main sports hall. 'Okay.' Mr Keytes stops by the doors and claps his hands. 'Everyone, listen. We've a few things to get through. Richard?'

Rich says goodbye to the boy he was talking to and joins us.

'I was just saying you've got a few things to tell us,' says Mr Keytes.

'Oh yes.' Rich looks at a piece of paper in his hand, then clears his throat like he's about to read the news. 'We're playing Foxley High in the first round,' he says. 'And we've drawn lots to see who plays who. So it's totally random. Rebecca, you're on table six, Chris, table twelve, Tom, table fourteen, Leah, table eighteen, I'm on table sixteen.' Then he looks up at me and adds, 'Felix, you're on table twenty.'

'But that's . . .' Chris reads over Rich's shoulder. 'He's playing Sam Paterson.'

'Yep.'

'Who's that?' I ask.

'Only the player who scored the most points last year!' says Chris.

'Wow!' says Jake. 'You'll get slaughtered!'

'Jake! That's not really going to help Felix,' says Mr Keytes.

'Just saying.' Jake glances at me.

It doesn't help, but Jake's right. I turn around and look for Granddad, but the doors have been pushed open and I'm being jostled through.

Inside, the sports hall has basketball ball hoops at both ends and in between them are loads of tables arranged in lines like when I take exams. And hundreds of boys and girls are standing between them, in smart uniforms, talking so loudly their voices echo off the walls.

Rich and the others push past me, then more children from another

243

school. I turn and look for Granddad again, but the only person I recognize is Jake.

'Break a leg, Felix,' he shouts above the crowd. But I don't want his advice. I want Granddad's.

'Felix!' I turn and see Granddad's hat above everyone else. 'You will be fine,' he says loudly. 'I will watch you from up here.' He nods up some stairs, then back at me. 'Just remember, do not look at them, just think of them as—'

A hooter sounds. Boys and girls push past me like they're late for a football match and they start to carry me with them.

'Think of them as what, Granddad?' I shout. I jump above the crowd to spot him, but all I see is an empty space on the stairs. *What was he going to say?*

I look at the two rows of tables. At the chessboards lined up on them and the clocks at the sides. *This isn't fair – why did I get drawn against last year's best player?*

I spot Rebecca across the room, talking to Chris. They walk towards me and I meet them in the middle of the hall.

'How did this happen?' I say. 'Can we swap?'

'What, so I get beaten?' says Chris.

'No,' I say. 'Maybe not with you, but with somebody . . . with Rich?'

'We can't,' Rebecca sighs. 'I know it doesn't seem fair, but it's a random draw – you don't get to choose.'

A bell rings out. Everyone stops talking.

'We've got to find our tables.' Rebecca points at the tables with numbers written on the corners. 'I am table six,' she says. 'And you're table twenty . . .'

I look around the room and try to see my table, but I'm panicking too much to count them.

'Felix.' Rebecca puts her hand on my arm like she's trying to make me relax. 'It's down there. Right at the other end.'

'Thanks.' I take a breath.

'Felix, it's okay. Don't worry. It's not all down to you; we're a team, right?'

'Right.' I smile weakly, then weave my way between the rows of tables, checking the numbers like I'm at the cinema searching for my seat.

I stop when I reach table twenty. My opponent is already seated. I keep my head down, trying not to make eye contact with him until we shake hands. I glance around the hall. Everyone else has reached their tables and are sitting ready to play. Everyone except Rich, who's grinning across the room, in my direction.

I look behind me, wondering if he's seen a friend, or his mum and dad up in the gallery. But all there is behind me is a massive white wall.

What is he grinning at?

I think of smoothing my face for zits or checking my flies.

Someone clears his throat, then holds out his hand. I reach out and take it, and look my opponent in the eye. Wait. I've seen him before. He's the boy I saw Rich talking to in the reception area. He holds onto my hand for too long. I try to pull it away. He lets go and his face cracks into a grin. He glances across the hall. I see Rich grinning back.

'So,' says my opponent. 'What are you going to play, the Sicilian Defence?' He laughs.

My heart jumps like a rabbit. Rich has told him the moves I use. It's a setup. They've fixed it. My head begins to throb. I don't know what to do. I want to get out of here, but I'm trapped, like I'm stuck in a cave in Tomb Raider with the walls closing in.

I stare across at Rich.

I thought we were here to win. I thought we were on the same team!

45

Tick, Tick, Tick

My opponent picks up a white pawn, then a black, and puts them behind his back.

This isn't right. This isn't right.

I look up at the viewing areas, see loads of parents, but not mine, just my granddad staring at me with Jake beside him eating a packet of crisps.

Rich has told him my moves. Help me! I try to transmit this thought across the hall. But Granddad stares ahead and Jake keeps munching.

I can't believe Rich has told this boy I use the Sicilian Defence. If I thought I had a tiny chance, even that's gone now because my opponent knows all the opening moves I'm going to make. I could switch to another. I should switch to another, but which one?

My heart beats fast as the walls creep in. *Don't panic, keep calm.* I close my eyes, check the rules in my head . . .

Don't eat before playing.

I haven't.

Don't make eye contact with your opponent.

Don't—

I lean forward and hold my head in my hands.

'You need to choose,' says my opponent.

'Left,' I say, without looking up.

'Then you're white.'

'Okay,' I say under my breath. 'Okay.'

I hear the sound of chess pieces being placed on the board. I glance up and stare at the clock – just like the one in *Pawn Sacrifice*. I need to make a move. I need to make a move then start the clock. I clench my fist.

'Head as clear as the sky, heart as calm as the sea.'

I know, Granddad, but my heart is pounding!

'Then imagine.'

Imagine what?

'A wooden box.'

What?

The clock ticks on to fifty seconds, fifty-one seconds, fifty-two, fifty-three, fifty-four, fifty-five.

'Imagine your opponent is . . .'

Fifty-seven, fifty-eight, fifty-nine.

Help me, Granddad!

'Imagine your opponent is the Mechanical Turk.'

I pick up a pawn and move it to e4.

There, that's my first move.

'Don't forget the clock.'

What?

'Don't forget the clock.'

I hit the clock.

'Pretend he's a faceless man in a box. A wooden box with no heart but with clunky arms.'

I know.

The wooden box moves a pawn to c5.

Stops the clock.

I move my knight to f3.

Stop the clock.

The wooden box moves its knight to c6.

Stops the clock.

I move a pawn to d4.

Stop the clock.

The wooden box takes my pawn on d4.

Stops the clock.

My knight takes a pawn on d4.

The box moves a pawn to g6.

I've seen these moves before; Granddad warned me about them one evening – it's the Accelerated Dragon variation of the Sicilian Defence. I need to think fast. I need to think clearly. What did Granddad tell me to do? What . . .

Got it!

I move a pawn to c4.

I wait for the wooden box to make its move, but no hand appears, no chess piece moves. It's like it is thinking extra hard. I've just played the Maróczy Bind, but it's like the box doesn't know how to respond to it.

I wait until eventually it moves its knight to f6.

Stops the clock.

It's cat versus mouse, me against wooden box. It tries to trap my king while I try to trap its king too.

More moves ... another ten each, and all the time I'm thinking three moves ahead until ...

Knight to c3.

Pawn to d6.

Pawn to f3.

Knight takes rook on d4.

Queen takes knight on d4.

'Check,' I say. 'Checkmate.'

'That's impossible!' my opponent mutters. 'Impossible.'

I feel a smile creep across my face. I thought it was impossible too. I imagine a wooden box, with wooden arms sticking out of it, whirring round like its circuits have been crossed.

I stand up and hold out my hand.

I've won. I've beaten the computer!

'Yes! Felix! YES!' Jake's jumping all around me like an excited Labrador.

Rebecca is smiling. Chris is smiling. Tom is smiling. Leah is smiling.

'Yes! Yes!' Jake is pumping his fist and jumping up and down in front of me.

250

'Okay, Jake,' says Mr Keytes. 'This is a chess game, not a football match. But well done, Felix,' he adds, patting me on the back. 'Great effort.'

This does feel like a football match. I feel like I've run the length of the pitch and smashed the ball in the back of the net.

Jake wraps his arm around my neck.

'Knew you would do it,' he says. 'Never in doubt.'

I pull myself away from him. I feel as happy as he is, so happy I don't want the day to end, but right now the only person I want to celebrate with is Granddad.

I look up to the viewing area and search for him, but all I see are exit signs and empty seats. He must be on his way down.

Rich stands in front of me, holding his hand out begrudgingly. 'Well done,' he says. I shake his hand without thinking.

I've just won my third game in a row and I feel so good that I'm laughing inside. Now all I want is to see Granddad and give him a hug, but I can't spot him anywhere because the hall is buzzing with pupils and teachers. I ask Rebecca how she did. She tells me she had one win, one loss and one draw, and she's quite happy. I tell her I'm happy for her, then a blonde girl wearing a blue school uniform walks towards us.

'Well done,' she says to me.

'Oh . . . thanks,' I say.

She gives me a quizzical look. 'You played me in the second game.'

'Did I?'

'Yes,' she says. 'You captured my bishop and my knight on moves twelve and fourteen.'

251

'I'm sorry,' I say. 'I can remember doing that, but I don't—'

'Remember me?'

'No,' I say. 'Sorry.'

'It's okay.' She smiles. 'You looked like you were in a trance.'

'He was.' Rebecca laughs, then asks the girl, 'How did your team do?'

'I'm not sure,' she replies. 'I think we had eight wins, seven losses and three draws, so we won't win. The teachers are working it out now.' She nods towards a table in the corner where a group of teachers are gathered with clipboards and pens. I blow out my cheeks. I want to know if we've won, but I want to see Granddad too. I search through the crowds but I still can't see him. He's taken so long to get down that he must have gone to the toilet.

Jake pats me on the back, tells me well done for the twentieth time. Behind us I hear Rich and Chris working out how many points we have – Chris says he and Rebecca both got two and a half, Leah got one and Tom didn't get any. Then Rich says he got three and a half, and 'he' – meaning me – got four. He works out that we've got thirteen and a half points, that we might not win, but we've got a chance.

The group of teachers nod at each other, then part.

'Here's the result,' says Rebecca, tugging my arm

One of the teachers picks up a bell and rings it. I look around the hall. All the groups of pupils have gone quiet and are standing with their teachers. My group does the same, except we stand with Rich because for some reason Mr Keytes isn't here.

'Okay,' says the teacher who rang the bell. 'First of all, I want to thank you all for coming and making this a wonderful tournament.'

I take a deep breath and look at Jake and Rebecca. I've won all my games, but it would be brilliant if we won the tournament.

'In third place,' says the teacher, 'with twelve points is ... drum roll?'

All the groups stay quiet, like they're too nervous to rap their hands on the tables or stamp their feet.

'Come on, drum roll, everybody,' says the teacher. The hall rumbles with people tapping the tables and stamping their feet. 'Fairfield High!'

A group of boys and girls in grey blazers turn and smile, patting each other on the shoulders. Some look happy they came third, some look disappointed they didn't win.

'We got thirteen and a half,' Rich whispers. 'We beat that! We're either first or second.'

'And so, the runners-up,' says the teacher. 'This was a very close thing. Very close indeed.' Rebecca nudges me. Chris and Leah look at each other. Rich has got his fist clenched. Jake's so wide-eyed he looks like he's going to explode.

I glance behind me for Granddad. If I've won I want him here, but the only person I see is Mr Keytes standing by the door with a serious look on his face like he's just found out we've been disqualified.

'And the runners-up are ...'

Mr Keytes beckons me.

Does he mean just me, or the whole team?

He beckons me again.

A big roar echoes around the room, but I didn't hear who it was for, because as I walk across the basketball court it's as though I'm moving in slow motion through a wall of noise.

Mr Keytes steps aside and lets me through the door.

'What is it, sir?' I asks. 'Did I do something wrong?'

'No.' Mr Keytes shakes his head. 'You've done nothing wrong. It's your granddad.'

'What? What's the matter?' I look down the corridor in panic. 'Where is he?'

'Outside,' says Mr Keytes. 'He's being looked after in the ambulance . . . Felix!' Mr Keytes makes a barrier with his arm. 'Felix, please don't panic. The right people are looking after him now.'

'But, you don't understand. I need to see him.'

'Felix!'

I push Mr Keytes's arm away and run outside.

46

Blue Lights and Disinfectant

I sprint down the corridor. My heart beats twice as fast as my feet move and I dodge past people in the reception.

Get out of the way.

Get out of the way!

I push the sports centre doors open. There's an ambulance parked at the bottom of the steps with the back doors open. A paramedic in a green uniform is standing by the doors.

I jump down the steps.

'Granddad!' I yell.

'Whoa!' The paramedic holds me back. 'He's fine.'

'Then why's he in the back of an ambulance?' I try to wriggle free.

Inside, another paramedic taps a plastic tube that is going into Granddad's arm. 'Your granddad is okay.' She turns to me. 'But you're not going to help him if you panic.'

'But I am . . . Can you just let me see him?'

'It's all right, Martin, let him through.'

Martin lets go of me and I take a step into the ambulance. Granddad's sitting in a wheelchair with a blanket pulled up to his chin. His hat is squished on the ambulance floor.

'Granddad,' I say. 'Are you okay?' I wait for him to answer, but he can't because he's got an oxygen mask over his mouth. The smell of disinfectant creeps up my nose and reminds me of when I used to visit Grandma in hospital.

'Just sit quietly.' The paramedic points to a bench inside the ambulance. 'Your granddad's going to be fine,' she says softly.

They used to say that about Grandma too, but really she wasn't. I sit down, slowly. Granddad doesn't look fine. His face is as white as the moon and his eyelids are droopy. He lifts his hand.

'No, Francke,' says the paramedic, 'don't try to move or talk.' Then she turns to Martin and says, 'BP one hundred and eight over sixty-eight, HR ninety-six.'

'What does that mean?' I ask. 'Is it serious?'

'It means we're going to have to take your granddad to hospital,' she says. 'Is your granddad diabetic?'

'Yes. He's got a black bag in the car.'

'Great, that'll help me lots.' The paramedic stands up and starts to move Granddad further into the ambulance.

'Felix!' I look out and see Mr Keytes standing by the ambulance doors. Beside him, Jake and Rebecca are standing on tiptoes, peering in.

'Is your granddad okay?' asks Jake. 'Tell him I'm sorry I thought he was a spy.'

256

'Jake,' says Mr Keytes. 'We don't need silly stuff from you now.' He holds out his hand to me. 'Felix,' he says. 'I think it best you come with us.'

'But my granddad,' I say. 'I don't want to leave him.' I look back at Granddad. His tie is skew-whiff and his best suit is creased. He tries to speak, but all I hear is a muffled mumble.

'What's that, Granddad?' I ask.

'Francke,' says the paramedic, 'I know it's frustrating, but for the moment it's best you leave the mask on and try not to speak.'

Granddad shakes his head irritably, like a bee just went into his ear. Granddad mumbles again.

'BP one hundred and eight over sixty-two, HR eighty-two. We're beginning to stabilise now, Francke, but we'll go to the hospital to be safe,' the paramedic says calmly, which begins to make me feel calmer too.

'Can I talk to him before he goes?' I ask.

The paramedic looks at Granddad, like he's going to ask him, but Granddad's already pulling at his mask.

'Go on,' says the paramedic, smiling. 'Just a quick word.'

Granddad moves the mask onto his cheek and mutters something, but he's so breathy I can't hear.

I lean over him.

'It's okay, Granddad,' I say. 'I love you too.'

Granddad shakes his head and takes a deep breath.

'No,' he whispers. 'Did you win?'

47

Is It Okay to Pray Only When You Want Something?

Dear God . . . Dear God . . . Is it okay . . . Do you mind if . . .

I'm lying on my bed, staring at the ceiling with my hands on my chest. I've been thinking of a prayer for Granddad, but every time I go to start I hear Mum's voice downstairs as she talks to Dad on the phone. Part of me wants to listen, the other part of me wants to wrap a pillow around my head and block it all out.

Dear God . . .

'Is he awake?'

I know I haven't prayed since Grandma was ill.

'Is he talking?'

And I know that didn't work.

'Does he know you're there?'

But I'm sure you tried.

'I'm sure he'll be okay.'

And ...

'One minute ...' For a moment Mum's voice gets louder as she walks into the hallway. 'Yes. I know. I'll move into the sitting room.'

Click.

Mum closes the sitting room door.

The news must be bad because this is what it was like in the days before Grandma died. Dad calling Mum, Mum calling Dad, Dad coming home, whispering in the kitchen, whispering in the dining room, whispering in their bedroom. I didn't want to listen, but you don't have to hear everything to know when someone is really ill. I didn't want Granddad to go to hospital on his own, but Mr Keytes said I was too young to be left alone at the hospital. It was so quiet in the minibus on the way back that all I could hear was the rush of the wind and the rumble of tyres on the road. Rebecca said she was sure Granddad would be okay, and Jake said the same, but there was no way they could know. They were just hoping like me.

I roll over onto my side. See the pieces of paper with Granddad's writing scrawled across them: the chessboard, drawings of the chess pieces with the moves written beside them – *Pawn, can only move forward, two squares first move, then only one. Bishop, can only move on the diagonal. Rook, can only move horizontally and vertically.* I close my eyes. Normally I would keep seeing the squares, but now all I can see is Granddad, wrapped up in a blanket in the back of the ambulance.

'Felix ... Felix ...' Mum knocks gently on my door. 'Can I come in?'

I wipe my eyes on my pyjama sleeve and roll over to face the door.

Mum pushes the door open slowly.

'I just thought I'd give you some news on Granddad,' she says softly.

'Is it his heart? Like Grandma?' I ask.

'We're not sure,' she says as she walks in and sits at the end of my bed. 'He's sleeping now, but Dad says not to worry and he'll call again in the morning.'

'I knew he shouldn't have driven to watch me play ...' My voice begins to crack. 'He did feel dizzy earlier in the week. I should have said something.'

'Hey.' Mum gives me a caring smile. 'You're not to blame. You know what your granddad is like, he's so stubborn. Even if we'd said not to, he'd have gone, and besides, it's you who cheered him up these past few weeks.'

I force a smile. I'd rather he'd been grumpy and be sitting at home, not happier and in hospital.

'I wish I'd never even started playing,' I say.

'Come here,' says Mum, holding out her arms.

I lean forward and she wraps her arms around me.

'He'll be fine,' she whispers. 'You wait and see. He'll soon be picking you up from school again in that pink car. You won't be able to wait to get into it!'

'I don't think I'd go that far!' I sniff.

Mum laughs. 'Well, that sounds like my Felix is back,' she says.

I smile weakly and she hugs me again. I wish my granddad was back too. Mum pats my back, then strokes my head like she used to when I was younger.

'He'll be fine,' she says softly. 'He's a tough old bird.'

'I hope so,' I say, even though I'm not sure Granddad is as tough as she thinks.

'He will be,' she says, letting go of me. 'Tell you what, I'm just going over to feed Samson. Did you want to come?'

'I'm in my pyjamas.'

'That doesn't matter,' Mum smiles. 'I just thought it would be good for you to be doing something.'

'No, it's okay,' I say. 'I'll stay here.'

Mum walks to my door, then stops. 'Just try to get some sleep,' she says. 'And we'll see how he is in the morning.'

'Okay.'

Mum's footsteps fade away as she walks down the stairs.

I lie back on my bed. She was trying to help, but going to Granddad's house when he's not there would be horrible. It would just be an empty shell, with Samson walking around looking for him like he did for Grandma for a few days after she died. And sometimes it was scary too, because Samson would suddenly stare into the hall like he'd seen a ghost. I bet Samson is missing Granddad too, and it's not just for the food.

I close my eyes and for a moment I hear Granddad's voice again in my head: *'a1, b1, f1, g1, this is a file, this is a rank. c1 ...'* I sigh. *'d1, e1, this is the bishop, it moves on the diagonal, this is a rook, it moves in straight lines.'* I hear Granddad so clearly it's like we're in the garden with the sun shining on us as we cut the grass.

I fold my hands on my chest. *Dear God, is it okay to pray only when I want something? I know it didn't work for Grandma, but do you mind if I try again?*

261

48

Stage Fright

'Stable,' whispers Jake. 'That's good, Felix. It means your granddad's like Everton; he's not going to win the league, but he's not going to get relegated either.'

'I know,' I say, 'but he's still ill.'

'Yes. But he's not going to d—'

'Shush.' Rebecca nudges him. 'We've got to go on stage soon.'

I'm standing behind the stage curtain with Rebecca, Jake and the rest of the chess team. Mr Mclugash is telling the whole school that whoever is jamming toilet rolls in the boys' sinks and flooding the toilets will be caught and punished, so they best own up now. Then he pauses and stares like he's expecting someone to put their hand up. No one does, so he starts talking about Year Nine's trip to York, but his words start to jumble in my head because my heart is beating fast and my palms are sweating. I've never been on stage before and I definitely didn't think I would be today – I didn't think I'd even be in school. I wanted to stay at home, but after Dad phoned and said Granddad was doing okay, Mum said school was the best place for me, because it would stop me thinking about him. And she's right, because all I can think about now is how to stop my legs shaking. I peer around the curtain. The whole school are in the hall, like the rows and columns of an army. I'm usually one of the pupils looking at the stage, but now hundreds of faces are looking in my direction. And it makes me want to disappear.

'So here they are.' Mr Mclugash holds out his arm. 'The school chess team!'

Rich brushes his blazer with his palms and walks onto the stage, followed by Chris.

'Go on!' Rebecca pushes me in the back. I try to move but my feet are superglued to the stage.

'Felix!' Jake urges. 'Move!'

I stumble forward.

'They may not have won,' says Mr Mclugash, 'but they were runners-up against some very tough competition, so let's give them a round of applause.'

Rich stops in the middle of the stage and we face the school. Everyone is cheering and clapping and the teachers are lined up behind us clapping too. Rebecca gives me a nervous smile. I can't smile back because I'm shaking like a penguin on an iceberg. I look at my feet, then at Rebecca again. My face is burning, but now I can't stop myself grinning as the clapping and whistling keeps on. This doesn't happen to me. This happens to Hannah Mills when she collects the Debating Society trophy, and Florrie Price for winning the school writing competition, and Luke Harvey when he gets yet another certificate for gymnastics. Last time he was on stage because he qualified for the county, although Jake always says his triple flips look more like forward rolls. But now it's my turn to be up here, to know what it feels like to be good at something, and it's a feeling I hope I have again.

'Okay.' Mr Mclugash holds up his hand and the clapping and cheering slowly dies away.

'So, Richard,' says Mr Mclugash. 'Would you like to tell us all what happened?'

Rich smiles, then pulls out some notes from his blazer pocket, like he's a politician about to give a speech.

'So,' he reads. 'I'm the captain of the school chess team and yesterday we went to Cheltenham Sports Centre for the Inter-Schools Championship. In the first round we played Foxley High and I won my match and we beat them three–one. In the next round we played Huntsville Grammar. It was a close match, but I won my game and we beat them three–two. In the next round we played . . .'

'Me. Me. Me!' Jake hisses in my ear. 'We played too!'

'I know,' I say under my breath. 'Or at least *I* did.' I turn and look at Jake. 'Hey, what are you doing up here anyway?'

'Don't know.' Jake smirks. 'Just am!'

I shake my head slowly. Rebecca smiles as she does the same. We all smile. They are my equal best friends and it's brilliant that we are all on the stage together.

'So we didn't win the tournament,' Rich continues, 'but we played really well. I drew my match in the last round so we ended as the runners-up.'

264

'Well.' Mr Mclugash takes a step forward. 'I think it was a wonderful effort, so let's give them another round of applause.' He claps his hands. Rich walks in front of us and starts to lead us off the stage.

'One moment!' says Mr Mclugash.

Rich stops walking and I bump into the back of Rebecca.

'We're not finished yet.' Mr Mclugash beckons us back. 'We've got another announcement, haven't we, Mr Keytes?'

We all edge back onto the stage.

Mr Keytes steps forward. 'Yes,' he says. 'We've got some good news, because even though Southwick High didn't win, one of our team did do rather well.'

Rich straightens his tie.

'Brilliant,' says Jake. 'He gets the credit for everything.'

'I know,' I whisper.

'Yes, Felix . . . Come over here.' Mr Mclugash holds up his arm.

What? Me!

I must be hearing it wrong, but then I see the whole school are staring at me.

It can't be me. I feel like I want to slip through the trapdoor and disappear under the stage.

'Don't be shy, Felix. Come here.' Mr Mclugash beckons me.

My heart beats double fast and my face feels like it's going to catch fire.

He's only ever spoken to me when I've been in trouble.

Go on! Rebecca mouths.

'Go on, you idiot!' Jake pushes me in the back.

I take one step, then another. *What have I done?* I keep walking, but my feet are numb and the stage is a blur.

Mr Mclugash shakes my hand, then turns me to face the school.

'I imagine a lot of you know Felix,' he says. 'Sometimes for the wrong reasons!' He opens his eyes wide.

Someone giggles.

Mr Mclugash glares at Jake. 'As I was saying ... sometimes it's for the wrong reasons, but today it's for a good reason. Because even though our team aren't the champions, Felix here won every one of his matches and ... I'm not sure if he knows this yet ...'

Knows what?

'Because he accumulated the most points, he has been chosen as the school representative to play in the National Finals in ... what ... two weeks' time, is it, Mr Keytes?'

'Ten days,' says Mr Keytes, holding up both hands.

What? National Finals, I think to myself. *How did that hap—*

'Great,' says Mr Mclugash. I don't have time to think how it happened, because Mr Mclugash is now shaking my hand and presenting me with a piece of paper.

Everyone in assembly starts clapping again. I try to read the piece of paper, but the rest of the team have gathered around me.

'Brilliant,' says Rebecca, smiling.

'Amazing, Felix.' Jake pats me on the back. 'Amazing.'

'Well done,' says Chris.

'Well done,' says Leah.

'Yeah, well done,' Rich says, like the words are stuck in his throat.

I take a deep breath, then another.

266

I'm in the National Chess Finals!

I can't wait to tell Granddad. If only he was well, I'd run to the square right now to tell him and Mum and Dad all about what I've done.

'No, Richard. Let's have Felix in the middle.' Mrs Lemon runs around in front of us and takes a picture with her phone.

'We'll put it on the school website and . . .' she says. I try to hear, but the rest of her words get lost in the cheers. I look down at the piece of paper. A smile creeps across my face and my chest fills with air.

FELIX SCHOPP

SCHOOLS NATIONAL CHESS FINALIST

Even I can stand still long enough to read that.

49

Hugs and Soppy Films

'Felix,' says Mum, putting her hand on top of mine. 'We really are so proud of you.'

'Yes.' Dad puts a chip in his mouth. 'It's amazing. Who'd have thought it, the boy who hated chess ends up going to the National Finals? It's like a Hollywood film.'

'Yes,' says Mum, beaming. 'Aww, come here.'

'What, again, Mum?'

'Well, it doesn't happen often.' Mum hugs and kisses me for what feels like the twentieth time. 'You've done so well.'

'Yes, matey,' says Dad, munching a chip. 'Seems like you didn't spend all your time firing canon balls from a tree. But no, seriously, Felix,' he chomps. 'I mean it. I'm really proud of you – can't wait to tell the blokes at work tomorrow.'

I smile and look up at the clock.

'So can I call Granddad at the hospital now and tell him?'

Mum looks at her watch. 'I don't know. It's gone seven. The doctors said he needs to rest and you know how your granddad hates talking on the phone.'

'But he needs to know,' I say. 'It might make him feel better.'

Mum and Dad exchange looks, like, *What do you think?*

'Okay,' says Dad. 'I took him Mum's old mobile but you know what he's like with phones. He may not answer.'

'He'll want to talk to me.' I smile. 'He followed me all the way to Cheltenham!'

Dad punches the number in, then hands me the phone.

I push back my chair and walk into the hallway.

'Don't tire him out,' calls Mum.

I put the phone to my ear and listen to the dialling tone. The phone clicks then I hear a rustling sound.

'Hi, Granddad,' I say excitedly. 'It's me, Felix!'

The rustling sound starts again, stops, then I hear the rush of wind, like someone breathing.

'Granddad?' I walk into the sitting room. 'It's me, Felix!'

'Oh, Felix. I am sorry.' Granddad's voice sounds weak and far away. 'I dropped the phone.'

'It's okay, Granddad,' I say. 'I just called to tell you that I'm going to play in the National Chess Finals, in Birmingham.'

'Birmingham,' says Granddad. 'I am thinking this is wonderful.'

'I know, Granddad. It is. I need to practise. Dad said you might be coming out on Wednesday. I could come over after school—'

'Felix!' Mum shouts. 'What did I tell you?'

'It's okay, Granddad, it's just Mum.' I walk over to the window. 'She says you won't feel like playing, but I know you will.'

'Well, I *am* feeling a little tired,' says Granddad. 'And . . .'

'And what, Granddad?'

'Well, you know I don't trust the phone.'

'It's okay, Granddad,' I say. 'It's only me here . . . well, and Mum and Dad. But we could always talk in code.'

I wait for an answer, but all I hear is Granddad breathing again.

'Granddad? Are you there?'

I look at the screen. The green icon is still lit. I listen again. Silence.

'Granddad,' I say, beginning to panic. 'Are you there? Granddad?'

'Yes,' says Granddad. 'I am thinking.'

Phew, he's thinking.

'I am thinking . . . I am thinking . . .'

'Yes, Granddad?'

The Dutch Attack?

The French Defence?

The—

'Con-fi-dence,' says Granddad so slowly it's like it's three words.

'What's that, Granddad?'

'Con-fi-dence is all you need. Above everything I taught you, con-fi-dence is the most important thing. Everything will take . . .' He starts to cough and I hear a nurse ask if he wants a glass of water.

The phone goes quiet.

'Granddad,' I say. 'Are you okay?'

I hear people talking in the distance, then the shallow breathing again.

270

'Felix, are you still there?'

'Yes, Granddad.' I sigh with relief.

'I need to go now. But everything will be fine.'

'Okay, Granddad,' I say. 'Love you.'

I wait for him to say it back, but all I hear is the shallow sound of his breathing.

The phone goes dead.

I stare at the screen.

'Tell your granddad, me and Dad will be visiting ...' Mum walks in. 'Felix, what's wrong?'

I turn around.

'I don't know, Mum,' I say slowly. 'He's gone.'

'What do you mean, gone?'

I hand her the phone. 'I just told him I loved him and he put the phone down.'

'He's tired, Felix, and you know your granddad is like your dad when it comes to expressing his feelings.'

'Yeah,' I sigh. 'It's just he didn't sound the same.'

'He'll be fine. Don't you worry. He'll soon be back over there making you eat sausages again.'

'Hope so.'

'He will!' Mum puts her arm around me and gives me a hug. 'Tell you what, let's have a movie night, and I'll go into work later tomorrow so I can take you to school in the morning.'

'It's okay, Mum,' I say. 'You don't have to.'

'No, we will,' she says, looking at Dad as he comes into the room. 'You deserve it, and we've not all been together for ages.'

271

'Yeah.' Dad nods. 'I'm up for that. What shall we watch? I think there's a new series of *Daredevil* on Netflix.'

'Well, that's not quite what I had in mind,' says Mum. 'Let's see if there's anything else.'

'Oh no, here we go.' Dad rolls his eyes as Mum walks towards the TV. 'Not another romcom, *Legally Blonde* or *Bridget Jones*, again.'

I smile. I don't care what we watch, just as long as we all sit down together. Mum is right, it has been ages – it's like everyone has been zapping around at a million miles an hour since Dad's business went bust and, of course, after Gran died.

Dad sits next to me on the sofa as Mum sorts through the DVDs.

'*Love Actually*?' she asks.

'No,' says Dad.

'*Along Comes Polly?*'

'No.'

'Oh ... I know ... *Frozen!*'

'Mum!' I lie back on the sofa and laugh.

I haven't done that for days.

50

Plan B

'I guess he won't be going zip wiring then?' whispers Jake.

I glare at him.

'What? I'm only saying ...' Jake shrugs. 'I was looking forward to it.'

'Who said you were going anyway?' I say. 'And besides, I'm not worried about zip wire. I'm not even worried about chess.'

'Boys.' Mr Andrews leans over our table. 'How are those graphs coming along?' He turns Jake's book towards him and sighs. 'Jake,' he says. 'We're supposed to be reflecting triangles on the y axis, not plotting the Milky Way.'

Jake laughs. 'I'm trying, sir.'

'Yes,' says Mr Andrews. 'You really are ... Now come on, why don't you take a leaf out of Felix's book and get some new-found concentration to apply to your maths ... ? Oh, and I think it's brilliant by the way.'

'But you said it was the Milky Way,' Jake says, confused.

'I meant Felix,' he says, turning to me. 'I'll be supporting you in the finals.'

'Thanks, sir.' My heart swells in my chest. I'm used to teachers telling me off, not telling me how well I've done.

'Thanks, sir!' Jake says in a high-pitched voice as Mr Andrews moves away.

'What?' I ask.

'You're turning into Rebecca. But I guess that's okay. If it's just a bit.'

I look down at my work. I've been so worried about Granddad that I thought it would get worse, but in geography I put my hand up and answered a question about rock erosion and deposition. Then when I went to read with Mrs Hudson she had to stop me to let Michael read, because I had read two pages already and was going to read another. If Granddad made some tweaks so that chess helped my schoolwork, they seem to be working, even from his hospital bed. I wish he was home so I could go and see him straight after school. But I can't expect him to play chess as soon as he comes out. I could practise more with Rebecca or play online. I have to come up with a plan. But chess is the last thing I should be thinking about because the most important thing is that Granddad gets well.

'We need a plan,' says Jake as we walk down the corridor towards chess club.

'A plan?'

'Yes, now your granddad isn't around, we need another plan.

But don't worry, I'll come up with something – after all, I am your coach.'

I laugh.

'It's true,' he chuckles. 'You'd be lost without me. You'd be like a boxer without his trainer, or a football team without its manager, like Pep Gwady ... Gwady ... what's his name?'

'Guardiola.'

'That's it, Felix.' Jake pats me on the back as we walk into the library.

Rich and Chris are already playing a game. Rebecca waves at us from a table in the corner. Chris nods, but Rich pretends he doesn't see us as we walk past them.

'Didn't think you were coming,' whispers Rebecca.

I sit down next to her and sigh.

'What's wrong,' she asks.

'He's panicking,' says Jake. 'His granddad is too ill to play and he feels bad that he doesn't feel really bad and he feels even worse because all he's worried about is chess.'

'How do you know all that?'

'It's obvious,' says Jake. 'He's been walking round like he's lost a dog.'

I stare at the chessboard.

'So he feels guilty?' says Rebecca.

'Yeah, that's it. Guilty ... So *you* need to come up with a plan.'

'I do?' says Rebecca. 'I thought you were his coach.'

'I am, but even great coaches get help. Even Pep Gwady ... Gwady—'

'Guardiola,' I sigh.

'Yeah. Even him. But whatever you come up with will only be temporary because Felix's granddad will be home soon and then he'll take over again.'

Rebecca shakes her head as she takes the chess pieces out of the box.

'How is your granddad, anyway?'

'I think he's okay. But he's got to stay in hospital for a while.'

'That's good.' Rebecca smiles. 'Well, not *good* good, but you know what I mean.'

'So what's the plan?' asks Jake.

Rebecca calmly puts the chess pieces on their squares.

'Well?' Jake asks again.

'It's obvious,' she says, looking at me. 'We play.'

51

Uh Oh!

'It's your move,' Rebecca whispers.

I stare at the chessboard.

'Felix, it's your move.'

'I know . . . I know this.'

'It's just lunch break is going to be over soon.'

I'm at chess club with Rebecca, again. Yesterday she said all we had to do was play, and we did, but moves that usually take me seconds are now taking minutes. She beat me and I don't think she was even trying because she sacrificed her rook like she was deliberately trying to lose just to make me feel good. But it hasn't worked because I'm playing terribly again today.

I lift my hand and hover it over the board.

Pawn to b4?

No.

Bishop to c6?

No.

I put my hand back down on the table.

Pawn to d4?

Pawn to h4?

No, it's useless. I can't think of my next move because there are too many other thoughts getting in the way. Granddad is coming out of hospital today and all I want to do is go home and wait for him. Last night I walked around the square three times and every time I passed his house I looked at the windows and imagined he was peeping through the curtains and waving at me, but there wasn't even a sliver of a gap. Samson was huddled up on the doorstep because he'd been locked out all day. There was no sign of Granddad at all. It was like an alien spaceship had landed and taken him away.

Rebecca opens a packet of crisps, really loudly like she's trying to get my attention. I glance up at her. She nods at the board.

I blink, trying to make the board come into focus, but I've been staring for so long that all the squares are blurred.

Pawn to g4 or pawn to e4?

Rebecca leans across the table.

'Felix,' she whispers. 'You've run out of time.'

'Again,' I mumble.

'I thought with Jake playing football, you might be able to concentrate better,' she says.

'Me too.'

Rebecca looks at me for a long time like that will make me talk, but it doesn't work.

I glance around the room. Since the Inter-Schools Championship we've got four new members so there are now six chessboards scattered on tables around the library and all of the players have their heads down, working out their next moves, except for Rich who's grinning across the room at me like he's been waiting for my next move too.

The end-of-lunch bell rings.

I grab my bag off my chair and walk between the tables. Rich stands up.

'Lose again?' he asks. 'What happened, have you run out of moves?'

My blood boils in my veins, but I don't want to reply because if I say anything I feel like I'll cry. I keep walking.

'Oh, I get it,' shouts Rich. 'Now you're in the National Finals, you think you are too good to play with the rest of us!'

I stop and stare at him. My chest goes tight and my blood pumps through my fist. I walk back to Rich and look down at his board. He smirks like he's daring me – daring me to swipe all the chess pieces off his board.

I draw my hand back and . . . someone grabs it.

'Come on, Felix,' says Rebecca. 'Let's go.' She pulls me away but I'm still staring at Rich.

'Hope you get your A game back for next week,' he says with a smirk.

'I will!' I snap. Everyone looks up from their chess games, but their faces and the books on the shelves blur as I make my way towards the door.

Ahead of me, some Year Eights are gathered around the noticeboard talking with Mr Keytes. I put my head down and go to swerve around them.

'Ah, there he is . . . Felix! I was just on my way to the library to see you. Felix!' Mr Keytes steps out into the corridor and blocks my way. 'How are you feeling?'

The Year Eights step aside as he turns me towards the noticeboard. 'I was just pinning it up.'

My heart sinks into my stomach as I read.

THE NATIONAL SCHOOLS CHESS
CHAMPIONSHIP IS NEXT WEEK!
JOIN US IN SUPPORTING FELIX SCHOPP!
ST MARTIN'S SCHOOL, 11TH MAY

'What do you think?' Mr Keytes grins like his enthusiasm might be catching. 'The whole school is behind you.'

Mr Keytes's words repeat in my head. The whole school is behind me. The whole school, packed into minibuses and coaches following me down the motorway, cheering and blaring their horns, all the way to Birmingham. And when we get there they'll all be watching me walk in, wishing me luck and patting me on the back because they think I'm going to win, but they don't know I haven't won a single match for a week. I've lost my game brain. I'm like Spider-Man without his webs, Thor without his hammer, Superman without his super powers.

I swallow hard, like I've got a golf ball stuck in my throat.

'Felix,' says Mr Keytes. 'Are you okay?'

I shake my head.

'No, sir, not really.'

52

What Mr Keytes Said

Mr Keytes said that it's okay to cry if you are worried about someone. It's okay to cry if you miss them. It just means you care about them.

Mr Keytes says he feels like it every day, that he still misses the person he loved and sometimes he feels like she's with him even though she is dead.

I told him that my granddad isn't dead, he's just not very well; that he hasn't been himself for ages because he missed my grandma loads, and still does. That's when I told Mr Keytes that I miss her as well. That Granddad's house feels empty without her and there's a big empty space inside of me too.

Mr Keytes said he knew this, but caring about someone when they are alive is as important as caring about them when they are dead and that we should take the chance to tell them how we feel before it's too late.

I said I told my grandma I loved her loads of times and I've told my granddad I love him as well. He said to make sure he knows I mean it, and that it shouldn't be something I just shout without thinking when I walk out of the door. He said lots of people do that, like when they add 'x' at the end of a text message. It's just a thing that's become normal, like people have trigger-finger at the end of a text – they just add the 'x' automatically.

I wasn't sure what he meant by that.

But I'm very sure that Mr Keytes misses his wife.

53

Teatime in Germany, Again . . .

'Now look where you're going or you'll spill the gravy.'

We're walking across the square to take Granddad his tea. I'm excited to see him, but I'm also nervous in case he's come home thin and pale like Grandma did. Mum says I'm not to be too noisy, that Granddad has had a shock, he needs to keep calm and I certainly shouldn't get him excited by talking about chess.

Granddad's TV is playing through the hall when we get there.

'Hi, Dad,' yells Mum. 'It's only me.' Then she nudges me to go in and see Granddad while she takes his dinner into the kitchen.

I peer around the edge of the door. The room is dark and quiet like always and Granddad is staring ahead at the TV.

'Hi, Granddad,' I say.

He turns his head slowly towards me. He looks thin and his eyelids are droopy like any moment he's going to fall asleep.

I walk slowly into the sitting room and sit beside him.

'Granddad,' I say quietly, 'I thought I'd come and see you.'

Granddad smiles.

'Yes,' he says. 'I'll be fine, but where—'

'Francke!' Mum bombs into the room. 'You've not taken your pills,' she says, pointing at two pills in her palm.

'But I drank the water,' says Granddad.

'Yes, but water alone won't make you better.' Mum blows out her cheeks and goes back into the kitchen.

Granddad sighs. I try to think of something to say, but all I can think about is how tired he looks and the only other thing I can think of is chess.

I look at the TV. Tomorrow it's going to rain in Hamburg, Münster and Stuttgart, but it's going to be sunny in Leipzig and Berlin.

'Looks like it's going to be nice in Berlin, Granddad,' I say, trying to fill the silence.

'Yes, I am thinking ...'

'Here.' Mum comes back in with a glass of water and picks two pills up off the coffee table. 'Now take these,' she says.

Granddad sighs again.

'I will,' he says. 'But the doctors said I should take them after meals.'

'Right,' says Mum. 'I'll get your dinner then.' She rolls her eyes as she walks out into the kitchen. I hear the sound of plates knocking against a dish, then a clunk as she closes the microwave door. Granddad leans forward.

'Felix,' he whispers. 'I am thanking God—'

'Did you want to sit at the table, Dad? Or shall I bring you a tray?' Mum shouts from the kitchen.

Granddad shakes his head and sits back in his chair. It's usually him who's barking orders but he's too tired to even argue with Mum.

'Table or tray?' shouts Mum.

Granddad takes a deep breath like we're at scuba again. I think he's going to shout, but then he says breathlessly, 'Tell your mum I'll have it on a tray.' I've never seen him like this and it's kind of scary not knowing what's wrong.

I get up and go into the kitchen.

'He says he'll have it on a tray,' I say.

'Good,' says Mum, then she looks at me, concerned.

'Felix,' she says. 'What's wrong?'

I try to speak but it feels like I've a tomato stuck in my throat. I swallow and try again.

'It's Granddad,' I whisper. 'He looks much worse than I thought he would and he keeps thanking God.'

'I know, love.' The microwave pings. 'But it's okay. The doctors wouldn't have sent him home if they didn't think he was all right.'

'But they did that with Grandma,' I whisper urgently. 'And the next week she died!'

Mum presses her hand against my cheek. 'That was different,' she says. 'Of course he's not been well, but we'll take care of him and he'll be fine.' She takes Granddad's tea out of the microwave and puts it on a tray. 'You bring the gravy and a knife and fork,' she says.

'Here you go, Dad,' says Mum as she enters the sitting room.

Granddad pushes himself up and Mum puts the tray on his lap.

'Now,' she says, 'is there anything else you want? Pepper? Salt?' Mum waits for his answer.

Granddad glances at me, then picks up his knife and fork. I wonder if he's thinking the same as me – about when we used the knife and fork as chess pieces the night he taught me the Sicilian Defence. I wish he could do it again, but he can hardly cut his meat let alone organize a chess attack. Then suddenly he looks up.

'Mint sauce,' he says.

'What?' says Mum.

'Mint sauce. I am thinking I would like some mint sauce.'

'We don't have any,' says Mum.

'Perhaps you could go to the shop and get me some.'

'Well, yes.' Mum looks at me, exasperated. 'If it means you will eat it. Felix, would you run to the shop for—'

'No,' says Granddad. 'I was thinking you could go.'

'But Felix will be quicker,' says Mum.

Granddad glances at me. 'Yes . . . he would,' he says slowly. 'But . . . could I have some Guinness too?'

'Guinness?'

'Yes,' says Granddad. 'The doctors said a little beer wouldn't hurt. But Felix is too young to buy it.'

Mum gives me a weirded-out look like she thinks Granddad has gone slightly mad, and I'm thinking that too.

'Okay,' she says warily. 'But do you need it right now?'

'It would be nice,' says Granddad. 'We could always reheat my dinner.'

'All right.' Mum swivels her eyes at me, like, *Felix, I need to talk.* I follow her out into the hall.

'I'll go and get it,' she says. 'But only so he'll eat. Just sit with him and make sure he's all right while I'm gone.'

'But, Mum,' I whisper. 'He's acting really weird.'

'He's just a bit confused after coming out of hospital,' she says. 'But I will phone Dad so he knows.'

She opens the front door and walks down the path.

I turn round and walk slowly towards the sitting room. I stop. Granddad's chair is empty. All that's left is his tray on the floor. I walk in to see if he's peering through the curtains.

'Has she gone?'

'What, Granddad?' I spin round and see Granddad sitting at the dining table. 'Granddad,' I say. 'What are you doing?'

He opens up the chess set.

'Come on, your mother has been driving me mad! I've been waiting for you to come over all day!'

'But . . . I thought . . . Granddad, you're supposed to be ill!'

'I was . . .' Granddad grins. 'I mean, I am, but you've the finals tomorrow.'

'Yes, I have.'

'Then take your blazer off and let's play.'

54

Worms in My Belly

'Are you sure you don't want us to come with you?' Mum's standing in the kitchen with a concerned look, like when Leo, my gerbil, died. 'Because we'd like to,' she continues. 'Dad said he's cleared the day.'

'Has he? Have you?' I say, surprised as Dad walks in. He's not taken a day off since Christmas.

'Yes, matey,' he says. 'The whole day.'

'See, think yourself lucky,' says Mum, smoothing down the lapels on my blazer, 'he didn't even do that for our tenth wedding anniversary.'

'Well, I tried,' Dad says sheepishly. 'But Rovers were in the play-off finals at Wembley.'

'Mmm.' Mum gives him a look like she still hasn't forgiven him. 'Anyway.' She stops smoothing my blazer to straighten my tie. 'I think we should come.'

'No, Mum,' I say. 'You really don't have to. I'll be fine and I know you're both busy.'

'Okay,' she says, smiling. 'But this time, win or lose, when you get back we are *definitely* celebrating in Nando's.'

'Okay,' I say. 'I'll do that ... but, Mum, that's too tight.' I loosen my tie. Mum would normally tell me off for getting stroppy with her, but she just stands there smiling with her head tilted, like when she's thinking of buying a dress in town.

I glance at Dad and see him smiling too.

'What?' I say. 'What have I done now?'

'Nothing,' says Dad.

'Then why are both acting weird?'

'We're not,' says Mum, edging towards me. 'We're just very proud of you.' She sniffs.

'Aww, Muuuum,' I say. 'You're not going to cry, are you?'

Dad puts his arm around her. 'No, she's fine,' he says, squeezing her. 'You go and get your bag and I'll take you to school now. Is Jake ready?'

'Yes,' I say. 'He messaged six times already.'

I turn into the hallway and take my bag off the banister. I know Mum and Dad are only trying to help, and I'm glad Jake and Rebecca are going, but the person I most want to be there is Granddad.

Last night he said he wouldn't wave me off because he wanted me to focus on the last move he taught me – the Yugoslav Attack. Like all the other moves, it was complicated, but I went over and over it in my head before I went to sleep last night. And I memorized Granddad's last words: 'You are ready.'

I hear the jangle of Dad's car keys.

'Ready, champ?' he says.

I open the front door and walk out onto the path. The sun shines brightly on the square and the houses. Everything is quiet and still, like everyone is still in bed. I look past our tree at Granddad's house. Samson is sitting by the front door and all of the house's curtains are closed. Out of the corner of my eye, I catch Jake running, cutting across the grass. I focus on Granddad's house again.

'You are ready,' he says in my head.

I nod slowly.

Yes, Granddad. I think I am.

55

Final

'Felix,' Jake whispers. 'It's like Hogwarts.'

'I know.'

'And some of them have got beards!'

'I know, Jake. You don't have to keep on.'

'And briefcases!'

'Jake!' snaps Rebecca. 'You're not helping.'

I puff out my cheeks and look up. As usual, Jake is exaggerating. This place isn't as big or as spooky as Hogwarts, but it does have huge pictures on the walls and a chandelier hanging from the ceilings, and it has big wooden doors that lead into the main hall.

I puff my cheeks again, as voices echo all around me. 'There are hundreds of them,' I say under my breath.

'What were you expecting?' asks Rebecca.

'I don't know,' I say. 'Just not this. It's like . . .'

'I told you, Hogwarts,' says Jake.

Me and Rebecca exchange looks, like for once Jake is right.

The Inter-Schools Championship was huge, but this is even bigger. The car park was jammed with school minibuses from all over the country – places like Liverpool, Manchester, Edinburgh and Carmarthen. Every region has sent their top player and they're here with their teachers, parents and friends supporting them. Some of them are wearing special T-shirts with the name of their school and a chessboard on the front. I haven't got a T-shirt, but Mr Keytes did bring our school's biggest minibus, and Mr Andrews followed in another which means all the members from chess club, including Rich, are here, as well as four students from the sixth form. For a moment, seeing the other parents makes me feel bad for telling mine not to come, but they might have embarrassed me like when Mum cried when I was a sheep in my primary school end-of-term play. But even that wouldn't be as embarrassing as what Jake is doing now.

'Felix, what do you think?' He grins as he holds up a banner he's made out of a bed sheet.

GO, FELIX! NATINAL CHESS CHAMP

He peers down at his banner. 'I tried to put the year on, but I ran out of space.'

'Is that why you missed the "O" out too?' says Rich, smirking.

Jake reads his banner. His face turns red as he spots his mistake.

'I think it's great,' says Rebecca.

'Yes,' I say, sticking up for Jake against Rich. 'It's cool.'

'Brilliant,' says Jake, wrapping it round his shoulders like a cape.

Rich shakes his head. I smile to myself. Jake can be really annoying, *and* embarrassing, but there aren't many friends who would cut up a bed sheet for you.

I head off through the crowds with Jake following behind. This is the second time I've been to the toilet since we got here. I went four times before I left home, then I had to get Mr Keytes to pull off the motorway three times so I could go in the service stations. I think it's because I'm feeling so nervous. So many people are depending on me – my granddad, my mum and dad, Mr Keytes, the teachers, the whole school. They say they are all behind me, but being in something like this is scary. It was easier when I was part of a team and not on my own. Granddad said I wouldn't be on my own, that he would be with me in spirit, but I can't feel his spirit, I can't even hear his voice in my head – maybe it's because he's one hundred and thirty miles away.

I reach the toilets. Jake says it's weird if we go in together, so he waits outside like one of Bobby Fischer's bodyguards. My path is immediately blocked by a queue of boys in smart uniforms, talking in posh accents. Granddad told me to block everything and everyone out, but over the rabble I hear the words 'capture . . . threat . . . defence'. One of the boys glances at me and cups his hand over his mouth like he thinks I might be listening in and stealing his tactics. Then they all look down at my scuffed-up shoes and start to grin. It's bad enough being in a strange place where I don't fit in, without someone trying to make me feel embarrassed about my clothes. But maybe they're playing mind games, like Granddad warned me about.

Part of me wants to tell them it doesn't matter how we dress, it's how we play chess. Part of me wants to just tell them to shut up. If

Granddad was here, he'd tell me to stay in control of my emotions, that no one wins if they lose their head.

I turn around and head back into the foyer.

'That was quick!' shouts Jake.

'I changed my mind.'

Jake runs after me. 'But you can't change your mind. I'm your coach. I passed up going to football for this.'

I stop walking.

'Jake, what are you on about? I changed my mind about peeing, not playing.'

'Oh.'

We push our way through the crowds and find Mr Keytes, who's talking to a teacher from another school.

'Ah, here he is.' Mr Keytes puts his hand on my shoulder. 'I was just telling Mr Givens about your new-found talent.'

Mr Givens smiles at me.

'It's wonderful to hear,' he says, 'and remarkable too, that you've mastered chess in such a short space of time. This tournament will be good experience for you.'

'Experience?' Jake butts in. 'Felix isn't here for experience, he's here to win. Aren't you, Felix?'

'Don't!' I nudge Jake.

'It's true. I'm his coach and he's been getting lessons from his granddad every night after school.'

My face starts to burn.

'Well, it's good to see someone has confidence.' Mr Givens smiles. 'I'll catch you later, Simon.' He shakes Mr Keytes's hand. 'And good luck, Felix, though I doubt you'll need it with your coach in your corner.'

Jake grins. I shake my head. It's great that he supports me, but what chance have I got anyway? Maybe I am only here for the experience. Maybe I should just run for the doors after all.

'Felix ... Don't look so worried.' Rebecca puts her hand on my arm. 'You'll be fine.'

'But everyone else looks like they've been playing for years and they've read loads of books. All I've done is play for six weeks with my granddad and watched a Bobby Fischer DVD!'

Rebecca puts her hand over her mouth.

'See, even you're laughing.'

'I'm not. It's just the way you said it.' She takes her hand down and suddenly looks at me, straight-faced. 'Felix. You've just got to believe in yourself as much as your granddad does. He wouldn't let you come here if he didn't think you could do it on your own.'

I take a deep breath. Then another. My chest begins to loosen, but immediately tightens as a hooter sounds and someone shouts, 'Can all the players make their way into the main hall.'

The main hall, I think to myself. *There's a bigger room than this!*

Mr Keytes stands in front of me. 'Well, this is it, Felix,' he says, sounding like Mum before she sent me in to have two teeth out at the dentist. 'Good luck, and don't worry about losing. Just do your best.'

'Okay.' I gather my breath.

'Yeah, good luck,' Rich sneers like he thinks I will need it.

I turn towards the hall doors. 'Take no notice of him.' Rebecca's walking alongside me. 'Just concentrate on your own game, don't worry about the others.'

'Yeah,' says Jake. 'And don't worry if you lose, because I'll make a bigger banner and fit the date on it next year.'

'Thanks, Jake,' I say. 'That helps lots.'

I inch forward in the queue. I feel as scared as I did when I went scuba diving with Granddad.

'Good luck, Felix!' Rebecca shouts. I try to look for her but the crowds are pushing me into the hall.

As the contestants fan out I see three long rows of tables full of chessboards, labelled A, B and C. They run the length of the room towards a big glass window at the end with a lectern by the side. I look up at the wooden rafters and beams, at the teachers and children taking their seats like Romans getting ready to watch the gladiators fight at a coliseum.

My heart thuds as I follow the contestants towards three whiteboards on the wall. As each one gets to the front they seek out their name and make their way to their table. I edge closer. The girl in front of me spots her name in seconds and moves away. I step forward and look for mine but I can't see it. Maybe everyone was so surprised I did so well in the Inter-Schools that they forgot to enter me.

I take a deep breath. I must be here somewhere.

Penelope Offiah

Christian Parker

Benjamin Lyons-Smith

Leah Patterson-Barnes

The names sound so posh that I feel like I don't belong. Felix Schopp, Felix S C H O double P . . .

There! Felix Shop: row C, table 14.

They could have spelt my name right. Still, it's not like they'll have to spell it again on the trophy.

I turn and walk down row C. Some of the contestants are already sitting down waiting to play. Others are standing quietly, like they are doing last-minute cramming for an exam. As I walk past them I realize that any one of these boys or girls could be my opponent and I don't want to make eye contact. I put my head down and count off the tables until I reach number fourteen.

I pull out a chair.

Me.

Table.

Chess set.

Clock.

That's all I need. I sit down and stare at the board.

The hall buzzes with voices.

The hall hisses with whispers.

Thud! Thud!

'Good morning, can you all hear me?'

Thud! Thud!

A man in a black suit is standing behind the lectern tapping his hand on a microphone.

'Yes? Great! Well, good morning, everyone, I'm Mr Trent, the head of the UK Chess Association, and this is just me saying welcome to our tournament and to tell you a few details.'

I should listen, but my stomach is flipping over and over the longer this goes on. I stare at the board, run over Granddad's rules in my head, but my thoughts get interrupted by Mr Trent telling us where the exits are and that in the event of a fire alarm we all have to follow signs towards the rectory car park. Then he tells us the format of the tournament which Granddad read ten times to me to drill it into my head.

'And that's it,' he says finally. 'Good luck, and may the best person win. On the sound of the hooter.'

Finally, this is it. This is it.

A hand reaches out in front of me. A girl's hand. I shake it. My opponent picks up two pawns. I draw white.

The hooter sounds.

56

Down, But Not Out

'It's okay, Felix, at least you won the first game.'

I'm sitting on a bench outside the hall. Jake is bending down in front of me talking to me like I'm a boxer that's just been knocked out. I've not actually been knocked out but it just feels like it, because after winning the first game I just got totally blown away in the second. I had my opponent in check after twelve moves but then I lost concentration.

'It was his Doritos,' I mumble.

'What?' Jake turns his head to hear me above the babble.

'He kept munching on Doritos.'

'What flavour?'

'What?'

'What flavour were they – Cool Original, Tangy Cheese or Heat Burst?'

'Tangy ... Jake, it doesn't matter what flavour they were.' I push him away. 'It was just the crunching noise he made when he ate them, and the smell.'

'We should get him disqualified. Mr Keytes!'

'Jake,' Mr Keytes sighs, 'I don't think he can get disqualified for crisp-eating. Besides, this is only a blip, and even if it's not a blip, if it turns into something bigger—'

'Like a blob,' says Jake.

'Jake!' Rebecca's sitting next to me. 'You're really not helping.'

'No, you're not,' says Mr Keytes, pulling a five pound note out of his pocket. 'Go over there and get us a drink and some biscuits.'

'I can't,' says Jake. 'I'm his coach. He needs me. Besides, I thought we were supposed to get a proper lunch.'

I glower at Jake. *How can he think of his stomach at a time like this?*

'Okay. Okay ... I'm going.' Jake turns away.

'I think I'd better go with him.' Mr Keytes glances at me, then at Rebecca. 'You stay here,' he says. 'And, Felix, don't worry about the last game. It's all going to be fine.'

I don't answer and look at the ground.

Mr Keytes is only trying to help, but he's wrong to tell me not to worry about the last game. Granddad says we always have to analyse them so we can learn from our mistakes and not make them again. I run through the moves again in my head. *Pawn to d4, pawn to g4, bishop to f7. Knight to rustle-rustle-munch-munch.* It was like radio interference zapping through my head. Then the clock started counting down, every second disappearing at the edge of my vision: *9:30 ... 29, 28, 27 ... Pawn to b4. Rook to h6 ... rustle-rustle-munch-munch.* It was only a boy munching Doritos, but I couldn't concentrate. I started to sweat like someone had plugged my body into the mains. *Munch-munch. Checkmate. What? Checkmate.*

I hold out my palms. My hands are sweating now like they did in the game. How did I let it happen? I should have blocked out the munching, pretended I was playing a computer. But I bet the Mechanical Turk never ate Doritos.

I shake my head slowly.

Granddad will be disappointed. I imagine telling him I got knocked out in the first round. He'd smile and say it was all right, but his eyes would give it away.

'I'm sorry, Granddad,' I mumble. 'I'm sorry.'

'Hey, what are you saying sorry for?' Rebecca's standing in front of me.

'Isn't it obvious? I'm going to get knocked out after three games.' I don't tell her it's not losing the game that I'm worried about. It's about losing the feeling of being good at something for once in my life.

I lean back and rest my head against the wall. Some of the contestants are already making their way back into the hall. Soon it will all be over. I can just get on the minibus and in two hours I'll be playing Forza in my bedroom.

'Felix.' Rebecca holds my arm like she knows I was drifting off. 'You can do this,' she urges. 'All you have to do is believe in yourself.'

'I know you're trying to help, but it's easier to say than do.'

'I know, but you've practised so hard. You can't give up now.'

The hooter sounds.

Rebecca looks at me for a long time like she's finally run out of words.

I push myself away from the wall.

'I better go,' I whisper.

Rebecca walks with me towards the doors.

Inside some of the contestants are in their chairs; some are standing with their arms folded like they are thinking, others are walking up and down the rows. There are sixty-four of us here and there can only be one winner. What was I thinking? I heard what Rebecca said, but I can't do this. I want to turn and run. If I don't play I'll never know if I would win or lose; that way I won't disappoint anyone, including myself.

Leaving Rebecca behind, I head into the hall. The room buzzes with players' and teachers' voices. No one seems to notice that I'm here. They won't miss me when I'm gone. All I've got to do is cross my name off the list and leave.

I walk over to the whiteboards.

'I believe in you. I believe in you.'

I know, Granddad, I just wish I believed too.

A teacher wearing glasses is standing beside the whiteboards, his eyes watching me as I reach into my blazer pocket and shakily search for a pen. Nothing. I search deeper, but all I can feel is a piece of paper that must be a page of my notebook or a detention note.

The teacher steps forward.

'You'd better find your seat,' he whispers. 'Or you'll get disqualified.'

'It's okay,' I say. 'I'm going to concede, I'm just looking for a ...' I pull the piece of paper out ... 'an envelope? What?'

I look at the light blue envelope in my hand. Then turn it over. On the front I recognize Granddad's scrawly handwriting.

The tenth thing I'd like to teach Felix.

'Young man, are you playing or not?'

I glance up. The clock says two p.m. All the contestants are sitting down at the tables, hands poised, ready to make their first moves. I look back at the envelope.

The tenth thing I'd like to teach Felix?

Granddad must have slipped it in my blazer last night. I slide my finger under the flap and pull out a piece of paper.

Felix,
I am thinking
about the tenth thing
I want to teach you
for a very long time.
And it is this:

I frown.

'Something wrong?' asks the teacher.

'I ... don't ... know ... It's a letter from my granddad, but it doesn't make sen—' I turn the paper over and smile.

Felix.
Never
Ever
Give
Up!

303

57

Knockout

It feels like all the lights in the hall have been turned off, except one. And it's burning down like a searchlight on my hair, through my head into my skull. The clock clicks slowly, like every second is a minute. I take a deep breath.

My heart is as calm as the sea. My head is as clear as the sky.

Tick.

Tick.

Tick.

It's just me sitting at a chessboard with the darkness around me. It's like I'm dreaming, like I'm in Granddad's sitting room back home.

I stare at the board. My knights have been captured. One of my bishops and one of my rooks too. The enemy has attacked me and left me wounded like a soldier on the ground. I hear the sound of gunfire and I can't see because there's smoke all around me, but with the gunfire I hear soldiers screaming and shouting for help. And I want to shout too.

Load the cannons.

Fetch our bayonets.

Get the medic. I'm hurt and I'm bleeding.

Pick me up and run for the hills.

But wait.

The smoke is clearing. The gunfire has ceased.

I look down at my stomach. The bleeding has stopped.

Never ever give up.

I lean on my rifle. I used up all the weapons Granddad gave me.

Tick . . .

Tick . . .

Tick . . .

Is it really over?

Is there nothing else I can do?

I lift up my head. See Jake. See Mr Keytes. See Rebecca. See hundreds of pairs of eyes around me, like cat's eyes shining in the dark.

Never

Ever

Give

Up!

I hover my hand over my king.

Check again.

Queen on d4. Bishop h6. Rook f6.

It's really over.

I move my queen to d6.

'Check . . . Checkmate.'

I stare at the board in silence. Check every piece on every square.

Check where my opponent could move his king or any other chess piece that could uncheck it.

But the king is trapped, and none of his army can save him. There's no way out.

My opponent lays his king on the board.

I stare at the board in silence.

One person claps.

Then another.

And another . . . until applause builds and echoes around the hall.

My opponent holds out his hand.

I stand up to shake it and look at him for the first time. He says something, but the applause drowns his words. I take a deep breath, then I feel a smile creep across my face. I feel like laughing. I feel like crying too. I feel—

'Yesss! Felix! You won!' Jake rushes from nowhere and nearly knocks me off my feet. 'You won, Felix!' he shouts in my face. 'You won! Unlucky beardy,' he says, turning to my opponent.

'I won,' I whisper to myself. 'I won!'

I clench my fist, see Rebecca beaming at me as she runs across the hall.

'I won,' I say, still not believing it.

'You did,' she says, hugging me. 'You did! See, I told you you could do it.' I try to tell her I can't believe it, but my body is shaking so much that no words come out.

'Congratulations, Felix.'

I spin around and Mr Keytes is smiling so much he's almost laughing.

'Well done, Felix.' I think that was Chris.

'Well done, Felix.' I think that was Tom.

So many people talking, so many people patting me on the back, I'm beginning to feel dizzy.

'Well done, Felix.' I don't know who that was.

'Well done, matey, that was—'

I spin around.

'Mum, Dad, what are you doing here?'

'As if we were going to miss this,' says Dad, putting his arm around my shoulder.

I wait for Mum to say something, but she's so excited that all she does is kiss me!

I wipe it away, but I'm so happy she's here.

'You were amazing,' she says eventually. I wait for her to add something like 'for once' or 'at last', but she just repeats, 'Amazing. Amazing!' and then kisses me again.

'When did you get here?' I ask. 'I never saw you come in.'

'You were too busy playing chess,' says Dad. 'I've never seen you so still.' He puts his hands on my shoulders like he's going to hug me, but then he just ruffles my hair and says, 'Well done, mate. Well done.'

'Did you want to call Granddad?' asks Mum, holding out her phone. 'It'll be late by the time you're home.'

I think for a moment. I want to tell Granddad, but he hates the phone and I really want to see the smile on his face when he hears I won. I go to tell Mum this but Mr Keytes interrupts me, saying, 'Felix, I'm sorry, but we have to move on. This is Mr Trent, the head of the UK Chess Association.'

'Very impressive play, young man,' says Mr Trent.

I shake his hand, then shake another person's hand, then another. Mr Trent hands me the trophy and says something, but my head is buzzing with excitement and I can't hear his words. I think I say thanks, but I can't even hear myself. Then Mr Keytes turns me around and I face a wall of people taking pictures with their cameras and phones.

'Smile, Felix.'

'Hold up the trophy, Felix.'

'This way, Felix.'

'Kiss the trophy, Felix.'

'Big smile.'

I try to smile, but I've been concentrating for so long that my face feels like a cracked eggshell when I do.

'Cool, isn't it, Felix!' Jake's grinning at me, leaning in so his face is in all the pictures. It is cool, it's more than cool, but it's happening so fast that I can't take it in.

A man wearing glasses and a suit walks over to me and shakes my hand.

'Congratulations,' he says, stepping in between me and Jake. 'I'm Hugh Harris, from *Chess Monthly*. Can we get a picture with just you and the trophy?' He guides us towards a banner that reads.

NATIONAL SCHOOLS CHESS CHAMPION
SPONSORED BY WEETOS

I stand in front of it and smile, but I've been smiling so much my face is beginning to ache.

'That's great,' says Hugh, snapping away behind his camera. 'Can you just tell me what it feels like to be the National Schools Chess Champion?'

'Umm, I haven't really thought about it,' I say. 'I didn't think I'd win, but I'm really pleased.'

'Pleased?' he says.

'Ecstatic!' shouts Jake.

'Yes.' I nod. 'Ecstatic.'

'That's wonderful.' Hugh lifts his hand and motions for me to move a little to my left. 'Brilliant,' he says. 'Now could you say something about how eating Weetos helped you?'

'Sorry?'

'Weetos.' He points at the banner. 'Perhaps something like, you eat them at home every morning before you go to school.'

'But I don't,' I say.

'But he eats a lot of German sausages,' Jake jumps in.

'That's fine,' says Hugh. 'I'll just put that you eat German sausages with Weetos ... Now, how about one with your teacher. Mr ... ?'

'Keytes,' says Mr Keytes.

Hugh drops his camera to his chest and takes out a notebook.

'How am I spelling that?'

'Keytes. Sounds like the poet, except it's spelt K E Y T E S.'

'And I'm his coach!' Jake jumps to my side. 'Jake Simms, that's J A K E, S I M M S,' he says, grinning as he puts his arm around my shoulder.

'Great,' says Hugh. 'Was it you who taught him castle queenside?'

'To do what?' asks Jake.

Hugh shakes his head like he's figured Jake has no idea what he's talking about. 'Felix.' He turns back to me. 'If you could just hold the trophy up ... That's it.' Hugh snaps one more picture. I put the trophy down on the table, then Hugh asks if he can ask me a few more questions.

I sit down and feel myself breathe for the first time since I won.

'So,' says Hugh, smiling, 'your teacher tells me you've only been playing a few weeks. How did you start playing?'

I tell him how Granddad made a list of all the things he wanted to teach me and that one of those things was chess.

'Wonderful,' says Hugh. 'What's his name?'

'Who?'

'Your granddad. What's his name? Is he here? Maybe we could get a picture.'

Hugh holds his pen above the pad, waiting for my answer. But even if Granddad was here, he'd hate to have his picture taken. He doesn't even open his curtains, so there's no way he'd want to be on the front of a magazine.

'No,' I say. 'My granddad's not here. And I don't think he'd like me to give you his name.'

'That's fine,' says Hugh. 'As long as we've got you and the trophy.' Then he shakes my hand and says the article will be on the *Chess Monthly* website by the end of the day.

I take a deep breath as he walks away. Finally I'm on my own. For the last four hours I've been in a trance, like a dream. *What have I done? What have I done?*

'You've won the National Schools Chess Championship. That is what you have done.'

310

I know, Granddad, I think, smiling. *I know.*

I've won.

I have won.

I've never won anything in my life, except for a minion with the claw machine in the games arcade at Swanage. I walk over to the table and pick up my trophy. I run my hand over the smooth metal, up the body, over the sharp edges of the cross on the king's head. It can only be about 15 cm high and probably weighs the same as a big bar of chocolate, but that doesn't matter.

I'd never have won it without Granddad. I'd never even have lifted a chess piece onto a square. I'd never even have got the pieces out of the box.

'It's a beautiful trophy.'

Yes, Granddad. It is.

58

When We Are Famous

Jake said I'm going to be famous. That *we're* going to be famous, and there will be a street party in the square at the weekend. He kept on and on about it in the minibus on the way home. He said there'll be tables and chairs on the grass by our tree and people will hang banners out of their bedroom windows that read: Well done, Felix, it's good to have you home. And then there's going to be a bus tour around the city, like City and Rovers do when they get promoted. And there'll be a statue of me like the one of Isambard Kingdom Brunel, and people will come for miles just to see it and they'll set up a giant chessboard by the docks.

He said we're going to be rich and live somewhere posh like Bath and we won't have to worry about the distance to school because we'll have chauffeurs to drive us in our Ferraris and Lamborghinis. And we're going to live in mansions next door to each other and we'll have a connecting tunnel, just for us, and massive TVs in every room. And all the time he was saying this on the way home, he was checking the internet on his phone to see if Hugh had put up the pictures on the *Chess Monthly* website. But they weren't there, so he made up his own headlines:

'Felix Schopp wins National Championships with his *genius coach*! *Amazing coach* helps boy conquer the chess world.'

That's when Mr Keytes took the wrong turning in the dark.

That's when Rich told Jake to be quiet.

That's when Rebecca went to sleep on my shoulder.

That's when I rested my head on the window and felt the rumble of the tyres as car headlights flashed by.

That's when I started smiling.

That's when I realized how brilliant being good at something feels.

59

Can't Wait Till Morning

I'm lying on my bed with my trophy on my chest. My heart beats so slowly and heavily that I can feel it vibrating through the mattress springs. I'm tired but I can't sleep because the day keeps zapping through my head – the journey to Birmingham, my nerves, the games, me wanting to concede, then everyone surrounding me, patting me on the back, shaking my hand. I've tried counting sheep, I've tried wrapping my head in my pillow, but the day just goes on, like a DVD stuck on repeat. And really, I don't want it to stop.

I jump as my phone buzzes on the table. It's so late there's only one person it can be. Jake said he's going to stay up all night until our pictures are on the internet.

I look at the screen.

Still not there. What's taking him so long? All he had to do
was write a few words and upload a picture.

I know, I reply. Must be busy. But I'm going to bed now.

You can't.

I want to get up early to see Granddad in the morning.

Okay. Leave your phone on Alert. I'll text you if it happens.

Okay.

I put my phone down and go to close my curtains. Across the square the street light is flickering outside Granddad's house. I can't wait to go over there in the morning. Me winning might make him feel better, and he definitely will when I show him the trophy. He's going to feel as happy as I do.

I pull the curtains and get into bed. I hold the trophy tight to me. It really is mine, but I can't stop thinking that any minute now Mum will come in and shake me awake and I'll realize that this day hasn't happened and I'm late for school.

I close my eyes. In my mind I can see the hall and I can feel the light shining down on me. And I can see the chessboard and my opponent's king lying across two squares. Then all around me I can hear the sound of a clock *tick-tick-ticking*. I screw my eyes tight and hug the trophy so hard it digs into my skin. The clock keeps *tick-tick-ticking*, and I wish it would *tick-tick-tick* faster so the morning would come.

60

Alerts!

BUZZ. BUZZ.

BUZZ. BUZZ.

My phone is buzzing and flashing in the dark.

I reach out and try to turn it off. My hand knocks against it and it falls onto the floor.

BUZZ. BUZZ.

What day is it?

Sunday.

No school. I didn't set an alarm.

I pick my phone up, squint at the screen – twenty-six messages?

It can't be.

I wipe the sleep out of my eyes – twenty-six messages!

Twenty-six messages, all of them from Jake.

Felix, wake-up.

Felix!

Felix!

Felix, are you awake?

Felix!

Felix, you idiot!

Felix!

I scroll down, but each time I do a new message arrives.

Felix, come on!

Felix!

Okay, I reply. I'm awake.

At last!

What is it?

Don't know how to tell you.

What?

Shall I call you?

No. We'll wake my mum and dad. What is it?

Your granddad.

My heart skips a beat. What about Granddad? Is he ill again? But how would Jake know?

What about him?

Can't tell you. Just look!

Jake sends another message, but this time there are no words, just an internet link.

https://schoolchesschampionship.com

I click on it. My screen lights up bright. I blink and refocus.
Wha—?
What?

Youngest ever schools chess champion wins using moves of Stasi commander.

Stasi commander? No, that's not right. Granddad told me everything about the Stasi, how they watched people all the time, went through

their rubbish, listened to their phone calls. They were spying on *him* –
he wasn't one of them.

I scroll down the page and see a picture of me holding the trophy.

Have you read it?

Another message from Jake pops up at the top of my screen.

I'm trying to!

I go back to the screen.

> We have our youngest ever National Schools Chess
> Champion. Eleven-year-old Felix Schopp beat off strong
> challengers from schools all over the country using the
> Spreebogen Variation of the Yugoslav Attack, a move
> only ever used by the former East German secret police
> commander Lionel Steiner, who famously disappeared
> after winning the 1962 World Championships in Berlin.

What's Jake on about? What's so urgent?

I read the article again. *Felix Schopp ... Spreebogen Variation ...*
Yugoslav Attack ... Lionel Steiner ... Commander Steiner—

My heart drops into my stomach.

Commander Steiner! The same name I saw on the identity papers
in Granddad's wardrobe.

It's him. Your granddad! He must have changed his name.

Jake! I'm still reading.

My throat feels like it's going to close over and my hands are shaking like I'm at the dentist. I read the first paragraph again and hope I'm reading it wrong. But the same name jumps out at me again – Lionel Steiner – and it's the same year that was written on the cards.

I read on:

> In a closely fought final with George Templeton from Richmond High, Felix used the Spreebogen Variation of the Yugoslav Attack, after castling queenside to combat his opponent's Dragon Variation of the Sicilian Defence. Felix said, 'I'm really happy to have won, but I couldn't have done it without my granddad's help.' Felix's teacher, Mr Keytes of Southwick High (Bristol), said, 'Felix has only been playing for a couple of months. He's a wonderful lad, and we are all very proud of him.'

Lionel Steiner . . .

I shake my head. It can't be true. But I recognize the word Spreebogen. Spreebogen Park; it was the place Granddad went through on the way to his sister's house. Why did he tell me that? After the things he said about people being watched all the time and tortured and then put into prison. He wasn't one of them. He was the one who put them there! But it can't be right. It can't be. My granddad would never do that.

Felix, what are we going to do?

I don't know.

Maybe we phone the police and get a reward.

It's my granddad!

You could still visit him in prison.

Jake, go away.

I drop my phone and lie back on my bed.

This isn't true. Me and Jake were only playing when we thought Granddad was a spy. But what if the things Jake said *were* true – the ripping of the paper, the camera on the lamppost, his curtains always being closed?

I jump up and turn on my laptop. I don't want to look, but I need to know. I type in 'Lionel Steiner'.

From Wikipedia, the free encyclopaedia

Lionel Steiner. Commander in the Stasi (former East German secret police). World Chess Champion

1962. No image available. 1943–? Status and whereabouts unknown.

I don't want to read any more, but I can't help it. I sit back in my chair. Images flash through my head. The soldiers, East German spies with binoculars who put wire taps on the phones, the Berlin Wall.

It was just a game, a stupid game in the park, but what if it was real all along?

I close my laptop down and lie on my bed.

My granddad wasn't just a spy, he was a Stasi commander.

61

What Do I Do?

6.33. Granddad's bathroom light switches on.

6.36. The bathroom light goes out.

6.53. The hall light turns on. His shadow grows big through the glass as he walks down the stairs.

7.00. The front door opens and he lets Samson in.

7.35. He goes outside and checks the gnomes, then stares across at my house. I duck down.

7.36. I peer up over the windowsill. Granddad has disappeared, but a white car has just turned into the square. Perhaps it's one of his friends from the GFG who has seen the internet and they've come to pick him up.

'Felix ... Felix!' I jump as Mum comes into my room. 'I said me and Dad are going out and ... and what are you doing on the floor?'

'Nothing,' I say. 'I just lost a pen.'

'Mmm.' Mum looks at me suspiciously. 'Anyway, we're going to a car boot sale – do you want to come?'

'No,' I say. 'I'm busy.'

'Yes, and maybe you can get busier by clearing the mess out from under your bed. Do that before you go and see your granddad. He's up and about.' She nods towards the window.

'I know,' I say.

'Then why haven't you been over there? You know how excited he'll be by your news.'

'I will ... in a minute.'

'But I thought you'd be desperate to tell him.'

'I am,' I say. 'I'm just ... doing something else.'

'Okay,' Mum says like she's surprised.

I listen to her footsteps go back down the stairs, then peer out of the window. The white car is parked just down from Jake's house and Granddad is nowhere to be seen. I reach for my laptop. I've been reading and rereading the *Chess Monthly* website, ever since Jake sent the messages. I've been hoping that it was a mistake, or maybe someone from school hacked into their computers and put the article there as a joke. But how could Granddad have got the move? Lionel Steiner disappeared; Wikipedia said so. The only way my granddad could have got the move is to be him.

I press refresh and hope the article disappears, but the screen reloads with the headline and the stupid picture of me grinning with the trophy and the same words: 'secret police commander ... disappeared ... World Championships ...' Granddad told me bits about his past, but it's like there was a whole chunk of years missing from the middle.

But he is still my granddad. He's the person who is always there to pick me up in his pink car, who makes me tea, gives me sausages, goes to the shops and buys Nutella especially for me because he knows that I like it. But even more than that, in the last few weeks I've gone from thinking he was just a grumpy man to seeing how happy he can be, and realizing how much he loved Grandma and me. And he was the only one who truly believed in me too. He didn't just teach me how to play chess; he made me feel good about myself. I grab my trophy and stand up. My granddad might have been a spy, but I still love him.

62

Confrontation

The trophy is gripped tight in my fist as I walk across the grass.

My feet are moving but I can't feel the ground. Out of the corners of my eyes I can see the houses and some people in their gardens, but the only thing I see clearly is Granddad's front door.

I stop at his gate and gather my breath. My phone buzzes again. It'll be Jake telling me not to do it, but he's too late because I'm already at Granddad's front door.

I raise my hand to knock, then stop. What if I disturb him? He might be packing up his things into a suitcase. Someone from the GFG might be in there with him, giving him new identity papers to help him escape. But I have to knock, because even if Granddad has done those things I want to see him one last time before he leaves.

I knock on the door and peer through the glass, waiting for Granddad's silhouette to appear in the hall. But there's nothing. I put my head against the door, listening for the boom of the TV or the brass band music playing in the kitchen.

Still nothing.

Weird. Maybe he's already left, or my imagination has gone wild and he's just out the back doing some gardening or working in the shed.

I walk round the side of the house and stop on the patio. The shed is closed and there's no sign of Granddad in the garden.

I try the back door handle. It turns and I slowly open the door. Samson squeezes in front of me and runs to his bowl.

The kitchen is quiet and there's a half-drunk cup of tea on the worktop. Granddad never leaves tea. I wonder if he's had one of his turns and gone to bed to recover.

My blood thuds in my ears as I walk into the hallway. I listen for Granddad, his radio, his TV, but all I hear is my breath and the tick of the clocks.

'Granddad,' I shout. 'It's me, Felix.' My voice echoes up the stairs.

Still nothing. He's really disappeared, just like Lionel Steiner did all those years ago. But he'd never have gone without his car. And he'd at least leave a note for Mum and Dad. And after all the things he said about trust and honesty, there's no way he'd have left me without saying goodbye.

I turn and walk into the dining room. The chess set is on the table with all the pieces on their squares ready for a game. I look to my left. My heart stops. Granddad's sitting in his chair in the dark. I wait for him to say something, but his head is back on the cushion and his eyes are closed.

He's asleep. He hasn't packed his bags and left after all.

I step towards him with my trophy behind my back. I don't want to give him a shock, but I have to wake him up to find out the truth. Samson's collar jangles as he walks through the hallway. I stop. Granddad opens his eyes and blinks in the dark.

'Ah, there you are, Felix,' he says, smiling. 'I've been waiting for you for ages, but I must have dropped off.'

'I-I-I know, Granddad,' I stammer. 'I just ... I was tired and couldn't get up.'

My trophy digs into my fingers. I thought that this would be the happiest moment, but my head is so mixed up with Stasi and spies that all I want to do is cry. I look down at the ground.

'Hey!' Granddad pushes himself out of his chair. 'It is okay if you lost, as long as you tried your best.'

I shake my head as he walks towards me. 'No, Granddad,' I mumble. 'It's not that ... I won.' I pull my trophy slowly out from behind my back. 'I won.'

'You have won!' Granddad's face lights up like it's been hit by the sun. 'You have won! Felix, I am so proud of you.' He puts his hand on my shoulder and shakes me. 'Very proud, but why aren't you happy? I know,' he says. 'It is the adrenalin. It has left you tired like it used to do me. Sometimes after a big game I would sleep for two days.'

I nod like it could be that, but it's not. I want to say something now, but Granddad's got the trophy in his hands and is smiling at it like it's him who's won.

I force a smile as Granddad walks over to the sofa. 'Come and sit here,' he says, tapping the seat beside him. 'Tell me all about it.'

I want to tell him that I know who he is, but my tongue is as twisted as the thoughts in my head.

I have to say something.

I have to say it now.

I take a deep breath, but I could suck air in like a whale and it wouldn't help. After our falling out and then making up by the tree, Granddad said that we need to trust each other and that we can talk about anything, but I can't talk about this.

I sit down beside him.

'Tell me everything,' says Granddad. 'Don't leave out any details. I'm interested to know everything as I have been stuck in this room.'

I stare at the floor. If I don't start talking soon, he's going to guess there is something wrong, and if I tell him about the tournament maybe he will tell me on his own – after all, he's told me lots of things lately that I never knew. But nothing as big as this.

Eventually my words start to come out. I tell him it took two hours to get to Birmingham and I ate sandwiches and drank plenty of water. And when we got to the school it was massive and looked like Hogwarts and he smiles and tells me he doesn't know what that is. And as I explain I find myself thinking that he looks too kind and friendly to be a Stasi commander, but then I've never met one so how could I know. It would be easier if I'd found out he was a secret Arabian knight that turned into a cheetah or a leopard. At least I could look at his skin for evidence of his spots or stripes. But there's nothing. Not even a number tattooed on his wrist or hand. He's just the same old Granddad, who's smiling at me as I tell him I lost the second game because my opponent was eating

Doritos, then nodding approvingly as I tell him the moves I made in the rest of the games.

'Wonderful,' says Granddad, leaning forward. 'Now, the final, tell me about the final.' He rubs his hands together like he's warming them by a fire.

This is when I have to tell him I know. After I tell him I used his move, that's when I tell him I know he's Commander Steiner. But I can't do it.

'It was just another game, Granddad,' I say.

'Nonsense,' he says. 'A final is not just another game.'

I lump back against the cushions.

'What's wrong?' asks Granddad. 'Is there something you are not telling me? Did your opponent just concede? This is fine if he did. It means you won the game with your mind.'

'No, Granddad,' I say. 'It's not that.'

'What is it then?'

I swallow hard. 'Granddad, I got cornered, and I was desperate, I was trapped.'

'And?'

'And I used the special move: the Yugoslav Attack.'

'Good,' says Granddad. 'But why are you so unhappy?'

I take a deep breath. Then another.

'Felix?' Granddad leans in front of me.

'Because I know who you are,' I blurt. 'You taught me the Spreebogen Variation, there's only one person who's ever used that move. I know you're Commander Steiner.'

'Who?' Granddad looks up at me.

'Commander Steiner. A commander in the Stasi. Look, it says here.' I reach into my pocket and show Granddad my phone. 'See!'

Granddad fumbles for his glasses but his hands are shaking so much he can hardly find his nose. I wish I hadn't started this. He might be a Stasi commander, but he's my granddad and I don't want to upset him any more than I have.

I start to pull my hand away.

'No.' Granddad grips my arm tightly and squints at the screen. I hold my breath as he reads the headline out loud.

'*Youngest ever schools chess champion wins using moves of Stasi commander* ... What?!' Granddad pulls the screen closer. '*Felix Schopp beat off strong challengers from schools all over the country using the Spreebogen Variation of the Yugoslav Attack, a move only ever used by the former East German secret police commander Lionel Steiner.*'

Granddad leans forward. 'Commander Steiner,' he whispers. 'I never thought I'd have to say his name again. I ... I ...'

My heart beats as fast as a rabbit's. I wish I could take it back, but it's too late now.

'I'm sorry, Granddad,' I say. 'I didn't want to believe it, but you mentioned the Spreebogen when you told me about your sister, and I saw his name on the cards in your wardrobe—'

'No. It is wrong!' Granddad snaps. 'It is wrong! *This* is wrong!' He jabs his finger at the screen. 'This is not what happened. He stole my move! Steiner stole the Spreebogen Variation from me.'

63

Final Curtain

Bump.

  Knock.

  Bump.

  Thud. Thud. Thud.

  Bump.

  Knock.

  Thud. Thud. Thud.

These are the noises coming through the ceiling. Granddad told me he needed some time on his own, that he needed to think, but he's been in his bedroom so long that I really think he must be packing a suitcase to go back to Germany.

I walk over to the window and peer out between the curtains. Two girls I don't know are doing handstands by our tree, Mum and Dad are unpacking things they bought at the car boot sale and Jake's riding round the square on his bike. He wants me to go out, but Granddad was so upset when I told him about Commander Steiner that I don't want to leave him alone.

Bump.

Knock.

Thud. Thud. Thud.

I look up and follow Granddad's footsteps across the ceiling.

Click.

Knock.

Thud. Thud. Thud.

I walk back towards the sofa just in time to see Granddad's hand gripping the banister as he walks down the stairs. I want to believe he's not the commander, but why would he be leaving if he wasn't?

I sit on the sofa with my head in my hands. I imagine him putting on his long coat, listening for the clink as he picks up his car keys and the click of the latch on the front door.

But there's no sound, just the clocks *tick-tick-ticking* from everywhere like they are built into the walls. Is this what spies do? Just disappear without even saying goodbye?

A shadow creeps across the doorway. I lift my head slowly. See Granddad's worn slippers, then his brown trousers, and his blue jumper that Grandma knitted for him. And tucked under his arm is the box file I saw in his wardrobe.

He smiles as he steps towards me.

'You remember I said we should trust each other?' he says softly.

'By the tree, Granddad?'

'Yes.' He sits down beside me and puts the box file on the coffee table. 'Well, I am thinking, I should trust you now.'

Granddad opens the lid slowly.

'This . . .' he says. 'This is something I have only told one person, and that was your grandma.'

'Not even Dad?' I ask.

'No, not even your father.' Granddad sighs as he looks into the box. 'Felix, this box contains a sad story, one that I don't like to think of, but . . . but . . . Perhaps I should just show you what this box is.'

I stare down at the box. There are hundreds of questions in my head, but it doesn't feel right to ask one now.

Granddad reaches in and pulls out the black and white picture. He holds it in front of me between his fingers. I hold the other side to stop it from shaking.

'This picture was the last that was taken with my father. It is also the last chess tournament I ever played. I was seventeen and it was taken after I won the German Youth Chess Championship in 1960. Like Bobby Fischer, I was the youngest chess champion of my country and everyone thought I would challenge for the World Championship like he had. I loved playing chess, it was my passion – pitting my mind against other players was the best feeling in the world. I used to play on my own in my room all the time, all day and night, but it ended up with me not being able to see my father again.'

'How, Granddad?' I turn and see tears welling in Granddad's eyes.

'Do you remember what I told you about the Berlin Wall, how they built it overnight in Berlin, my city, to split the people in the East from the West?'

'Yes, Granddad,' I say. 'They built it the day you tried to go and see your sister.'

'Yes. Well, my father was a military journalist. He wrote about battles and new developments in weapons, the latest tanks and guns. He had access to military information, and one morning the Stasi arrived at our house and accused him of passing information to the armies on the other side of the Wall, in the West. My father said it wasn't true, but one day he went out of the house and my mother saw some men bundle him into a delivery van. We did not hear from him for weeks until we were told he was in a Stasi prison camp in East Berlin. I was not allowed to visit him, but we heard from other people that the rooms had no windows but lights that were kept on all day and night to deprive the prisoners of sleep. Sometimes they would suddenly let my father out and he would come home. He never told us what happened in there, but he had sores on his head and his bones showed through his skin.'

'That's terrible, Granddad,' I say.

'Yes.' Granddad stares at the picture. 'And it was a cruel trick, because each time my father thought it was over, only for them to then arrest him again. He lost his job, and my mother too. She and I were placed under house arrest – never allowed to go out, never allowed anyone to visit. We lost contact with my aunties and uncles, all of our friends. I was forced to give up college. At night the soldiers would come and wake us. My father was not talking, so the Stasi came and interrogated us. They said they would torture my father if we did not tell them everything we knew, but we knew nothing. There was nothing.'

I try to think of something to say, but all I can think is how horrible it must have been.

Granddad reaches into the box.

'These are our identity cards. We had to carry them all the time, and these . . .' He reaches back into the box. 'These are the security passes for me to go and see the head of the prison camp, Commander Steiner.'

'You went to see him? . . . You went to *see* Commander Steiner.'

'Yes.'

'So you're not—'

'No.' Granddad shakes his head slowly. 'I am not Commander Steiner.'

I let out a big breath of relief. 'But why did you have to go and see him?' I ask. 'You were only seventeen.'

'Because the commander was crazy about chess. He was a grandmaster who played at all the big tournaments in Europe. He found out I was the Youth Champion. He wanted to play me. I did not want to, but they threatened to torture my father more if I didn't. The Stasi took me to his office. It had huge wooden doors that opened into a room that was as big as your hall at school. It had just one desk in it – the commander's desk with a chessboard set out on it. And he was standing behind the desk, waiting for me in his uniform, many medals on his chest. He told me to sit down and play, even though I knew you do not play games with the enemy. But when your father is being tortured in a room only metres away, you will do anything. I made the mistake of beating him. I thought he wouldn't want to play any more, but instead it made him want to play me more. He made me teach him moves in exchange for not sending my father to another camp far way, near Poland.'

'But he was a commander,' I say. 'He couldn't play chess all day.'

'But he could,' says Granddad, 'that is the point. In East Germany, if you were a good athlete – a runner, a swimmer – or if you were good at anything at all, the government would help you. And because of their mental strength, chess players were treated like kings. So of course I played the commander, to help my father. We played every day, sometimes twice, and he took me with him to play tournaments in the East with the Russians. I was not allowed to play, I was just there to help him prepare before every game and replay them after. I taught him every attack I knew, invented new ones and taught him those too, and he won every tournament in the East. I thought I'd fulfilled my side of the bargain, that maybe instead of threatening to send my father to Poland he would let us all go. He said he would, but only if I helped him win the World Chess Championship in 1962, that was being played in West Berlin.'

'The other side of the Wall?'

'Exactly.' Granddad nods. 'The other side of the Berlin Wall. They took me to see my father; he was even thinner and had so many bruises I could not see the white of his skin. My father said I should not believe the commander's promises, that no matter what I did, he would be tortured in prison for ever. Then my father made me promise him one thing – that when I was on the other side of the Wall, in West Berlin, if I got the chance to escape I should run away and join my sister. I told him I didn't want to, but he said my mother and I would never be released either, that we might go to prison too. I should try to escape to the West now, because I might never get the opportunity again.'

'But you'd have to leave your parents behind?'

'Yes.' Granddad swallows hard and reaches into the box. He shows me a picture of a man in an army uniform with lots of medals. It looks like he's in a hotel foyer surrounded by other men in uniforms and dark coats. Just like in *Pawn Sacrifice*.

'This is the hotel where we played. To get there we had to drive through Checkpoint Charlie. It was a border point where the East of Berlin met the West. I sat in the car that followed the commander. There were guards with guns up on the watchtowers, and even more standing on the border, in front of the Wall with the barbed wire on top. We stopped at a barrier where the guards checked our papers. For a moment I thought we weren't going to be let through, but then the barrier lifted and we drove on. The Wall was now behind us and at that moment I felt so sad because I realized that if I did as my father asked, I may not see him or my mother again ... So this ...' Granddad's finger shakes as he points at the picture. 'This is the commander ... And this ... this is me.'

I peer at the crowd in the background and see Granddad as a boy looking back at me. He looks so nervous and lost in the crowd.

'There were bodyguards everywhere,' Granddad continues. 'Even if I'd tried to escape like my father wanted, I couldn't have, because they followed the commander and me everywhere we went, to every game. For three days, I helped the commander prepare in the mornings, playing chess in his room, and even in our heads as we went down in the lifts to the main hall. He won his first four matches and was in the semi-final against a military general from Russia. They had never played each other before and the commander was very nervous. He demanded I tell him my best moves, something no other player would know. If I helped him reach the final, he wouldn't just not send my father away, he would release him and remove my mother's house arrest the next day. That evening was when I taught him my best move. That's when I taught him . . .'

'The Spreeborgen Variation,' I say slowly.

'Yes.' Granddad nods. 'You see, Felix, the Yugoslav Attack wasn't his, it was mine. And he used it the next morning to beat the Russian general. Afterwards we went back to his room. The commander was happy. Everyone was drinking and celebrating, even the bodyguards. That was when I asked him to keep his side of the bargain. I'd helped him to the final; now he had to release my parents. But he looked at me like I was talking backwards. "I have to win the final first," he said.'

'That's not fair,' I say.

'No,' says Granddad. 'It was not fair and that night I lay awake thinking. Even if I helped the commander win, there would always be something else that stopped him releasing my parents – another game, another championship. He couldn't be trusted. I wanted to call my father and tell him what had happened, but even if the Stasi allowed him to talk, I knew they would be listening.

'That night was when I decided I would do as my father said. I should escape to the West. I knew of the risks, and that I may not make it. I'd heard many stories of people being shot trying to get over the Wall. But even though I was already over, I was still surrounded by guards with guns. The next morning, as the commander and I made our way through the lobby for the final, with reporters shouting questions and cameras clicking and flashing, I saw my chance – a gap between the commander and the bodyguards that I could escape through. The guards wouldn't shoot me, not in broad daylight, not with the whole world watching. I ran through the gap, out of the hotel doors and onto the pavement. The street was full of people walking and cars blaring their horns, stuck in traffic. I could not trust any of the people just in case they were Stasi, so I ran through the traffic as fast I could without looking back. Eventually I slowed down in a suburb of the city where the streets were quiet, and that evening I made my way across the city to my sister's house in Heinz Hoffmann-Straße. And I saw her for the first time in over a year.'

'Wow, Granddad,' I say. 'It's so exciting it could be a film.'

Granddad gives me a weary smile.

'Yes,' he says. 'It could be a film, but unfortunately it is true and it does not end well.'

'But you escaped,' I say. 'You wouldn't be here now if you hadn't.'

Granddad smiles again. He said the story does not end well, but why? From the sad look in Granddad's eyes, I suddenly think I know the reason.

'He didn't let him go, Granddad. Did he? The commander never let your dad go.'

'No.' Granddad shakes his head slowly. 'He sent my father to that place near Poland. My mother never saw him again. I never saw my father again. All we had were two letters from him, saying he didn't want us to worry because he was okay. But he wasn't okay. One year later, my mother received a letter from the Stasi, telling her that my father had died. They never said when or how.' Granddad takes his glasses off and wipes his eyes on his sleeve.

'I have never been able to forgive myself,' he says. 'My mother came to live with me after the Wall came down, but I should never have left her and my father behind. I should have helped the commander win the final.'

'But it wasn't your fault, Granddad. He still might not have let them go.'

'I know,' says Granddad. 'I know. And now you know everything. Why I kept it secret for so long, why I keep the curtains closed, why I could not play chess for sixty years. Not until now . . . with you.'

'So why did you suddenly want to teach me?' I ask. 'After all this time?'

'Because I realized something . . . something your grandma said before she died. I realized what she meant.' He nods at the picture of Grandma on the mantelpiece.

'What did she say, Granddad?'

'That we should always share our loves with the people we love.'

Granddad moves his fingers to the middle of the picture of the commander and slowly tears it in half, then tears it again, and again. I don't know what to say. I can't even imagine what it must have been like for him to have been locked away from his friends, never allowed out. I can't imagine what it must have been like to run away and never see your dad again.

I want to tell him I'm sorry about what he had to do; I want to tell him I'm sorry for thinking he was the commander. How could I have thought such a terrible thing?

I open my mouth.

'Granddad, I . . . I'm . . .' I only have to say two words, but my throat is so tight that the second one won't come out.

Granddad wraps his arms around my shoulders.

'It is okay,' he says, hugging me. 'Sometimes it is okay to say nothing.'

'I know, Granddad, but I just want to say sorry.'

Granddad rests his head against mine. 'You don't have to say sorry,' he says. 'You have made me happy for the first time in a very long time. I have loved playing chess with you, but most importantly I have loved having you here with me.'

'I've loved it too, Granddad.'

'What, even me picking you up in Grandma's pink car?' He lets go of me. 'It's okay – maybe I will park further away from now on.'

I laugh as I wipe my eyes on my sleeve. 'Maybe,' I say.

Granddad closes the box slowly, then picks up my trophy. The silver flashes against his face as he turns it round. 'It's a splendid thing,' he says. It's like closing the box means it's the end of the story, that he doesn't want to talk about it any more.

Granddad turns the trophy round and reads the engraving. 'Felix Schopp. National Schools Chess Champion. Yes, that is you,' he says, smiling. 'You definitely won.'

'No, Granddad,' I say. 'We *both* won.'

'Yes.' Granddad smiles again. 'In a funny way, I think we both did.'

I wait for him to say more, but from his huge sigh I think he's exhausted after telling me his lifetime in one day.

I look up at him.

'Thanks, Granddad,' I say.

'For helping you become a chess champion?'

'No, for *everything*.'

Granddad smiles down at me. 'I am very proud of you, Felix,' he says. 'I hope you are proud of yourself.'

'I am, Granddad,' I say. 'I feel great.'

'And I hope your mum and dad are too.' Granddad's eyes start to water.

'They are,' I say brightly, trying to cheer him up. 'Mum says you've got to come with us for tea because we're going to Nando's to celebrate.'

'Okay,' he says. 'If that's what you would like.'

'I would,' I say. 'So are we going to have a game now?'

'Of course . . . But there is something I must do first.' He nods as he walks past me into the sitting room. I think maybe he needs to rest, or he's going to pick up the TV remote and check the morning weather in Germany, but he walks straight past his chair and stands in front of the curtains. I think of following him. I want to know more about the Wall, like why they took it down, but I don't think this is the right time to ask because Granddad has been staring at the curtains for so long it's like he suddenly wants to be alone.

I put my trophy down gently on the table without making a sound. I think Granddad should have it in his house for one day.

I edge towards the door.

'You don't have to go,' says Granddad like he's reading my mind.

'But I thought . . .'

'No, I do not want to be alone. I have been sitting here alone too long. I miss your grandma, but she would be mad at me for sitting here in the dark for so long.' Granddad pauses on his heels like he's a long jumper gathering himself before the jump. Then he steps forward, lifts up his arms and pulls back the curtains. The sunlight bursts in, turning his grey hair white, turning the red walls pink, making pieces

343

of dust sparkle as they float in the middle of the room. He steps back, takes a deep breath, and then another, like he's stepped outside on a cold winter morning.

I walk forward and stand next to him. As I look up I can't tell if he's smiling or squinting in the light. He takes another deep breath like he's about to say something important. I wait, but all he does is let the breath out as Jake cycles by. He's nosing at the house so much he's heading straight for Granddad's car. For a moment I think he's going to smash into it, but then he swerves at the last minute. I don't think Granddad's even noticed because he's just staring straight ahead.

'Granddad,' I say. 'What are you thinking about?'

Granddad lowers his head and looks at the lawn. 'I am thinking it is a beautiful day for—'

'Ah, no, Granddad,' I say. 'Not the grass! I know it needs cutting, but do we have to do it again?'

'Humph.' Granddad's face cracks into a grin.

'Not the patio slabs!'

'No, not the patio slabs. Even I didn't enjoy that.'

'What is it then?'

Granddad puts his arm across my shoulders.

'I am thinking it is a beautiful day for zip wire.'

64

Zip Wire

'I don't think I can do this.'

'It's okay,' I say.

'But it's very high.'

'I know.'

'Felix, you know I said we had to be honest with each other?'

'Yes.'

'And trust each other?'

'Yes, Granddad.'

'Well, trust me, I am being honest when I tell you I really do not like heights!'

'It's okay. You've got the harness around you and there are people waiting for you at the bottom.'

'Maybe I will go back down. We're holding people up.'

'Granddad.'

'Yes, Felix.'

'Just jump!'

'Aaaaaaaaaaaaaaaaaaaaaaaaaaaaaaaaaaaaaaaaaargh!'

Acknowledgements

This story was a while in coming, so I'd like to thank:

Sam Drew and my daughter Lois for helping me get unstuck. (Yeah, yeah, and you Tallulah, for keeping up our appearances in Nando's.)

Jon Bentley-Smith, for his brilliant words of encouragement and leading me to discover The Mechanical Turk.

Lucy Rogers for doing what good editors do.

Clare Wallace for keeping me sane.

Roy Ludlow, for checking and triple-checking all the chess moves, in his chess room and the pub.

Casey Ball (aged 10) from Oldfield Park Juniors, Bath, and Kerrie Grant, who sat down with me and gave me a great insight into the challenges they face and the brilliant ways they overcome them. (Casey, I hope you love secondary school. Kerrie, good luck at uni).

Big thanks to Bob Schopp for a long walk along the beach when I told him about Felix and he kindly agreed I could borrow his surname. And thanks to all the teachers who lent me their names for this book. Of course the story and its characters are all a work of fiction, but once I nailed the names the book took shape.

Anna Funder, for her amazing book, *Staziland*, that did so much for my understanding of life in the eastern area of Germany during the Stazi era.

I'd also like to thank all the wonderful schools I've visited in the last two years. Your pupils, teachers and librarians are amazing and help me to keep going. Special mention to Mr Hunt and all his staff and pupils at Springwood Heath Primary, Liverpool. I am proud to be the Patron of Reading at one of the most special places on earth.

And finally, thanks to my Dad, who on summer's days patiently waited until after 3pm to knock on my writing room window, to go for a walk, or just chat. I hope he is some place good and feeling as proud as I am about this book.